A Man Called
SUNDAY

Center Point
Large Print

Also by Charles G. West and available from
Center Point Large Print:

Mark of the Hunter
Long Road to Cheyenne

**This Large Print Book carries the
Seal of Approval of N.A.V.H.**

A Man Called
SUNDAY

Charles G. West

CENTER POINT LARGE PRINT
THORNDIKE, MAINE

This Center Point Large Print edition is published in the year 2015 by arrangement with New American Library, an imprint of Penguin Publishing Group, a division of Penguin Random House LLC.

The text of this Large Print edition is unabridged. In other aspects, this book may vary from the original edition.
Printed in the United States of America on permanent paper.
Set in 16-point Times New Roman type.

ISBN: 978-1-62899-804-7

Library of Congress Cataloging-in-Publication Data

West, Charles.
A man called Sunday / Charles G. West. — Center Point Large Print edition.
pages cm
Summary: "Luke Sunday is relieved of his position as an army scout after his opposition to the army's attack on a peaceful Cheyenne village. Desperate for work, he agrees to guide a couple across hostile country to the Gallatin Valley"—Provided by publisher.
ISBN 978-1-62899-804-7 (hardcover : alk. paper)
1. Outlaws—Fiction. 2. Indians of North America—Fiction.
3. Large type books. I. Title.
PS3623.E84M36 2015
813'.6—dc23
2015035620

For Ronda

CHAPTER 1

Chief Scout Ben Clarke looked over the group of Crow Indians who had volunteered to act as scouts for General George Crook's winter campaign against the hostile Sioux. Principal among the hostile leaders, Sitting Bull and Crazy Horse had refused to obey orders from Washington to report to the reservation, and it was now up to the army to punish them. As Clarke scanned the line of warriors standing before him now at Fort Laramie, his gaze was captured by one among them, and he paused to study the lean features of a lone white man. Dressed in buckskins from head to toe, the man would have passed for an Indian had it not been for the shock of sandy hair, tied in a single strand between his shoulder blades. A closer look revealed deep-set gray eyes that locked, unblinking, on Clarke's. "You're Luke Sunday, ain't you?" Clarke asked, certain the man could be no other. He received a single nod in response.

Ben Clarke was as informed as any white man in the territory, but this was the first time he had come face-to-face with Luke Sunday. He knew him only by tales he had heard from others who had chanced upon the man the Crows called Dead

Man. He would have dismissed the rare sightings as nothing more than tales the Indians had created, had it not been for verification by John Collins, the sutler at Fort Laramie. Collins said there was such a man named Luke Sunday who had come in his store a couple of times to buy .44 cartridges. He said the man was short on conversation and never lingered once his purchases were made. He didn't know where Sunday got his money to pay for the ammunition for the Henry rifle he carried, but he supposed it came from the trading of furs. Ben couldn't help being fascinated by the chance encounter with an Indian legend, so while the Crows were being issued ammunition and weapons, he called Sunday aside. "You speak English?" Clarke asked, not sure whether the man had been raised from childhood by Indians, as some folks believed.

Again, Luke nodded, then spoke. "I do," he said, somewhat surprised that Clarke had to ask.

It was Clarke's turn to nod thoughtfully. "Well, I wasn't sure since you came in with the Crows," he said. "I've hired on close to thirty white scouts for this campaign, some of 'em the best in the business. All of 'em claim to know the Powder River country like the back of their hands. What about you? You know the country between here and the Yellowstone?"

"About as well as the next man," Luke answered.

"I reckon there'll be plenty of opportunity to find out," Clarke said. "I've been runnin' scout details for the army for a helluva long time. How come I ain't ever run into you before?"

"I wasn't this low on money for cartridges till now," Luke stated frankly.

Ben took another few moments to study the man's face before deciding. "I reckon I'll take a chance on you even though I've already got more scouts than I'll probably need."

Although Luke's shrug in response might have seemed indifferent, he was genuinely grateful for the employment. It had been a hard winter so far, and what little money he had managed to accumulate was rapidly running out. He had no real quarrel with the Oglala Lakota. It was a Hunkpapa Lakota war party that had killed his parents. Now the Sioux were at war with the United States, so he felt no qualms about scouting for the army against them. He did find it odd, however, that Clarke said he was going to take a chance on him, as if he was going to interview each of the Crow scouts who volunteered. It didn't occur to him that Clarke meant to measure him against his proven senior scouts.

"I'm gonna send you out with Bill Bogart," Clarke continued. "He's worked for me before. Sometimes he's hard to get along with, but if you just do what he says, you'll be all right, I reckon." He turned and pointed to a large man with a full beard the color of pine straw. "He'll be scoutin' for Colonel Reynolds most of the time. You might wanna go on over and tell him I said you'll be ridin' with him and his partner."

Luke nodded, but hesitated for a moment. "All right if I collect my cartridges first?" he asked. Judging by the arming of the Crow scouts, he was concerned that the soldiers might run out of cartridges before he got his.

"I reckon," Clarke answered. Then out of curiosity, he motioned toward the ash bow strapped on Luke's back. "You any good with that thing?"

"I get by," Luke replied.

"Ben Clarke told me that I'll be ridin' with you," Luke announced as he approached the large man standing by one of the campfires, talking to a smaller, dark-complexioned man.

"Is that so?" Bogart replied, not particularly impressed by the sandy-haired man clad in buckskins. "What might your name be?"

"Luke Sunday," Luke replied.

"Luke Sunday," Bogart repeated, trying to recall. He turned to his friend and asked, "You ever hear of Luke Sunday?" His partner shook his head. Bogart turned back to the stranger. "This here's Sonny Pickens. Me and him has scouted for the army for the last five years. How come we ain't ever run into you before? I expect I know, or know of, every scout hired for this campaign, but I ain't never heard of you. Where the hell have you been scoutin'?"

"Round about," Luke answered without emotion.

"Round about," Bogart repeated, obviously amused. Then he glanced at Pickens and smiled. "Looks like we got us a greenhorn to break in, Sonny." Turning back to Luke, he said, "I'll let you ride with us, but the best thing you can do is keep your eyes open and do what I tell you, and maybe you'll learn somethin'." Luke shrugged in response. He wasn't out to impress the man or his partner. He had simply signed on for the pay and the supplies. Bogart continued. "We're fixin' to get goin' here as soon as the colonel gets his soldier boys in the saddle, so, Sunday, you can get started by saddlin' them two horses yonder." He pointed to a gray and a sorrel tied by the stream.

Luke figured that was about as far as he intended to be buffaloed. "How about if I shine up your boots before we go, too?" His deep-set gray eyes locked with Bogart's, so that his next statement would not be misunderstood. "I signed on as a scout. The sooner you learn that, the easier it'll be for us to get along."

A brief silence followed before Bogart responded. He was accustomed to throwing his weight around, especially with new hires, but this one had a lethal look about him that warned of potential trouble—much like the sensation of cornering a bobcat. Bogart was bigger by half than the rangy stranger, but he wasn't sure the contest would be worth the pain. After thinking about it, he forced a wide smile and, with an exaggerated wink for Pickens, said, "Damn, Sonny, he ain't as green as I thought. I expect we'd best get saddled up. We're 'bout to pull outta here, headin' to Fort Fetterman." He let it pass as a harmless incident, but Bogart still smoldered inside. He wasn't accustomed to anyone showing that much backbone when he stared them down. *I'll be teaching you a hard lesson before we're done,* he promised silently.

Designated the Big Horn Expedition, the campaign was under way, with General Crook's troops marching two days to arrive at Fort Fetterman. The fort was known as a hard-luck post by the troops stationed there, because of its desolate location. The fort was situated on a high bluff on the south side of the North Platte River above the valleys of the river and LaPrele Creek, where it was subjected to heavy snows and freezing winds during the long winters. Water had to be carried up the bluffs from the river, and the soil was unsuitable for growing fresh vegetables. So all supplies had to be brought in from Fort Laramie or Medicine Bow Station on the Union Pacific Railroad. Desertions were common.

Upon arriving at Fetterman, Crook was

informed that Sitting Bull and Crazy Horse had been reported to be in camp somewhere near the headwaters of the Powder and Tongue rivers. Anxious to catch the Lakotas in their winter camp, General Crook left Fort Fetterman on the first of March and headed north. Luke Sunday found that he was little more than a forward scout for the column, along with Bill Bogart, Sonny Pickens, and a few other scouts. His excellent knowledge of the country was not really needed since the column followed an oft-used government road through eastern Wyoming.

Five more days found the expedition at the ruins of Fort Reno, where Crook established his supply depot. Pushing on from Reno, the troops continued their march through the freezing country until the scouts came upon frequent travois trails left by many Indians, and all of them heading toward the Powder River. Convinced that he had found Sitting Bull's camp, the general divided his command and ordered Colonel Joseph J. Reynolds on a night march with three hundred men and rations for one day. Out in front of the column by about two miles, Luke and the other scouts searched for the hostile camp.

It was shortly before dawn when the scouts found a large Indian village on the west bank of the Powder River. From their position, high on a plateau that stood about five hundred feet or more above the village, it was difficult to see clearly through the fog that had settled upon the river. Bill Bogart had seen all he needed to see, however. "We'd best get right on back to tell Colonel Reynolds we found them Sioux he's been lookin' for," he said, his breath forming a white cloud as it struck the frozen air.

Luke Sunday wasn't ready to assume as much. From where the small party of scouts now stood, and it not yet daylight, he couldn't be sure whose village it was without a closer look. When the others immediately started to act upon Bogart's opinion and turned their horses back toward the way they had just come, Luke felt it his duty to speak. "Hard to say who that is down there on the other side of the river, with it being so foggy. Might be old Two Moons's village—Cheyenne— and he ain't at war with anybody."

"Horse shit!" Bogart responded. "I don't need to get no closer to know that's a Lakota village. Hell, I can smell 'em. We already know Sittin' Bull's camp is on the Powder, him and Crazy Horse, and that's sure as hell a big village down there. Couldn't be nobody else, so let's get ridin' and tell the colonel we found 'em, so he can hit 'em before they wake up good." He glared impatiently at Luke, halfway expecting his disagreement since he didn't know how far the newly hired scout would push the issue.

No one he had talked to really knew much about

Luke Sunday, and this bothered Bogart. Sunday had not volunteered any information about his past, and he was the kind of man a person would hesitate to question. Had he been inclined to ask, Bogart would have found that no one in General Crook's column knew much about the man—and only a few outside his command had rumored knowledge. There were a couple of different stories—both hearsay that came from the sutler's store at Fort Laramie—about his prior life before he arrived that day at the fort and signed on as an Indian scout. One story had it that he was kidnapped by a band of Cheyenne warriors when he was a baby. Others were certain that he was born to a Crow mother and father. That version failed to explain why, up close, he didn't look like an Indian, especially when you considered his light, sandy hair.

He had spent some time with the Cheyenne as well as the Crows. That much was obvious, because he spoke both languages well—when he spoke at all. A tall, rangy man of few words, Luke made no effort to fit in with the other thirty-odd white scouts hired by General Crook at Fort Laramie that February. With the exceptions of chief scout Ben Clarke, Louis Richaud, Frank Grouard, and a few others, most of the white scouts were little more than cutthroat drifters, cattle rustlers, bank robbers, and probably murderers. Luke had little in common with any of them, and seemed to be more comfortable with the Crow scouts, who called him Dead Man because of his seemingly lifeless gray eyes that looked at a man as if seeing right through his skull and reading his thoughts. That lifeless gaze was fixed now on the likes of Bill Bogart as the lumbering bully insisted to Luke and the other two scouts that they had found the combined camps of Sitting Bull and Crazy Horse.

"I reckon I'll move in closer to get a better look at that camp," Luke said after he thought the situation over. It made no sense to him to attack a village before you were certain about who you were attacking.

"You're a hardheaded cuss, ain't you?" Bogart retorted. When Luke made no reply, Bogart said, "Suit yourself, but we're ridin' back to get Colonel Reynolds. You go nosin' around close to that village and get yourself caught, and the colonel will most likely have your hide for givin' away his surprise—if the Sioux ain't already scalped you. And after he's through with you, I might decide to give you a good ass-kickin' myself." He hesitated for a few moments to see if Luke wanted to challenge the threat. When he did not, and just remained sitting passively on his horse, Bogart turned to the other scouts and said, "Come on, boys, let's get goin'. Let this jackass go see if he can get hisself scalped."

Luke waited a moment to watch them disappear

into the heavy fog rolling over the bluffs from the river below. When he could no longer see them, he took his horse's reins in hand and led the paint Indian pony along the snow-covered bluffs, looking for a good place to descend the icy slope. The thought occurred to him that the approach to the village on the west bank of the Powder was not going to be easily accomplished by six companies of cavalry with any element of surprise. The predawn darkness would make a surprise attack even more difficult for the horses to move with any sense of urgency over the broken terrain of shallow ravines and gullies that led down to the river. Picking a narrow ravine that promised a gentler descent, he led the paint down toward the water's edge to a clump of cottonwoods with a thick undergrowth of plum bushes. Leaving his horse there, he moved even closer to the edge of the water. From this point, he could see more of the village, as well as a large pony herd of maybe a thousand or more. Though it was sizable, he could not believe the village was big enough to be the combined Sioux camp the colonel searched for.

As he knelt there, an old man appeared on the opposite bank and settled himself to offer his prayers to Man Above. It struck Luke that he knew the old man, a Cheyenne chief called Old Bear. His instincts had been correct. This was Two Moons's village, as he had suspected. Knowing there was little time to stop Reynolds before he attacked a peaceful Cheyenne camp, Luke called out to the old man, "Old Bear!"

Startled, Old Bear looked right and left before spotting the tall, sandy-haired scout across the foggy river. He recognized him at once. "Ah, Dead Man," he called back. "What brings you to our village?"

Luke wasted no time in warning the old chief that a large column of soldiers was right on his heels. Old Bear assured him that his village was on its way back to the reservation and had no quarrel with the soldiers. "The soldiers think they have found Sittin' Bull's village and are plannin' to attack. I'll try to stop them, but you must prepare your people to defend themselves in case the soldiers won't listen to me." Old Bear was immediately alarmed, and quickly left to return to his village to warn the others. Luke hurried back to his horse. There was little time to tarry.

Within a mile, he met Reynolds's forward scouts, led by Frank Grouard with Bill Bogart by his side. "You need to tell the colonel that that ain't no Sioux camp," Luke sang out as he approached. "It's Two Moons's village—Cheyenne."

"He don't know what the hell he's talkin' about," Bogart said.

Grouard was not overly concerned one way or the other. "It don't make no difference," he said.

"It's too late now, even if the colonel did give a damn. He's already split the column up to take positions in front and back of the village. He's gonna fight 'em. Won't make no difference if they are Cheyenne. They're sidin' with the Sioux, anyway."

"Well, that don't make a helluva lot of sense," Luke protested. "These Cheyenne ain't headin' toward Sittin' Bull's camp. They're goin' the other way. Two Moons ain't lookin' to fight the soldiers, but if the soldiers attack his village, he sure as hell will—and I expect he'll figure he ain't got no choice after that but to join up with Sittin' Bull if the army ain't got no better sense than to attack him. So you're just gonna have that many more Indians to fight."

"Like I said," Grouard repeated, "it's too late to stop it now. We're gonna end up fightin' all of 'em, anyway, Sioux, Cheyenne, Arapaho. Hell, they're all hostiles." He turned to look at the column of troopers already approaching. "These boys is primed and ready to fight after so many days freezin' their hind ends off in the saddle."

Colonel Reynolds had divided his six companies into three battalions of two companies each. One battalion was sent to take positions on the ridge behind the sleeping village to cut off that avenue of escape. The second battalion was to be held in reserve, while the third was to descend the bluffs and launch the primary attack.

This battalion, headed by Captain James Egan and Captain Henry Noyes, made up the column just then arriving at the edge of the bluffs. Luke could see that Grouard was right; there was no chance of stopping the ill-advised attack on the Cheyenne camp. Still, he knew he had to try.

Leaving Grouard and Bogart, he rode back to meet Captain Egan. The captain was no more prepared to consider Luke's assessment of the Indian camp than the two scouts had been. He was frank, in fact, to inform Luke that, since this was his first expedition with a full-scale cavalry attack, he would do well to listen to the experienced voices of Grouard and Bogart. "I don't think there's any doubt that we've found the combined camps of Sitting Bull and Crazy Horse," he said, "and now we'll go about the business of teaching them a lesson."

Luke pulled his horse aside to watch as Egan led his company down the icy bluffs. Enraged by the deaf ear given to him by Egan, he felt a heavy sense of guilt for not preventing the attack on Two Moons's camp, but he realized there was nothing more he could do. As he had predicted, the horses had a difficult time maintaining any sense of purposeful progress as they slipped and slid down the icy gullies and ravines. By the time they had gained secure footing at the base of a deep ravine that stood between them and the Cheyenne camp, the Indians had been alerted to their presence, although with little or no time to prepare a defense. Consequently, they were forced to flee in the face of a cavalry charge through their village. Grabbing their rifles and ammunition, the Indians hurried their women and children to the ridge behind the camp to take cover. This was what Reynolds had anticipated. However, the battalion charged with the responsibility to cut off the hostiles' escape was unable to negotiate the rough terrain in time to be in place. As a result, the warriors were able to move up into the gullies and take command of the ridge. Soon they were able to lay a heavy barrage of rifle fire down upon the troopers who had now taken control of their village. The momentum of the battle changed at once as the Cheyenne snipers began to pick off the troopers from their vantage points above the village. Before very long, Colonel Reynolds was forced to withdraw his troops from the village to prevent further casualties. He ordered the village burned, including all supplies and weapons.

A disgusted witness to what the colonel would call a victorious battle when his column had retreated to report to General Crook, Luke Sunday had taken no part in the fighting. To his way of thinking, he had signed on to help fight hostile Sioux and had no cause to fire upon people he had once lived with, who had done him no harm, and had received him cordially in their village on several occasions in recent months. In his opinion, the Indians had taken the day, forcing Reynolds to retreat, and would now be emboldened to join their Sioux friends in their war against the army. The Cheyenne had not escaped without loss, however. Their tipis had been destroyed, and large stores of food and ammunition had been lost, as well as about eight hundred horses the soldiers had captured. *Well, Two Moons,* Luke thought as he took one last look at the destroyed village, *you mighta thought you were at peace, but you're at war now.* Disgusted by the army's attack on the peaceful village, he turned the paint's head away from the burning camp and followed the retreating troops.

CHAPTER 2

Colonel Reynolds ordered his weary command to withdraw twenty miles back to Lodge Pole Creek to rendezvous with General Crook. Already suffering from a night march before their attack on the village, as well as freezing temperatures, the likes of which Luke compared to the coldest in his memory, Reynolds's troopers were fortunate that the Indians had not come after them. By the time they reached the mouth of Lodge Pole Creek, horses and men were totally exhausted. It was close to nine o'clock that night before the troop went into camp. All food supplies were gone, the soldiers having been issued only one day's rations the day before, and there was precious little coffee left. Luke found it difficult to understand why the soldiers had destroyed great quantities of food in the Cheyenne village, without taking some to eat. He was baffled by a commanding officer who ordered all food, supplies, guns, and ammunition destroyed when his men sorely needed all four. They had managed to capture about eight hundred horses from the village. The ponies were left practically unguarded as weary sentries slept at their posts, causing Luke to speculate on how long they'd hold on to them.

Fires were built and what little coffee could be

found was put on to boil. Luke paused to share a fire with some men in Captain Egan's company. They were involved in a most earnest conversation regarding the fight behind them, and the fact that all of the dead had not been recovered. "I don't like it worth a damn," a skinny corporal with a heavy black mustache complained. "I know of three men that's still a-lyin' back there in that camp, and somebody shoulda been sent to recover their bodies before them savages cut 'em to pieces."

His comment brought forth a few grumbles from those gathered about the small fire and caused one of them to ask a question. "Has anybody seen Foster?"

No one had. "He was with me and Thompson when we set fire to those two tipis at the edge of the camp, and he went to help Bob Rivers after he got shot," one of the men said. "Bob got shot twice in the leg, and couldn't walk." He paused for a moment as if trying to recall. "I didn't see either one of 'em after that." As an excuse, he offered, "Them Injuns up on the ridge got the range about then and started pepperin' us pretty hot. There wasn't no time to think about anythin' but gettin' the hell outta there."

Genuinely concerned at this point, the corporal said, "I need to find out if they got back all right." He got to his feet and went to seek out Captain Egan.

Egan was equally concerned when informed that two of his men might have been left behind. After a quick investigation, it was confirmed that that was the case, so the captain went directly to advise Colonel Reynolds. As it turned out, the colonel had already been confronted with reports that his quick withdrawal had caused the abandonment of three of his dead. "That is bad news, indeed," Reynolds said to Egan in weary reply. "But there is little we can do about it at this late point. I'm sorry to say that it is highly unlikely your two men have survived after this length of time." When the captain started to protest, the colonel stopped him short, advising him that his supplies and ammunition were already low, and he had had orders to withdraw to Lodge Pole Creek to rendezvous with General Crook. "What's done is done," he said.

Luke listened when the captain returned to tell the skinny corporal that there was nothing that could be done to learn the fate of Foster and Rivers. The news was not well received by the small group of soldiers gathered about the fire, with some faintly subdued grumbling about the responsibility of their officers to recover the wounded and dead after every battle. The Indians' penchant for mutilating the bodies of their enemies was well known among the troopers. "I don't like it, either," Captain Egan told them, "but we were ordered to move on."

"I reckon I could go back and see if I can find out what happened to your two men," Luke volunteered. His announcement brought forth looks of surprise on the faces of those gathered around the fire. He had made no comment up to that point.

"That might not be such a good idea," Egan said, "riding back into that swarm of Indians. The minute they see you, you're a dead man."

"I don't plan on lettin' 'em see me," Luke replied.

Egan took a moment to study the scout's face, wondering if the man was just plain crazy. "All right," he finally said. "If that's what you wanna do, I don't see any reason to tell you no. But, mister, you'd best be damn careful, because nobody will be coming to help you. The column will be joining up with General Crook as soon as he shows up, and we'll probably head back to Fort Fetterman."

Luke drained the last swallow of coffee from his cup and said, "Much obliged." Then he asked the soldier who had last seen Foster exactly where he should look for the trooper named Rivers.

He was told that Rivers had been wounded while the troop was pulling back from the lower end of the Cheyenne village. "There's a deep gully about ten or twelve feet across, about forty yards shy of where that outmost tipi stood before we burned it. Rivers got hit when he was runnin' along the edge of it."

"I'll go take a look," Luke said. "Maybe they're hidin' in the gully, but the captain could be right. They're most likely dead." He went to fetch his horse, then disappeared into the night.

"That's the last we'll see of that crazy son of a bitch," the corporal commented.

"You're probably right," Egan said. "It wouldn't surprise me if he just hightails it somewhere as far away from that Indian village as he can get. He didn't take part in any of the action back there that I could see. I don't know if he has the stomach for fighting."

Bob Rivers pressed his body tightly up against the icy face of the gully he had been hiding in since shortly before nine o'clock the morning before. Cold, hungry, and in pain, he held his pistol in his hand. There was one cartridge left, and he planned to use it on himself when the time came. Why the Indians had not found him was a mystery he could not explain, but he knew they were bound to at any time, especially since it would soon be daylight. He had never expected to end up this way, alone and frightened, while his comrades left him behind. He had heard the warriors and the wailing women as they searched through the charred remains of their village, and on one occasion, the screams of a wounded soldier who, like himself, had been abandoned. He was determined not to give them the satisfaction of torturing him until death came for him.

He could only speculate upon what had happened to Calvin Foster. A man he had always thought of as a friend and one he could count on, Calvin had come to help him when his legs were shot out from under him. But when they realized that the company had pulled back, allowing the resurging warriors to counterattack, they knew they were trapped. They had no choice but to hide in the gully and hope to get an opportunity to escape after dark. Throughout the long day, they had waited for the warriors to find them, but somehow their hiding place had been overlooked. The bleeding had stopped, but he was afraid the leg was broken. One thing he knew for sure, he could not walk on it. With no better option, Foster had decided to go in hopes of finding a stray horse to carry them out of there. So once it was dark, he made his way down the gully, promising that he would return, with or without a horse. Now that it would soon be dawn, Rivers could not help wondering if Calvin had seen an opportunity to save his life and chose to do so instead of coming back for him. He had to admit that, had their positions been reversed, he might have given in to the impulse to do likewise.

Realizing that his desperate grip on his pistol had caused his hand to ache, he switched it over to his left hand and tried to relax the fingers on his right. The bitter cold made it difficult to flex the stiffened fingers, and he wondered then what had happened to his gloves. He had removed them when the attack was launched, knowing it was too cumbersome to try to fire his pistol while wearing them. They were not inside his heavy coat where he usually put them, and he couldn't remember much of anything that immediately followed the shots that tore into his leg. *Calvin, where the hell are you?*

Feeling the fear rising again in his veins, he switched the revolver back to his right hand, hesitant to tell himself what he knew now to be true. Calvin wasn't coming back. It would be daylight before much longer, and there was little chance that he would not be discovered. Even if he was not found, what would become of him? He couldn't walk. He had a weapon with one bullet. He could not hope to survive without help. *Maybe,* he thought, *I should try to crawl down the gully to the river and hide in the bushes.* With that in mind, he struggled to pull himself up between the rocks to see if anyone was near.

With a great deal of effort, he managed to raise his body high enough so that his eyes were above the level of the gully rim. What he saw was enough to stop his heart for an instant, rendering him paralyzed with fear. He wanted to drop back in the gully, but he was afraid to move lest the dark shadow slowly moving up from the bottom of the deep defile should see him. He could not see clearly in the dark bluffs of the river, but the outline told him that it was a warrior, and if he continued, he would pass right by him. The time had come for Bob Rivers—and he had to make the decision that was bound to mean the end of his life no matter which way he chose. Should he spend his last cartridge on himself, or use it to buy a little more time on earth after he alerted other warriors who heard the shot? There was no time left to decide. The warrior was almost upon him! He lifted the muzzle of the revolver to press against his temple, deciding on a quick death by his own hand instead of a long agonizing one in the hands of the Indians.

"Bob Rivers?" the voice, low and subdued, whispered.

Rivers choked back a sob in relief, almost unable to answer, his finger had already begun to tighten on the trigger. "Yes! God yes," he gasped when he could speak. "I'm Bob Rivers."

Luke knelt beside the wounded man. "My name's Sunday. I'm fixin' to get you outta here."

"Praise the Lord," Rivers whispered. "I thought I was a dead man for sure."

"Well, you still might be," Luke said. "Reckon you oughta pull that pistol down? If it was to happen to go off, I'da wasted a trip back here to fetch you." The hand holding the revolver dropped, suddenly limp. He had not been aware that he still held it to his temple. "How bad are you hurt?" Luke asked. "Can you walk?"

"No, I can't put any weight on it, else I'da sure as hell tried to walk outta here before now. I don't feel like I've got much strength left. I've been bleedin' a lot."

"I reckon I'll have to tote you, then," Luke said, "at least till we get back to my horse in the brush back down by the river. We're gonna have to hurry before it gets daylight, 'cause there's still thirty or forty warriors that are camped here. The rest of the village is gone—most likely to find shelter with Sittin' Bull or Crazy Horse on farther up the Powder. This bunch stayed behind to act as a rear guard in case the soldiers decided to go after the women and children, and half of 'em's fixin' to ride after your soldiers to try to get their ponies back."

"How do you know that?" Rivers asked.

"I heard 'em talkin' about it when I snuck up close to see what they had on their minds." He didn't bother to tell Rivers that before the ill-fated attack, he could have walked into the village and been welcomed. He couldn't take that chance now, since the angry warriors were out to kill any soldiers they found still alive. Even if some of them recognized him as a friend, and let him go, it was unlikely they would permit him to take the soldier out with him. "They didn't have enough ponies for all of 'em to ride after their herd," he continued. Reaching down, he extended his arm to help Rivers shift his weight onto his good leg. "Here, turn around and I'll squat down a little. I'm gonna give you a piggyback ride down this gully. Can you hold my bow in your hand and still hang on?"

Rivers said he could, and readied himself to climb on Luke's back. Once Luke had him up and had settled under the weight, he started making his way carefully down the snowy defile. "Did you run into Calvin Foster down near the river?" Rivers asked. "He went lookin' for a horse in the middle of the night."

"Was that his name?" Luke asked. "I ran across a soldier that was cut pretty much to pieces. Maybe that was Foster. I couldn't say, but from the look of it, they most likely killed him a few hours back. The blood hadn't froze yet."

Stunned, Rivers realized that it had probably been Calvin's screams that he had heard during the night. Suddenly feeling too weak to hold his head up, he let it drop on the broad shoulder of his rescuer. Aware of the sudden draining of the wounded man's strength, Luke said, "Don't drop my bow." He had no sooner said it than he heard his bow bounce off a rock and settle in the snow. Moments later, the arm around his neck relaxed and Rivers started to slide down to the ground. "Damn," Luke murmured, and quickly spun around to catch his burden. He stooped down and let Rivers's limp body fall across his shoulder while still holding his rifle in one hand. Before straightening up, he reached down and grabbed his bow with his other hand. "Damn!" he said again under the deadweight on his shoulder. "I wish to hell you'da waited till I got you back down this gully before you passed out."

It was a slow descent down the slippery defile with Luke giving thanks that Bob Rivers was not a big man. Carefully placing each foot, and bracing under his load as he stepped, he managed to make it down to the riverbank without tumbling. Successfully down from the ridge, he could not relax his vigilance, for now he was faced with the task of evading the twenty-five or thirty Cheyenne warriors gathered near the water's edge. There might even be one or two among them who knew him from prior visits to their camp. Looking up at the sky, he guessed that he had an hour or more of darkness. After that, he didn't give himself much hope of slipping away from the village without being seen. Another troubling thought came back to mind then. His horse, although a strong pony, had already been ridden hard. It was in no shape to race across the prairie carrying double. He needed another horse to carry Rivers, and there was only one place to get one. With a reluctant sigh, he lowered the unconscious man to the ground. *You better not be dead,* he thought, and bent low over him to make sure he was breathing.

Then he looked toward the group of warriors some fifty yards away, preparing to make an effort to recapture their pony herd. Judging by their actions, he guessed there was still much confusion and discussion as to the best way to accomplish the job with the few horses they had managed to save. His best chance was now, he decided, while they were still in a state of confusion. "Up on the ridge!" Luke called out in the Cheyenne tongue. "Wounded soldiers at the top of the gully, I think they have bullets left. I have no weapon."

His cries halted the discussion among the Cheyenne warriors as they all turned and strained to see the dark figure standing in the shadows of the cottonwoods that lined the river's edge. "Who speaks?" one of the warriors called back.

Thinking at once of the name the Crows had given him, Luke answered. "I am Dead Man of the Arapahos," he said, knowing that there were usually a few Arapahos as well as some Sioux in most Cheyenne villages of any size. "I am wounded in the leg, or I would go to kill them."

There was no need for further incentive for the angry warriors. They responded at once, hurrying toward the mouth of the gully. "How many?" one of them asked as they ran toward Luke.

"Two, maybe three," Luke answered, pointing with his arm up high against his face, and hoping it was too dark to see his sandy hair.

Filled with a savage desire for revenge, the

warriors took no time to talk to Luke. One who seemed to be the leader shouted to another, a young boy. "Little Sky, stay and hold the ponies." Then he led the others up the gully.

Guessing the boy was disappointed to be left behind, Luke said, "I am wounded and cannot climb up the ridge. I will hold the ponies, so you can go." In the darkness, Luke couldn't see the smile on Little Sky's face as the boy immediately followed, leaving him to guard the horses. With no time to waste, he picked the only pony with a saddle. It was a typical Indian saddle and blanket, but would be easier for Rivers than riding bareback. Had there been time, he would have tried to run the remaining horses off across the river, but he couldn't take the chance of some more warriors showing up before he was able to get it done.

When he led the pony back to Rivers, he found the wounded man trying to get up on his knees, the cold snow having brought him out of his faint. "Come on," Luke said. "I got you a horse. I know it's gonna be hard for you, but you've got to stay on him if you wanna make it back to your company."

Rivers nodded. "I'll make it," he promised, optimistic now that there was a horse to ride. Luke lifted him up in the saddle and he immediately fell forward on the horse. "I'll make it," he repeated, and wrapped his arms around the pony's neck. The horse, a shaggy sorrel, wasn't sure he liked the strange smell of the man on his back, or the one holding the rope bridle for that matter. He tossed his head repeatedly in protest, causing Luke to fear he was about to buck Rivers off, so he snatched a blanket off one of the other ponies and rubbed the sorrel's face with it. The familiar smell served to calm the pony down, enough so that Luke was able to lead it quietly downriver to the plum thicket where his paint was waiting.

"I know you're hurtin' a helluva lot," Luke said when he led his horse out of the bushes and climbed in the saddle. "I'll try to see what I can do to help you in a little bit, but we need to get as far away from here as we can. When those warriors find out there ain't no wounded soldiers at the top of that gully, they're gonna be lookin' for us in a hurry, especially the one whose pony you're ridin'."

There was no response from Bob, his only focus being directed toward holding on to that pony. Luke took the reins of Bob's horse and led him across the river, glancing back frequently, half expecting to see the suffering man slide off into the water. Thankful that he hadn't done so, he turned the paint's head south to follow a well-traveled trail along the eastern bank. He felt reasonably safe sticking to the common trail, where there were many tracks in the snow, because, like the Indian ponies, his paint was not shod. And he reasoned that the warriors would most likely storm off on the wide trail left by the retreating soldiers, assuming that he would be anxious to catch up with them. Instead of heading back to Lodge Pole Creek, however, he planned to follow the South Fork of the Powder for ten or twelve miles before cutting back to head straight for Fort Fetterman. His foremost thought was to get the wounded soldier to a place where he could get medical attention. In the meantime, he'd do what he could to ease Rivers's discomfort.

It was about an hour past sunup when the trail he had been following veered to the east, away from the river. "You doin' all right, Bob?" Luke asked.

"I'm still here," came the weak reply.

"Good. I ain't seen no sign of anybody on our trail, but just in case, I'm gonna leave this trail here—take us into the river for a little bit. The water's shallow near the bank, so we'll follow it a ways till we find a good spot to make a camp and let you rest up some."

After about a quarter of a mile up the river, he found a suitable spot in a stand of cottonwoods on the east bank. He dismounted, then helped Rivers down. "I'll have you a fire goin' in a minute," Luke said, "soon as I take care of the horses." With one arm around Luke's neck, Bob was able to hop on one foot over to a log, and stand there for a moment while Luke swept the snow off. Once he was settled, he managed to sit upright while Luke pulled the saddles off the horses and hobbled the Cheyenne pony to let them paw around in the snow to find grass. In a short time, he had a fire going close up to the cottonwood log with Bob sitting on a saddle blanket next to it, his back against the log. Luke stood over the wounded man then and said, "I reckon it's time I took a look at that leg."

By this time, the leg had swollen to the point where Luke had to cut the boot to get it off Bob's foot. Bob clenched his teeth, but could not prevent a few sharp gasps from escaping while Luke slit his trouser leg enough to reveal the twin wounds just above the knee. They looked as bad as Luke had feared, and he knew that Bob was withstanding a huge amount of pain. There were two entry wounds, but only one exit wound, which tended to confirm what Bob had thought—that his leg was broken. One of the rifle shots had gone right through his leg and was not a serious problem. The second bullet had done the damage, and had apparently struck the bone. He straightened up and gave Bob his prognosis.

"It don't look good," Luke began. "You need a doctor to try to fix that leg. I'll do what you want me to. It's your leg, but if it was mine, I'd open up those wounds and let 'em drain some of that swellin' outta there. They're tryin' to heal over, and there's one slug still in there and probably oughta come out. It'll hurt like hell, but I expect it'll feel a sight better afterward. Like I said, though, it's your leg, your call."

"I need to do somethin'," Bob admitted. "The way it's painin' me now, I don't think I can stand it till I get to a doctor."

"I sure as hell ain't no doctor," Luke repeated. "But like I said, if it was my leg, I'd open that one wound back up before it toughens up over that bullet."

Bob leaned his head back and sighed. "Go to it, then."

Luke heated his skinning knife in the fire until he felt he had killed most of whatever had accumulated on the blade. Then, after it had cooled down enough, he set to work on Bob's wounds. He worked slowly and as gently as possible while making the initial incisions, but when his patient passed out again from the pain, he went after the rifle slug in earnest. Reluctant to make the wound worse than it was already, he stopped probing when it became obvious that he was not going to be able to go deep enough to dislodge the bullet from the bone. "About all I can do," he muttered. His cutting had released a great deal of bloody fluid, however, that should ease the pain somewhat—until it built up again. But by that time, with a little luck, maybe he could get him to a doctor. Heating up his knife again, he cauterized the minor wound, but hesitated over the more serious one, thinking that it might cause greater problems for the surgeon if he cauterized it.

All done, he stood up over the unconscious man and considered his chances of recovery. In a few moments, Rivers came to, still in pain, although it was now a different kind of pain. "Damn," he forced through clenched teeth and raised his head, trying to get a look at the result of his rough operation.

"How long has it been since you ate somethin'?" Luke asked.

Bob had to think about it for a few seconds before recalling. "Night before last," he said.

"You've lost a helluva lot of blood," Luke said. "I need to find you some food to build your strength up. We've got a long ride to catch up with the army. I'm sorry I ain't got any coffee to give you, but I'll find somethin' to put in your belly." He picked up his bow and set out along the riverbank.

He knew his prospects for finding deer or antelope were pretty slim, but he saw quite a few holes in the bank that looked like muskrat lodges. He wasn't partial to muskrat, but it was nourishment, and that was the important thing at the moment. He had eaten it many times before when there was nothing else available. The meat had a taste similar to that of rabbit and the Indians seemed to enjoy it. "It'll do till I find somethin' better to hunt," he declared.

When he approached a bend in the river where a colony of muskrats appeared to have built a series of lodges, he crouched in the brush near the water and waited. The little beaverlike animals were most active early in the mornings and early evenings, but they were often about any time of day, so he waited. After a wait of approximately half an hour, he detected a stirring in a patch of lily pads, so he rose to one knee to watch it more intently. In another few moments, a muskrat appeared among the pads where it had been feeding. Luke notched an arrow and drew back his bowstring. *There's dinner,* he thought as he released the arrow.

They remained there by the South Fork of the Powder for the rest of that day. Luke made bandages out of an old shirt he carried in his saddlebag, and fashioned a splint for Bob's leg from cottonwood branches and straps made from muskrat hides, donated by several more of the little four- or five-pound critters. While the Cheyenne pony seemed well rested, Luke's paint needed the extra day before starting out on the long ride back to Fort Fetterman. As for Rivers, he appeared to be responding favorably to Luke's care, although he was still in a great deal of pain. The operation had succeeded in relieving much of the pressure around the wounds, and the nourishment served to lift his spirits enough to question his benefactor.

"How'd you know where to find me?" Bob asked while sucking the last little bit of meat from a tiny bone.

"One of the fellows in your company told me where he had seen you last," Luke replied. "He said he saw you when you got hit."

"I knew the captain wouldn't run off without sendin' somebody back to get me," Bob said, although he had thought he had been abandoned all during that long night when he and Foster had hidden in the gully. "I don't reckon I've thanked you for riskin' your neck to come after me. At least, I don't remember it if I did. I was outta my head there for a while."

Luke shrugged, but made no reply. He saw no purpose in telling Bob that Captain Egan had not sent him, but had written Rivers off as an unfortunate casualty of the botched attack on the village. Able to concentrate on something other than his wound now, Bob studied the sandy-haired man in buckskins closely. "I don't recollect ever seein' you around before you showed up in that gully last night. Tell you the truth, I thought you mighta been an angel."

"I ain't ever been mistook for one of them before," Luke said. "I'm one of the new scouts that signed on back at Fort Laramie."

42

"Well, mister, I'm mighty glad you did. What is your name, again?"

"Sunday," Luke replied. "Luke Sunday."

"Well, I'm pleased to know you," Bob said, extending his hand. "And I owe you a helluva lot." Then he repeated the name. "Sunday," he said. "Maybe you ain't no angel, but that's close enough."

Luke shrugged and shook his hand. "Maybe you'd better wait till I get you back to Fort Fetterman before you thank me too much."

The next morning, Luke helped Bob into the saddle again and they set out on a course almost directly east. Luke figured they were roughly eighty or ninety miles due west of Fort Fetterman. Although he had hoped to make better time, he found that the ride was taking too much of Bob's strength just to remain in the saddle. Added to the problem was the necessity to dismount every so often to keep stiffened joints from freezing. In Bob's case, this meant hopping for a few minutes while being supported by Luke. As a consequence, the miles covered in a day's time were far less than what Luke had hoped.

After the second day's travel, Luke set up camp when he came to a favorable spot by a creek that had frozen over. There were trees for shelter and firewood as well as cottonwood limbs to peel for food for the horses. He planned to make Rivers as comfortable as possible while he went in search of game. By this time, both men felt the need for food. Luck was with him, for he found a small herd of deer taking shelter in a grove of trees some two miles downstream from his camp. That night the two travelers feasted on fresh venison, with plenty left over to sustain them for the rest of their journey. Most of the next morning was spent in the construction of a travois, since Bob's leg was getting progressively worse, and he could no longer sit up in the saddle without excessive pain. Luke took the fresh deer hide and used it on the platform of the travois to help keep the cold from freezing the wounded man. Then he piled his blanket and buffalo coat on top of him. Satisfied that it was the best he could do for him, he set out to cover the remaining thirty miles to Fort Fetterman.

CHAPTER 3

It was late in the afternoon, in the midst of a heavy snowstorm, when Luke rode into Fort Fetterman, leading Bob's horse and travois with the half-frozen man aboard. Hard-luck fort or not, it was a welcome sight for both travelers. Stopped briefly by a picket, who thought it was an Indian approaching, Luke identified himself and then proceeded directly to the post surgery, where two orderlies took Bob off his hands. Luke hung around while the post surgeon examined Rivers to make sure he hadn't brought in a dead man. Afterward, Bob got the bad news that the leg couldn't be saved. Obviously distraught, he nonetheless took the prognosis calmly. "I'm afraid that bone is smashed," the surgeon said. "There's no way I can set it, and there are already some signs of gangrene setting in. I'm gonna have to take it off. To tell you the truth, the fact that you came in here half-frozen probably kept that leg from getting worse than it is now."

"That's hard news to swallow," Luke told Bob. "I'm sorry I couldn'ta done somethin' to save that leg, but I don't know what it woulda been."

"No call for you to apologize to me for anythin'," Bob quickly assured him. "You saved my life. If you hadn't come in that Injun camp after me, I'd be dead right now. And I'd a heap druther be a peg leg than a dead man."

"Well, I reckon I'll be goin' along now," Luke said in parting. "You take care of yourself. I'll see you after they get through sawin' on you." Seeing the glistening in Bob's eyes, he could see that the man was fighting to control his fear of the operation awaiting him, so he didn't linger, wishing to avoid Bob's embarrassment for failing to hide his emotions.

After he left the surgery, his first obligation was to take care of his horses, so he went to the stable to see if he could find some grain for them. Both were Indian ponies, used to living off grass, but grazing had been scarce, so he wanted to give them a good feeding. He was told by the sentry at the stables that grain was in short supply and there was none to be issued without the commanding officer's or the officer of the day's permission. "Fair enough," Luke said without complaint, and turned his horses out with the cavalry herd to find what grass they could under the snow. Afterward, he climbed through the back window of the stable, filled a bucket with grain, and took it to his horses. His paint showed its appreciation, having been fed oats before. The stolen sorrel didn't know what to make of the grain in the bucket at first, but consumed it gratefully after Luke poured it on the ground. Luke went back to the stable while the sentry was still out front, and returned the bucket. The paint's welfare was as important to him as his own. A man on foot in the middle of a rolling, snow-covered prairie wasn't much good for anything, he reasoned, and he felt the army owed him a bucket of oats. With his horses taken care of for the moment, he decided to go in search of coffee and maybe something to go with it.

"Well, I'll be damned," Bill Bogart blurted. "Look what the cat drug in." He grinned at Sonny Pickens and declared, "I reckon I owe you a dollar, Sonny. I swear, I never thought that jasper would show his face back here." Everyone gathered around the fire turned to see who Bogart was talking about. Not inclined to permit the tall, lean scout to quietly rejoin the group sitting around the campfire, Bogart continued. "Where the hell have you been while we was making the march back here?"

"Mindin' my own business," Luke replied flatly. His dislike for the boisterous blowhard was already growing in direct proportion to the number of times he found himself in the bully's presence. He figured that he had told Bogart and his sidekick, Sonny Pickens, what he was going to do when they had parted back at Two Moons's village. Turning his attention to one of the other scouts, he asked, "Any chance there might be some coffee left in that pot?"

"Sure," Jake Bradley responded. "If you've got a cup, help yourself." Jake was typically as easygoing a man as you would likely find in any camp, but he was not above egging Bogart on. It was apparent that Bogart had a bone in his craw when it came to the new man in the fringed buckskins, and he thought it might be entertaining to see how far Bogart might take it. No one knew much about Luke Sunday, so it might also be interesting to see if he would be buffaloed by the bigger man. It didn't take long to find out.

"Much obliged," Luke said, and dumped his saddle on the ground. He took a minute to get his cup out of his saddlebag, then filled it from the pot resting in the coals of the fire. Settling himself off to one side of the fire, next to Jake, he pulled out a strip of the venison he had fire-cured several days before and started working on it. He happened to glance in Bill Bogart's direction and had to wonder why the big man glared at him so hard. Indifferent to the blowhard, and seeking to avoid any unpleasantness, he chose not to meet his gaze. It was not enough to discourage Bogart. In fact, it served to further get his goat.

"I'd like to know just where the hell you've been," Bogart started. "You bragged about how you was gonna go back to that Sioux village and find out what happened to them two missin' soldiers. Now you show up settin' around our fire and chewin' on deer meat. Looks to me like you just went huntin'."

"Don't matter how it looks to you," Luke replied calmly, determined to enjoy the first cup of coffee he had had in a while, but he had to set Bogart straight on one thing. "Like I told you before, that was Two Moons's village, Cheyenne. They weren't Sioux."

"The hell they weren't!" Bogart blurted. "The colonel said they was—the general said they was—and I say they was. You callin' me a liar?"

Luke refused to rise to the bait for a few minutes longer, intent upon finishing his coffee. His hesitation was interpreted as weakness and served to encourage Bogart's bluster. The stocky bully threw his head back and forced a loud chuckle. "You wouldn't know one Injun from another'n if they was wearin' signs." He turned to his attentive audience then. "Well, boys, we're lucky to be ridin' with a genuine hero who was gonna charge into that Sioux camp and save some poor soldier boys. Only he musta run up on a deer instead. I hope the deer didn't put up much of a fight."

Luke took the last bite of his venison, licked his fingers, and drank the last swallow of coffee before reacting to the taunts. "You've been ridin' me pretty hard for some reason I can't understand," he said in a matter-of-fact tone. "Now I expect it's about time you got off my back, you loudmouthed son of a bitch." His frank remark brought smiles of anticipation to the faces of the other men witnessing the potential altercation. It had the effect they had all anticipated.

"What?" Bogart spewed, his face flushed, nearly matching the color of his beard. "Why, you yellow-bellied half-breed! You'll answer for that!" He lunged to his feet, and those closest to him backed quickly away to give him room. Some there had seen him riled before in barroom fights and knew what to expect. When angry, Bogart was transformed into a raging bull, literally pawing the snow-covered ground with his feet, in preparation to charge. "By God, it's time you was saddle-broke, and I'm fixin' to ride your ass into the ground."

Of the half-dozen spectators to the pending whipping, all moved back away from the fire, save one. Luke continued to sit where he was. Although his eyes measured the bull about to attack him, there was no sign of emotion on his face, one way or the other. This was not the first time he had been threatened by a formidable adversary. He had faced down a grizzly bear and a wounded buffalo bull before, as well as mountain lions in the past. All were dangerous when fighting on their terms. He had survived before in contests such as this by not fighting on their terms.

"Get on your feet," Bogart commanded, his huge fists doubled.

"Go to hell," Luke replied calmly, still sitting by the fire. "I ain't got time to fool with you."

"Why, you . . . ," Bogart sputtered, astonished by the casual response. "Get up and fight like a man, or I'll stomp your ass right where you sit." When Luke still made no move to act, Bogart lost all vestiges of patience. In full fury, he charged the seated man, aiming to deliver a kick in Luke's ribs with his heavy boot.

Quick as a cat, Luke sprang to life, still by the fire, but up on his haunches now, crouching while the lumbering bull barreled toward him like a mindless cannonball. Still he waited until Bogart drew his foot back to deliver the blow intended to crack Luke's ribs. As the boot was launched, Luke quickly sprang to the side, like a matador evading a bull's rush. He grabbed the boot with both hands and yanked as hard as he could. Caught off balance, and standing on one leg, Bogart went down hard on his back, struggling to free his captured foot while Luke dragged him toward the fire. Realizing what was about to happen, Bogart kicked awkwardly at Luke with his free foot, but it was to no avail. Luke's grip was too strong. Bogart roared out his rage as he was dragged across the campfire and was stopped in the middle of it, and held there long enough for the flames to catch his coat on fire.

When Luke finally released his captive, Bogart rolled out of the fire, yelling in pain as he crawled off in the snow. Not content with the lesson administered, Luke grabbed a flaming branch from the fire and followed on the heels of the scrambling bully. Placing his foot in the middle of Bogart's broad rear end, Luke flattened him on his face. When Bogart rolled over on his back to extinguish the flames eating his coat, Luke went to work with the burning branch. It was not heavy enough to do serious harm to the brute, being more the size of a stout whip, but it was enough to administer a sound whipping to the head and neck, leaving stinging smut-blackened stripes with every blow. When Bogart tried to roll away from the humiliating beating, he was kicked off his hands and knees to go down again to receive more from the whip. Stunned and confused, he finally lay still, facedown, with his arms wrapped around his head seeking protection from the blows.

Luke tossed his switch aside and pulled his skinning knife from his belt. He grabbed Bogart by his hair and pulled his head back, the knife pressed against the big man's forehead. Then he bent close to Bogart's ear. "I didn't ask for this, so this better be the end of it. If you come after me again, I will take your scalp."

If Bogart still retained the bluster to reply, he didn't get the chance, because at that moment Captain Egan walked up to the scouts' fire. "What in hell's going on here?" Egan demanded.

"Nothin' much," Jake Bradley quickly replied,

"just a little horseplay goin' on, is all—lettin' off a little steam."

That was explanation enough for the captain. Since they were civilian scouts, and not enlisted men, he really didn't care if they killed each other. When he moved closer to the fire, which was scattered somewhat by then, he recognized Luke Sunday. "Sunday," he said, "you're the man I'm looking for." Again, all eyes turned to stare at the rangy scout. Egan continued. "I just wanted to tell you that was a helluva thing you did, going into that hostile camp and bringing Private Rivers out alive. He's gonna lose his leg, but you saved his life—damn good work. It's a shame about Foster, but there wasn't anything you could do about that."

"No, sir," Luke replied. "If I'da been a couple hours earlier, I might have."

Egan studied the serious face for a few moments, wondering if it was ever expressive. He decided not. With a shrug of his shoulders, he spun around to return to his tent. "Well, I just wanted to let you know somebody appreciates what you did at great danger to yourself." With that he disappeared into the darkness of the parade ground, leaving a small group of chagrined scouts staring after him.

No one said anything right away, and not for a few minutes after that. Not surprisingly, Jake Bradley was the first to speak. "Well, I reckon that pretty much settles where Mr. Sunday was for the last few days." He glanced at Sonny Pickens and received a shrug in response.

There was not much anyone could say when it was apparent how wrong they had been in judging the somber scout. Bogart sat in the snow, still dazed by the violent reaction of the man he had thought to teach a lesson, his heavy woolen coat still smoking from his encounter with the fire. Almost as stunned as he, Sonny Pickens walked over to stand next to him. "Well, Bogart, I reckon you taught him a helluva lesson," he remarked facetiously while he threw a handful of snow on a small lingering flame near the big man's shoulder. Feeling he had worn out his welcome, Luke picked up his saddle and left to seek out the Crow scouts he had ridden into Fort Laramie with.

Still sitting in the snow, a trickle of blood making its way down into his beard, Bogart stared after the departing scout, mortified, his anger smoldering. "This thing ain't over," he muttered so low that only Sonny overheard him. "You'd best be mindful of your back, Injun lover."

General Crook's ill-fated campaign against the friendly Cheyenne village was enough to convince him that he would be better off waiting for spring before taking the field again. In spite of reports from Indian scouts in the weeks that followed, confirming what Luke had claimed, Crook never admitted his attack had been upon a peaceful Cheyenne camp. He maintained that he had raided Sitting Bull's camp. With his decision to wait until spring to mount another campaign, when the new grass would sustain his horses, and the ground would thaw, he released most of the scouts he had signed on. The Crows, with whom Luke was encamped, decided to return to their village. He might have gone with them, had he not received an offer from Ben Clarke to stay on at Fetterman.

The campfire incident with Bill Bogart, even after Captain Egan's compliments, served to distance Luke even further from the other white scouts. His preference to camp with the Crow scouts fed fuel to the aura of mystery that surrounded the man.

Ben Clarke was intrigued by the rangy white scout, however, so he asked him to stay on. Still needing the money, Luke accepted, in spite of his disgust for the attack waged against the friendly Cheyenne camp. There wasn't a great deal for him to do while the army was encamped there, so he spent much of his time hunting, which saved him from having to survive on the army's cooking. Since his skills with his rifle, as well as with a bow, were unsurpassed, he always had deer and antelope to share with anyone who wanted it. His biggest challenge then was how to battle the boredom of the hard-luck post that was Fort Fetterman. Unlike many of the soldiers, he felt no attraction to the "hog ranch" located near the fort with its questionable assortment of *soiled doves,* but it was the only place a man could get a drink of whiskey. And every once in a while Luke enjoyed a couple of shots of rye whiskey. It was on one of those raw wintry nights when he decided he would spend a little of his money to indulge in something to warm his belly.

It was his first visit to the so-named hog ranch, so he paused at the door to look the crowded room over. His glance shifted from the bar, across the room, to the tables in the back where a few rough-looking women were surrounded by soldiers desperate for female companionship. Something caught his eye as his gaze skimmed by the tables, and he shifted it back again to recognize Bill Bogart and Sonny Pickens seated at a table in the corner. As was his usual manner, Bogart held court over a handful of soldiers and civilian scouts in his typical boisterous way. Thinking it the wiser thing to do, Luke started to turn around and leave his drinking to another time. On second thought, however, he decided he had a hankering for a drink of whiskey now, and there was no point in letting the possibility of a confrontation stand in his way. Bogart's attention seemed to be pretty well occupied by the questionable pair of women seated at his table, so Luke made his way quietly over to the bar.

"What'll it be?" the bartender asked.

"If you've got any decent rye, I'll take a shot of that," Luke replied.

"Well, I've got some rye," the bartender responded, "but if it was decent, it wouldn't be in a place like this, would it?"

"Reckon not," Luke said, "but I'll try a shot of it, anyway." He watched while the bartender took a shot glass from a tray of once-rinsed glasses and poured his drink. About to indulge, he stopped when the glass was inches away from his lips, interrupted by the booming voice from the back table.

"Hey! Can't no Injun buy liquor in here!" Bogart roared.

Luke hesitated for only a second before tossing his whiskey back, and returning the glass to the bar. "I'll have another one," he pronounced calmly.

Startled by Bogart's outburst, the bartender took a closer look at the buckskin-clad scout as the barroom became suddenly quiet. "Hell, you ain't no Injun, are you?" When Luke made no response, the bartender spoke in Bogart's direction, "He ain't no Injun."

"The hell he ain't," Bogart insisted loudly, "and Cheyenne at that. He ain't got no business in here with white men."

Confused at this point, the bartender stood poised with the whiskey bottle suspended over

Luke's glass. "Pour it," Luke said, his voice still calm, but spoken with quiet authority. He had still not looked in Bogart's direction, but he heard the scraping of the big man's chair as it was pushed back from the table. In spite of the warning he had given Bogart when the two of them had tangled before, he knew it was going to come to this eventually as long as they were both working as scouts. Undecided, the bartender seemed frozen with the bottle hovering over the empty glass, his eyes locked on the bull-like monster storming toward the bar. Luke reached out slowly to place his finger on the neck of the suspended bottle and pressed it gently down until the whiskey flowed out to fill his glass.

"You ain't gonna drink that in here!" Bogart fumed. All the anger and humiliation that had built up in his gut was bound now for release. He grabbed for Luke's arm.

Luke easily avoided the attempt to grab him. "You're right, I ain't," he said, and tossed the whiskey in Bogart's face.

Sputtering and swearing, Bogart took a step back, frantically trying to wipe the stinging liquid from his eyes with his shirtsleeves. "Come on, you Injun-lovin' son of a bitch," Bogart challenged. "I've got somethin' to settle with you, and we might as well get to it—man to man, fists or knives."

"It ain't hardly a fair fight," one of the soldiers

in the crowd gathered around the bar exclaimed. "He ain't but about half your size, Bogart."

"That's his tough luck," Bogart replied. "He shoulda thought about that before he crossed me the first time. Now he's got to pay up." Turning back to Luke, he demanded, "Fists or knives? Choose one or the other. If you don't, I'm gonna hammer you into the floor anyway, so you might as well get ready to take a whuppin'."

Remaining deadly calm during the inflamed bully's ranting, Luke said, "Knives."

The bartender, having regained his wits, spoke up then. "Take your trouble outside. I don't need my bar all tore up."

"Outside! Take it outside," one of the soldiers directed. A sergeant, he was accustomed to ordering the enlisted men around. Equally accustomed, the crowd of soldiers took up his cry and pressed in around the two combatants, pushing them toward the door, everyone eager to see the fight. The sergeant quickly took it upon himself to referee. "It's gonna be a fair fight, no guns, and each man with one knife."

The two antagonists were literally swept out the front door by the crowd of onlookers to be deposited in the open yard of the hog ranch. "Get rid of the revolver, Bogart," the sergeant ordered. "You, too," he said to Luke. "Let somebody hold that rifle for you." Grinning at Luke, Bogart drew a large bowie knife from the scabbard, unbuckled the gun belt he wore, and handed it to Sonny Pickens. Luke looked around him at the eager faces before entrusting his Henry rifle to a young private standing on the inside of the circle. "Back up some on that side," the sergeant continued to direct. "Give 'em some room."

Like a great cat patiently watching its prey, Luke stood on one side of the circle while Bogart shifted his bowie knife back and forth from one hand to the other in an effort to intimidate his adversary. Although prepared to react instantly, the tall, rangy scout appeared to be relaxed, almost casual in his manner. It was not unlike facing an angry bear, Luke decided, except he figured the bear would be smarter than the hulking brute that was now advancing toward him, waving his knife back and forth. Bogart paused for a few moments, waiting for Luke to make a move. When he did not, Bogart interpreted the scout's lack of aggression as fear. With a roar like a charging grizzly, he suddenly lurched forward with his knife thrusting like a sword. Luke easily avoided the attack, stepping quickly aside to deliver a sharp hatchetlike chop across Bogart's arm with his knife. Bogart roared again, this time in pain as Luke's blade opened a gash in his fore-arm. He stumbled quickly away to prevent further damage.

Circling warily now around the dead-calm man in buckskins, Bogart was suddenly struck with the realization that he should never have challenged Luke to a fight with knives. The sandy-haired scout was too quick, but it was too late to opt for fists, so he was going to have to go through with his boast. He glanced down at the blood already soaking the sleeve on his right arm, and it served to spark his anger once more. After circling Luke again, feigning thrusts with his knife, Bogart lunged when he thought Luke wasn't expecting it. He was wrong again, and paid for it with a slash across his belly, causing him to disengage from the combat as before, fully aware of the hooting and hollering of the spectators.

His face still completely devoid of expression, Luke watched the big man as he stepped away from him and stuck his hand inside his torn shirt to feel his wound. He could read the angry confusion in Bogart's eyes, but it was tempered now with caution as the surly brute was faced with the prospect of being cut to pieces. Luke was also aware of a change in the crowd watching the fight. There was a perceptive shift in the cheering and encouragement for the bigger man, for it seemed apparent that Bogart was far outclassed in the art of knife fighting. They no longer chastised him for picking a fight with a smaller man, but rooted openly for him to corner the elusive scout.

Buoyed up by the crowd's encouragement, Bogart advanced upon his opponent again, but this time he did not charge blindly, pausing instead to anticipate Luke's response. This time he was able to react when Luke stepped aside to avoid the expected charge and was successful in slashing Luke's shoulder. His triumph was short-lived, however, for he received a long slash along the side of his neck in retaliation. Wincing with the pain, he tried to grab Luke's knife arm only to land on his back when Luke ducked under his outstretched arm, thrust his shoulder into his stomach, and lifted the heavy man in the air to dump him on the ground. In an instant, Luke was on top of Bogart, his knife at the stunned man's throat. "This business between you and me is done," he threatened, "or I'm fixin' to open up your throat right now."

Before Bogart had a chance to yield, a .44 revolver spoke and a bullet snapped by Luke's ear. With no time for him to think, his instincts took over and he dived off Bogart and rolled over and over to the feet of the startled young private holding his rifle. In the confusion of the moment, the crowd of spectators scrambled for safety as another bullet kicked up dirt beside Luke. Luke managed to grab his rifle before the private ran for his life. Turning toward the source of the gun-shots, he discovered Sonny Pickens, pausing to take better aim for another shot. Without consciously thinking about it, Luke cocked and fired the bullet that hit Sonny in the heart a split second before Sonny could squeeze the trigger.

"Yeah, that's why I came lookin'
Clarke had already heard the complai.
both Major Potter and Bill Bogart, an
account of the killing at the hog ranch. He i.
feeling there was another version of the incide
so he had made it a point to talk to a Sergea.
McKim, who claimed to have been a witness to
the fight. "You ain't makin' it easy for me to keep
you on the job," Clarke commented.

"If you're talkin' about that little set-to at the
hog ranch last night," Luke replied, "I didn't start
it. And it wouldn't have been much more'n a
little knife fight if that sidekick of Bogart's hadn't
tried to kill me. He didn't leave me much choice."

"Well, that's pretty much what Sergeant McKim
told me," Clarke said, "and that's the only reason
I talked Major Potter outta sendin' a detail of
soldiers to slap some irons on you and haul you
off to the guardhouse. It's a damn good thing I'm
in good with General Crook. That's the only
reason you're still on the payroll and not in the
guardhouse." He didn't tell Luke that he had
convinced the general that Sunday was the best
scout he had, Indian or civilian.

"When I saw you ridin' along the bluffs, I
figured you was comin' to fire me," Luke said. "I
figured I'd be movin' on before a bunch of
soldiers came lookin' for me."

"You're lucky the army has got more important
things on its mind right now than a little shootin'

66

As startled as anyone, Bogart rolled over on his
belly and prepared to get to his feet, but was
stopped on one knee by the sight of his friend
Sonny, sprawled flat on his back. Without
thinking, he reached for the pistol that he no
longer wore, realizing then that it lay on the
ground beside Sonny's body. Fearing that he was
next, he jerked his head around and met the deadly
gaze of Luke Sunday and a Henry rifle aimed at
him. "You kilt him," Bogart blurted.

"Just as dead as hell," Luke replied soberly.
"Now I reckon it's up to you to decide if you're
wantin' to go with him."

"I ain't got no gun," Bogart protested. He
figured his only chance was to get his pistol and
get off a shot before Luke expected it. "If it's
gonna be a fair fight, you have to let me get my
gun."

"I'm tired of playin' your little games," Luke
said. "You either leave that pistol where it lies and
walk away from here, or I'm gonna shoot you
down where you stand."

The drama playing out now was too much an
attraction for the frightened spectators, and they
gradually drifted cautiously closer with the
prospect of witnessing a second killing. Finally
one of them had the courage to speak. The
sergeant who had sought to referee the knife
fight said, "This wasn't meant to be no killin'."
He aimed his plea at the solemn scout holding

63

the rifle on Bogart. "A few cuts and scratches, and maybe somebody gets slit good, then somebody calls, 'Enough,' and it's over. It don't call for killin' anybody."

Luke didn't take his eye off Bogart as he answered the sergeant. "He tried to kill me—twice—so I shot him. And I'm gonna shoot this one if he doesn't walk away and leave me alone."

Turning back to Bogart then, the sergeant said, "You'd best do what the man says, Bogart. One killin's been enough."

Fearing for his life moments before, Bogart now felt that the sergeant had saved his bacon, so there was a return of some of his bluster in an effort to save face before the spectators. "He ain't got no stomach for facing me with a gun in my hand," he boasted.

"Don't be a damn fool," the sergeant said. "He'll shoot you down, just like he said."

"Yeah, Bogart," one in the crowd said, "he'll shoot you down just like he did your friend." The comment was repeated by several of the other soldiers. The fact that Pickens had tried to kill Luke first seemed to have been forgotten.

Relieved to have the opportunity to walk away with his life, Bogart said, "Well, I don't like it, but I ain't willin' to commit suicide if I ain't gonna get a fair chance."

"That's using your head," the sergeant replied. "You go on. We'll take care of your friend's body.

64

xpect the officer of the day will be lookin' is to see what must be done about it. He's bo o have heard the shots."

"There'll be somethin' done about it," Bog spat in one final show of bravado. "I'll guarar that."

"I'll handle this," the sergeant said as Bog got to his feet and walked away. Then he turn to Luke and said, "I expect you'd best come w me."

Luke slowly shook his head, then replied, expect not, Sergeant. I reckon I'll be on my way. With his rifle cradled in his arms, ready to fire if anyone threatened to stop him, he walked through the ring of onlookers to the paint pony at the end of the hitching rail. Once in the saddle, he slid the Henry in his saddle sling and, urging his horse with his heels, loped off into the night.

"You lookin' for me?"

Startled by the sudden voice behind him, Be Clarke couldn't help jumping. "Damn!" h exclaimed when he turned around to find th sandy-haired rifleman standing on the side of th deep gully. "You scared the hell outta me." Whe his words were met with the usual stoic expre sion from the unemotional scout, he continue "Yeah, I was lookin' for you where I thought yo had a camp in the bluffs, but you were gone."

"I moved it last night," Luke said.

65

between two civilians off post," Clarke said. "You're still on the payroll, but there's a lot of folks that think you shouldn't be. I'm gonna send you with a column of wagons to pick up supplies at Medicine Bow. I figure it might be a good idea if you were gone for a couple of weeks to let things between you and Bill Bogart simmer down a little bit."

It was not with a great deal of enthusiasm that he greeted an assignment to accompany a wagon train leaving the fort to pick up supplies at Medicine Bow on the Union Pacific Railroad. On the other hand, he could see that it was a wise decision on Ben Clarke's part. He wasn't satisfied that his trouble with Bill Bogart was over. It was bound to come bubbling to the surface again, but he felt sure there would be no challenges from the bully for a fair fight of any kind. Next time it would likely be a bullet in the back. If he hadn't needed the money, he would have struck out for some other part of the country.

One of the other scouts retained by Clarke was also sent with the wagons, Jake Bradley. Bradley was the only one of his scouts that had no real animosity toward Luke, as far as he knew. There was really no need for scouts at all. The trail south to Medicine Bow was well known by the teamsters, but it was a matter of routine to send scouts with every expedition.

On a chilly morning in early spring, the train, consisting of twenty-five wagons with canvas, set out from Fort Fetterman. A fifteen-man detail headed by Lieutenant James Findley was assigned to escort the wagons. Another wagon train set out the same morning, this one bound for Fort Laramie and accompanied by Bill Bogart, and was a far easier trip than the road to Medicine Bow. "Looks like ol' Bogart got his pick of the trains," Jake said, well aware of Bogart's favored status with the major. "I ain't surprised you got the trip to Medicine Bow, but what the hell has he got against me?" The Medicine Bow Road was a rigorous test for horses and men alike, crossing the Laramie Hills, four river crossings, and miles of canyons and treeless flats. Luke listened to Jake's complaints, but voiced none of his own. He was at home in all parts of the territory. Some just took a bit more effort to survive in. As far as he was concerned, all life was like the different parts of the country—sometimes it was easy, sometimes hard. Still, he felt it was part of his job as a scout to advise the lieutenant, so he did.

"I expect it ain't necessary to tell you that it's better'n a fifty percent chance some of those mountain passes are still piled up with snow," he told Findley. "It's awful early in the spring yet. You might wanna take another way around the Laramies."

As his column formed up, Lieutenant Findley

paused to consider Luke's advice. He had never ridden with either of his two scouts, so he was not inclined to put complete faith in the pair until he had more experience with them. Based on what little he knew about Luke Sunday and Jake Bradley—one a potential troublemaker, the other a lackadaisical ne'er-do-well—he was inclined to stick to well-known trails. "We're going to follow the common road to Medicine Bow. What I want from you two is to range a mile or two ahead, so you can let me know if there's anything for me to be concerned with. I don't expect any trouble, but I damn sure don't wanna be surprised by some stray hostile raiding party. Understood?"

The lieutenant's orders were fine by Luke. He merely nodded his understanding. Jake took it upon himself to speak for them both. "Sure thing, Lieutenant. We'll keep our eyes open. You never can tell, what with the weather lettin' up a little bit now, some of Sittin' Bull's boys mighta snuck back figurin' to catch us when we ain't expectin' it."

Findley favored Jake with a patient smile. He didn't expect to meet up with any trouble this close to Fort Fetterman and Fort Laramie. "Just see that you do," he said. He stared at the broad back of the sandy-haired scout named Sunday as the two men went to their horses. He didn't know much about the man except the fact that he had shot one of the other scouts, but Captain Egan had praised him for rescuing one of his men after the Powder River raid. He had also heard of an altercation where Sunday had dragged another scout into a campfire and threatened to kill him. So he wasn't sure if he had a dependable scout or a troublemaker along on this detail. One thing for sure, he decided, the man seemed to have no friends in the entire regiment. He sighed and returned his attention to getting the wagons under way.

Findley was wrong about Luke's lack of friends. He had one friend in the camp, one eternally grateful to him. Luke had gone by the hospital the night before to see how Bob Rivers was getting along. Bob had been in good spirits in spite of the stump where his right leg had been. "I'm already gettin' around pretty good on these crutches," he had said, "and the carpenter is workin' on a peg leg for me. I'll be dancin' a jig over at the hog ranch by the time you get back from Medicine Bow. Wait till them gals see me spin around on my peg leg." Bob's comment caused a sight seldom seen by any of the soldiers or scouts at the fort when a smile of amusement formed on Luke's ever-serious face. When he got up to leave, Bob had grabbed his sleeve and his expression sobered. "Don't think for a minute that I ain't grateful for what you done for me. I'll never forget it, and that's a fact."

Suddenly uncomfortable, Luke had nodded, his

somber expression returning. "Well, take care of yourself," he had muttered, and quickly took his leave.

As Lieutenant Findley had anticipated, there was no trouble encountered on the trip to Medicine Bow Station as far as hostile Indians were concerned. As Luke had cautioned, however, there was still heavy snow in the canyons of the Laramie Mountains, which made for a difficult passage, even for empty wagons. It caused Findley to give some thought to the return trip to Fort Fetterman with loaded wagons. The going proved somewhat easier once the hills were behind them and they passed through the Little Medicine country. The last forty miles took them across the Laramie Plains and involved four difficult river crossings, poor grass, and no wood for their campfires. There was a great deal of complaining from the army teamsters and cavalry troops by the time the column reached Medicine Bow just before noon.

It had been a while since Luke had been to Medicine Bow. The last time the town had been little more than a shipping point on the Union Pacific Railroad. This time there was considerable growth in the station in the form of saloons, bawdy houses, a general store, and an army warehouse. There were not many permanent residents in Medicine Bow, and most of them worked for the railroad, or managed the local business establishments. Standing apart, some several hundred yards from the freight depot, Luke noticed a lone wagon, obviously encamped, and a team of two horses hobbled nearby. Close by the wagon, a man and a woman sat before a campfire. The scene struck Luke as peculiar. *Maybe they're waiting to catch an eastbound train,* he thought, *after they found out they couldn't make it in this hostile land.* He paid it no further mind while he pulled his paint pony to the side and watched the troopers prepare to bivouac while the lieutenant went to the depot to arrange for receipt of the supplies.

"Lieutenant, sir," Sergeant Branch, the ranking enlisted man, said, as Findley started toward the door. "Some of the men are wantin' to know if it's all right to visit one of the saloons to cut some of the dust in their throats. It's been a long, dry ride for the last two days."

Findley paused, not surprised by the question, but somewhat amazed that any of them had money to spend. Although the men had been scheduled to receive their pay a day before leaving Fort Fetterman, he had ordered a delay in their payday until the detail returned there. Consequently, he felt assured that the men would have very little money to spend on whiskey, or anything else, and there would be little danger of desertion, always a concern with troops stationed at Fort Fetterman with its lack of creature comforts. In addition, the delayed payday was incentive to return to their base. Giving Branch a stern look, he said, "All right, Sergeant, but you can tell them anybody not fulfilling their duty might find themselves making the trip back in chains, walking behind the last wagon. I want these wagons loaded first, a guard detail set for tonight, and the detail ready to roll after first light in the morning."

"Yes, sir," Branch replied. "You don't have to worry about that. I'll see that your orders are carried out. I doubt if anybody's got the price of more'n one or two drinks, anyway."

Standing close by, and hearing the conversation between the lieutenant and his sergeant, Jake Bradley turned to Luke and grinned. "That don't sound like a bad idea," he said. "I reckon I've got enough to buy a couple of drinks myself. Whaddaya say?"

Luke gave the idea a moment's thought before replying, "I reckon, maybe one or two, but not till after supper." Unlike the soldiers in Lieutenant Findley's detail, he and Jake had received their pay on the scheduled payday. His hesitation was due to his natural tendency to hold on to his money to ensure the ability to purchase things he needed to survive, like coffee beans and cartridges for his rifle. He was not completely sure he liked scouting for the army, especially after his first engagement at Two Moons's village. And he was convinced that he might quit his job if he continued to witness a similar lack of good judgment on the part of other officers in command. If that happened, he was going to need his money.

"I reckon I can wait till then," Jake conceded reluctantly. His attention turned then to the wagon parked near the railroad tracks. "I wonder what those folks are waitin' for. I can't tell a helluva lot from here, but the woman don't look too bad, does she? She looks pretty young, too. They look like they've been travelin' a ways, and there ain't nobody with 'em. Sure seems strange." Not really interested, Luke glanced briefly at the couple by the wagon before turning away, intent on watering his horse before the teamsters and the cavalry troops muddied the one available creek with their horses.

John Burnett looked past Lieutenant Findley to see the man and woman approaching his office. He paused then in the process of verifying the paperwork on the shipment of supplies to be loaded to inform Findley, "Here's some folks that's been waitin' to talk to you, Lieutenant," he said, and nodded toward the open door. Findley turned to follow Burnett's gaze, then stood waiting.

"Lieutenant," Burnett said when the man and

his wife entered the small office, "this here's David Freeman and his missus."

Findley extended his hand to Freeman. "Lieutenant James Findley," he said, then nodded toward the woman. "Ma'am," he acknowledged. "Did you want to talk to me?"

"Yes, sir, I do," Freeman replied. "I'm hoping you'll let me hitch on to your wagon train when you head back north. Mr. Burnett said you'd most likely be pulling outta here in the morning."

"Well, I expect that's so," Findley said. "We'll be heading out in the morning, right enough." He looked the man and his wife over carefully. "Where is it you're heading?" Before Freeman could answer, Findley asked, "How'd you get this far by yourselves?"

"We weren't by ourselves when we got to Medicine Bow," Freeman replied. "We came here with four other wagons, all of us heading for the Yellowstone and the Gallatin Valley, but the others turned back, decided it was too dangerous to try to get through."

"But you didn't," Findley said. "Maybe it would have been smart to listen to your friends and go on back to where you came from."

"Cheyenne," Freeman said. "There ain't no future for us back there. The piece of land I was trying to farm was dry as a bone. The little creek we had all but dried up. We had to get out or starve. I got word from my brother in Montana

Territory and he said there were some fellows building a new town, called Coulson, just starting up on the Yellowstone. It's gonna be an important town for certain—just right for a steamboat stop, and the railroad is coming that way before long, too. My brother said him and a few others were moving east to get closer to the town. According to him the river flats around there are fertile and prime for farming, and he said there ain't no real trouble with the Indians there anymore."

Findley paused to think about that for a few moments. Maybe the man was right, as far as Indian trouble was concerned. The army, and General Crook's command in particular, was making ready to take to the field again, in concert with two other columns, to entrap the Sioux and Cheyenne in the Powder River country. Maybe this town of Coulson that Freeman referred to was far enough removed from the Powder, Tongue, and Big Horn to be out of harm's way. The problem for a lone wagon like Freeman's was to make the journey through the Powder River Valley safely, so he didn't have to ask what Freeman was looking to him for. "I understand why you're trying to get to the Yellowstone," he told him. "But this detail, this wagon train, is only going from here to Fort Fetterman. Now, I have no objection if you want to go with us that far, but I must warn you that you'll be on your own from Fort Fetterman on. There will be no troops available to escort you to Montana."

Now it was Freeman's turn to pause and consider that. He had hoped that the lieutenant might suggest the possibility of some military protection beyond Fort Fetterman. A few days before, he had been determined to continue, even after the other wagons turned back. Now he was not so confident that it was the safest thing to do. He glanced at Mary Beth and found an expression of genuine concern on her face. "Well, sir," he said to Findley, "I 'preciate what you're telling me. I reckon I'll talk it over with my wife before we decide."

"You're kinda gambling on that land still being available, aren't you?" Findley said.

"Well, maybe a little, but my brother is hoping to buy up as much of that land as possible, and he'll have a place for us."

"You folks must be well fixed for finances," the lieutenant remarked.

"My brother is," Freeman was quick to reply. "He was one of the lucky ones at Last Chance Gulch up at Helena. Mary Beth and I don't have but a little to make a start."

"I wish I could promise you an escort to the Yellowstone," Findley said, talking mainly to Freeman's wife, "but you're welcome to go with us to Fort Fetterman."

"We'll talk it over," Freeman said, "and if we

decide to keep going, we'll be ready to roll in the morning when you pull out."

"Good enough," the lieutenant said, and walked with them to the door.

The discussion between David and Mary Beth Freeman started as soon as they were outside the station door. With no knowledge of the country beyond the North Platte River, the young couple found it a difficult decision to make. Married just eighteen months, they had never been faced with a choice that might mean the difference between life and death, so their deliberations continued until bedtime that night. With Mary Beth's assurances that she was willing to risk facing whatever dangers might lie beyond Fort Fetterman, David decided to prepare his wagon to roll at first light. "There's a chance for a good life ahead of us with your brother and the others," Mary Beth said, "and a dead certainty that there's nothing behind us in Cheyenne."

CHAPTER 4

Roll call proved Lieutenant Findley correct in his speculation that his men were too short of cash to finance any serious drunks. Every man was accounted for, even the teamsters, with only the few cuts and bruises usually associated with the rough saloons in Medicine Bow. Among those who did have enough money to buy more than a couple of drinks was Jake Bradley. Complaining of a bad head, he pulled his horse up beside Luke's paint to wait for the wagon train to pull out of Medicine Bow. "I swear," he commented painfully, "that bartender musta put some kinda poison in that whiskey, as bad as my head hurts this mornin'. How come you ain't sufferin' like me?" He paused a moment when he encountered the disinterested gaze from the ever-stoic scout. "Where were you last night, anyway?" It occurred to him that he had not seen Luke since he joined a group of the army teamsters at a back table.

"I went to bed," Luke replied indifferently.

Jake shook his head in mock amazement. "I swear, you're a regular hell-raiser, ain't you?"

"I had a drink," Luke responded dryly. "That's all I wanted." In Jake's opinion, there was something untrustworthy about a man who didn't like to get drunk every now and then, and he said as much. To which, Luke responded, "I got things I need to buy with my money, and one of 'em ain't a head like you're totin' on your shoulders this mornin'."

"Damn," Jake replied with a forced chuckle, "next thing I know, you might take up preachin'."

"I might," Luke said in the emotionless tone Jake was becoming accustomed to, "if somebody offers to pay me to do it." He turned the paint's head toward the column of wagons that had now begun to pull out, and nudged the Indian pony into a comfortable lope. Jake sighed and followed.

Luke returned David Freeman's nod when the two scouts rode past his wagon. He had not given the couple in the wagon much thought beyond wondering what they were doing in Medicine Bow. It appeared now that they were going to Fort Fetterman with the train. It didn't concern him, so he didn't waste further speculation on it as he loped past on his way to the head of the column.

"You know a better way back to Fetterman than hauling these wagons through those mountain passes?" Lieutenant Findley asked when the two scouts pulled up beside him.

"The only easier way is to go around those mountains," Luke answered, "but it'll be a slight longer trip."

"How much longer?" Findley asked.

"Two days, maybe," Luke said.

Findley took a moment to decide. He wasn't

sure how much he could rely on the new scout's knowledge of the country. Deeming it better to trust that the wagons could make it back the way they had come, he decided not to venture farther west in an effort to bypass about fourteen miles of canyons and peaks. "We'll go back the way we came," he told his two scouts, and sent them out ahead of the column. It was all the same to Luke.

The column proceeded with little trouble through the Little Medicine country, slowed down only by the multiple river crossings. Trailing along behind the army wagons, which were pulled by four-horse teams, David and Mary Beth Freeman were able to maintain their position with their two horses. Once, however, at a particularly difficult crossing, they were hesitant to commit their team to the water after the army wagons had churned up the riverbed so badly that their wheels were sunk almost to the hubs. It was at this time that they had their first encounter with the sandy-haired scout dressed in animal hides.

Watching the river crossing with minimal interest, Luke sat his horse on the far bank while the teamsters, encouraged, complained, and cursed the horses as they struggled to pull their loads to the other side. He let his gaze wander to the small farm wagon, pulled by two horses, that was waiting its turn to enter the water. His advice had not been solicited by the lieutenant as to the best place to ford the river. Instead, Findley had chosen to ford where wagon trains had always crossed this particular river. If Luke's opinion had been asked, he would have suggested a crossing about fifty yards upstream where the river bottom was firmer. Seeing David Freeman hesitating now as the last army wagon descended the bank to follow those before it, Luke guided his horse toward the smaller wagon.

"I ain't so sure my horses can pull us across," Freeman volunteered when Luke came up beside him.

"I ain't, either," Luke replied. His dry comment did little to encourage Freeman to act. Both husband and wife stared at the rangy scout, the uncertainty shining in their faces. "Follow me," Luke said, and started upstream along the riverbank. When Freeman hesitated, Luke looked back and prompted, "Come on." David hauled back on the reins and pulled his team around to follow the man on the paint Indian pony, not sure if he should or not.

About fifty yards upstream, Luke wheeled his horse to a stop on a sandy stretch of the bank. "Just follow me and you won't have no trouble," he said, then guided the paint into the water.

David followed and found the crossing to be much easier than he had anticipated. "Why didn't the soldiers cross here?" he asked Luke when he drove past him.

" 'Cause they're soldiers, I reckon," Luke replied. "That's the same crossin' they've always used. That's the way soldiers do everythin'."

Once his wagon was up on the opposite bank, David called after the scout, now riding back toward the head of the column. "Much obliged." Grateful to the quiet man for making a crossing that had promised to be difficult much less stressful, David was drawn to observe Luke Sunday more closely during the remaining days of the journey to Fort Fetterman. "He's a strange one," David remarked to his wife. "He doesn't talk very much, to anybody, but when the lieutenant wants to know something, he always asks Sunday, instead of the other one."

"He may not be very sociable," Mary Beth said, "and he looks like a wild Indian, but he certainly came to help us cross that river. I know we don't know the man very well, but the soldiers seem to trust him." She paused. "As much as you can trust any drifter, I guess."

"I was thinking how valuable a man like him might be to come along as a guide to the Yellowstone if the army decides they can send a few soldiers to escort us through the Powder River country. He sure seems to know the land." He didn't express it to Mary Beth, but he was really thinking that Lieutenant Findley might have spoken truthfully when he said there would be no troops spared to escort them beyond Fort Fetterman.

● ● ●

The trip back to Fetterman was uneventful as anticipated with the exception of a light snowfall in the Laramie Mountains that added to the already poor conditions of the canyon floors. The layer of snow had to be broken by the cavalry escort before the wagon teams could plow through the frozen slush beneath. The trip of about eighty-five miles from Broken Bow required over a week to complete, two full days of which were spent on the fourteen-mile stretch through the mountain passes. Food rations were depleted when they were still a couple of days short of their destination, but fortunately Luke and Jake tracked a small herd of deer that had sought shelter in a narrow pine-covered ravine. They were lucky enough to kill three of the herd before they scattered up the mountainside. The carcasses were a welcome sight for the hungry soldiers, and Luke made sure to cut a sizable portion of the fresh meat to take to the couple in the farm wagon.

"I thank you for seeing that we got some of this meat," David Freeman said when Luke walked the venison over to their wagon. Luke merely nodded in reply as he handed the rump portion to him, turning at once to return to his campfire.

"Yes, thank you," Mary Beth called after him. "That was very thoughtful of you, and we appreciate it." Luke turned long enough to nod in her direction, then continued on his way.

As he stood beside his wife, holding the generous chunk of venison, David was prompted to chuckle. "He's a sociable cuss, ain't he?"

"Sometimes I want to shiver when he looks at me," Mary Beth commented, "with those eyes that look like they're dead."

Her remark reminded David of something he had heard from one of the soldiers and caused him to chuckle once again. "You know what the Crow Indians call him? Dead Man, that's their name for him."

"Well, that's a good name for him. That man frightens me," Mary Beth said. Then after a moment, she added, "But I'm certainly glad to get the meat." After another pause, she reflected, "I guess I could have offered him some of our coffee."

The wagon train rolled into Fort Fetterman in time for supper on the night of April 15, where they found the post busy making preparations for a June campaign against the hostiles. His mission completed, Luke went immediately to find Colonel Reynolds, assuming that he was still assigned to the colonel's troop. He found the colonel's headquarters tent, but not the colonel. Instead, he found Bill Bogart and another scout, a man called Wylie, whom Luke had had very little contact with. They were standing leisurely by a campfire, drinking coffee, and talking to a major Luke had never met. Of slight build, almost dainty in fact, the officer stood in sharp contrast to the hulking Bogart, who glowered darkly at Luke when he stepped down from the saddle. "This here's Sunday," Wylie commented dryly, as if he had been the topic of their discussion with the major.

The officer looked Luke up and down as if evaluating him. "I'm Major Potter," he said. "I'm in command of this troop now. I think Ben Clarke wanted to talk to you as soon as you got back."

Luke nodded thoughtfully. Clarke had mentioned a Major Potter, but Luke wasn't interested enough to wonder why Colonel Reynolds was no longer in command. "You happen to know where I can find Ben Clarke?" he asked.

"Where he's usually at," Bogart quickly answered for the major, his tone thick with sarcasm, "pretty damn close to General Crook."

Luke ignored the caustic remark, looked at Major Potter, and said, "Much obliged. I'll go find him." He stepped back up in the saddle.

As soon as he was out of earshot, Bogart commented to Potter, "I'm sure surprised he even showed his face around here again after he killed Sonny Pickens and what he done over on the Powder when we fought them Sioux."

Potter stared after the man a few moments longer before speaking. "Captain Egan seems to think Sunday's a hero for going into that camp after Private Rivers."

"Yes, sir," Bogart said. "I've heard talk about that, about how he slipped into that camp and saved Rivers, but I think them Sioux was long gone by the time he got there. Besides, I expect if them Injuns was Cheyenne, like he claims, he wouldn'ta had to sneak in to bring that boy out. And I was there when Colonel Reynolds was tryin' to sneak up on that village. Captain Egan's hero was tryin' to tell ever'body that it was a Cheyenne village, when the colonel and ever'body else knew it was a Lakota camp, full of rifles and ammunition. Ain't that right, Wylie?" He paused for Wylie's nod of affirmation. "He's hooked up with Sittin' Bull and that crowd of Sioux somehow, 'cause he sure acted like he didn't want us to attack. And I ain't heard nobody say they saw him shoot at any of them Injuns." He paused again to judge the effect his words might have had on the major. "I can tell you I'm gonna damn sure watch my back around him," he continued.

Potter seriously considered Bogart's condemnation of the man. Having just been given command of the troop, after Colonel Reynolds's reprimand and relief of command, Potter was not interested in having any source of friction under him. Reynolds had been censured and threatened with court-martial for his failures in his attack on that village on the Powder, and the damning fact that he had left wounded men behind when he withdrew. He formed a picture of Luke, dressed head to toe in animal skins, his sandy hair the only thing that prevented his passing for an Indian. He had come into the job as a scout with a group of Crows, but could it be possible his sympathies, as well as his allegiance, lay with the Sioux? Maybe he might be a threat to warn his Sioux friends of an impending attack. *That wouldn't be good,* Reynolds thought. *So why risk it?* He decided then to reject Luke as a scout, for it was obvious that Bogart and Wylie didn't trust the man.

Ben Clarke glanced up from his camp, about thirty yards from General Crook's tent, to see the rangy scout approaching his fire. He waited for Luke to dismount before greeting him. "I saw you come ridin' in—took you a little bit longer than I figured. Have any trouble?"

"None worth speakin' of," Luke answered. "There was a lot of snow in the mountains. That slowed us down, else we'da most likely been here two days ago." He moved up close to the fire and squatted on his heels. "A major back there—I done forgot his name—said you wanted to see me."

"Major Potter," Clarke said. "He took over for Colonel Reynolds. Yeah, I wanna send you back to Red Smoke's village to bring those Crow scouts back here. This parade is gonna be ready to move in about four days, so they need to be here now."

Luke nodded his understanding. "Oughta be

back here in two days," he said. Red Smoke's camp was on the North Platte, about halfway between Fort Fetterman and Fort Laramie. It would take him but one day to reach it.

"Good," Clarke said. "Get yourself somethin' to eat tonight, and start out at first light in the mornin'. The general wants to get all those back that went home after the battle on the Powder."

"I'll tell 'em," Luke said. "It'll be up to them whether they wanna come back or not."

"You even think like an Injun," Clarke commented with a chuckle. "Tell 'em they'll be paid and supplied with ammunition."

Luke shrugged. "I'll tell 'em," he said, well aware of an Indian's tendency to change his mind if the day didn't suit him.

"Tell 'em there'll be many horses to capture," Clarke said. "That oughta bring 'em."

"I'll tell 'em." He got up to leave.

As he led his horse back toward the ordnance warehouse, he saw the settler, David Freeman, on his way to the general's tent. He couldn't help wondering what the man and his wife planned to do, now that they had reached Fort Fetterman. The thought didn't occupy his mind very long. He was hungry and ready to make his camp and roast some of the venison he had left.

Freeman noticed the tall, lean man leading the paint pony toward the edge of the compound and offered a brief wave of his hand, but Luke was too far past to notice the greeting. The thought occurred to David that the solemn cavalry scout seemed always to be alone, even when in the midst of hundreds of soldiers. His thoughts returned to the purpose of his visit to the general's command post as he approached the gathering of officers assembled to confer with General Crook.

Freeman was received politely by the general and his staff, but the meeting was brief. Crook offered his sympathy for Freeman's plight. However, Freeman's request for a small escort for him and his wife was swiftly denied. As part of the three-pronged campaign to settle the hostile Indian problem, Crook told him that he could not spare a single man to see the couple safely to the Yellowstone. It was a bitter pill for David to swallow, but one he had been warned to expect. There was no one to blame but himself for being stranded in this desolate outpost on the North Platte River. He could have turned back with the others at Medicine Bow. Walking back to his wagon to give Mary Beth the bad news, he anguished over what he should do. One thing he was sure of, they could not stay there at Fort Fetterman, but the thought of returning to the bone-dry piece of land near Cheyenne was out of the question as well. He was prone to pushing on to find the new town of Coulson, but he could not in good conscience subject Mary Beth to a journey that might be filled with danger.

His despair was evident to the point where Mary Beth guessed the outcome of his audience with the general by the look on his face. "He turned us down," she stated when he squatted next to the fire and warmed his hands. He nodded in reply. "Well, what are we gonna do?" she asked.

"I don't know," he answered. "We're stuck between a rock and a hard place. All these soldiers are fixin' to march outta here soon, and he said he couldn't spare a man to help us."

A determined woman, Mary Beth considered their plight for a few moments before asking, "Do you think you could find Coulson?" She was of a mind to continue their quest, equally reluctant as her husband to return to their failed efforts in Cheyenne.

"I don't know," David replied after some hesitation. "I reckon anybody could find the Yellowstone River from here. Just by heading north, you'd have to run into it somewhere. I don't have any idea where the Gallatin Valley is, or that little town they're talking about. What I'm more worried about is whether or not there are hostile Indians between here and there, and which way to go to avoid running into them."

Mary Beth studied her husband's face carefully. Clearly he was uncertain about what they should do. She could not be critical of him because he was not stalwart in his conviction. He had no knowledge of this country or the Native Americans who dwelt there. But what would they do? "We'll think about it for a day or two before we decide what is best," she said. "You said the horses should be rested for a couple of days, anyway. Maybe when they're rested enough to move on, we'll have decided." She looked at him and smiled encouragingly.

As he had promised, Luke was back from Red Smoke's village after two days, accompanied by only a few warriors, far short of the number that had originally volunteered. Ben Clarke was certain the Crow scouts would eagerly embrace the opportunity to fight their old enemies, lured by the prospect of capturing many of the Sioux and Cheyenne horses. Spotting Luke Sunday ride in with only four Crow warriors, Clarke went directly to meet him.

"Looks to me like all them Crow scouts decided they didn't have the same fire they showed before," Clarke remarked, his disappointment obvious. "What the hell happened to the rest of 'em?"

"They're still comin'," Luke said. "When I got to Red Smoke's camp, most of the men were gone huntin'. Some of the younger boys spotted a small herd of buffalo north of their village, so they couldn't pass up the chance to pack away that much meat. I found 'em about five miles west of the Lightning River. They'll finish the hunt and meet you where Fort Reno used to be on the Powder River."

Clarke smiled, relieved. Then he changed the subject abruptly. "You still think that was a Cheyenne camp Colonel Reynolds attacked on the Powder?"

"I don't think it, I know it was," Luke replied, surprised that Clarke asked the question. He was still amazed by the colonel's insistence that he had struck Sitting Bull's village.

"Reynolds is sure it was a Sioux camp," Clarke said. "So are his officers, and Bill Bogart said it was. He's got an arrow with Lakota markings on it to boot."

Luke slowly shook his head. "I ain't sayin' there weren't a few lodges of Lakotas in the camp, but it was Two Moons's village. I talked to Old Bear, so I'm tellin' it to you straight. There was no sense in attackin' that village. All it did was to send them to join up with Sittin' Bull and Crazy Horse."

"All right," Clarke said with a weary sigh, knowing that Luke was telling him the truth. "It don't make no matter who's right, 'cause we'll be fightin' all of 'em, anyway, Sioux, Cheyenne, and some Arapaho." He decided to quit stalling before giving Luke the bad news. "Ain't no sense in beatin' around the bush," Clarke continued. "You won't be ridin' with Major Potter's troops when we pull out. He's decided he don't need nobody but Bogart and Wylie and some of the Crow scouts."

A knowing smile crept slowly across Luke's face. "Bogart and Wylie, huh? I expect those two mighta had somethin' to do with it." He turned to loosen the girth on the paint, wondering what Clarke was getting at.

"Captain Egan wanted you to ride with his company," Clarke went on, "but Potter told him you were a troublemaker and he didn't want trouble between his scouts."

"Don't make much difference to me," Luke said, "long as they're payin' me, I'll ride with somebody else."

Clarke grimaced and shook his head, reluctant to say what he had come to say. "Well, that's just it. They said there wasn't no use to keep you on, 'cause they had enough Crow scouts ridin' out front, lookin' for them Sioux camps."

Although Luke was normally unemotional to the point of indifference, the impact of Clarke's words was evident on the face of the imperturbable scout. "Can't I ride with the Crow scouts?" he asked. He was not that eager to accompany the expedition, but he earnestly wanted the money.

"I'm sorry, Sunday, I'm gonna have to let you go. We've got more'n enough scouts for this campaign, and even Crook is convinced that you're a troublemaker—ever since you had that trouble with Pickens—and you told Bogart you was gonna scalp him."

"Pickens shot at me first," Luke protested. "What was I supposed to do?"

"You're right," Clarke agreed. "I don't figure you for a troublemaker. I just think you're damned unlucky. And if it was up to me, hell, I'd keep you on for sure, but, dammit, the major, and the general, too, see it the other way. And on top of that, they think you're too damn friendly with the Cheyenne. I've got no choice but to fire you."

Disappointed, but never one to fret over the way things happen, Luke retightened the girth strap he had just loosened, and prepared to step up in the saddle. He was thinking that Clarke could have come right out and fired him instead of pussy-footing around it. He would have told him so, but it occurred to him that the chief scout was sincere in his profession of regret. So instead of telling him to go to hell, he said, " 'Preciate it, Ben."

Clarke backed a step away to give him room to turn his horse while he deliberated on whether or not to make a suggestion. "Wait a minute, Luke," he decided. "There's a greenhorn settler that's tryin' to get himself and his wife up to the Yellowstone. He was hopin' General Crook would send some soldiers to escort him, but Crook turned him down."

"I know the people," Luke said.

"That's right, the ones come in with you from

Medicine Bow. Why don't you go talk to him? He ain't got no idea how to get where he wants to go, and I expect he might be glad to have you take him—maybe pay you for your trouble."

"I don't know—maybe," Luke replied. At first thought, he was not keen on the idea. Playing nursemaid to a greenhorn and his wife was not something he thought he'd be good at. They never should have left the wagon train they started out with before dropping out at Medicine Bow. He thought the matter over while he rode up to the fort, and by the time he reached the sutler's store he had decided against approaching David Freeman. He turned his thoughts to other things. There were supplies he needed before he said good-bye to Fort Fetterman, and he had just enough money left to buy some of them.

The largest portion of any amount of money he had always went toward the purchase of cartridges for his Henry rifle. With the balance, he bought coffee beans, flour, and salt. "How much do I owe?" he asked the sutler's clerk. When the clerk gave him the figure, Luke carefully counted out his money, making the cost of his purchases with only a few cents to spare. "There you go," he said. "I was thinkin' on havin' a glass of beer, but I didn't leave enough to pay for one."

"I'll buy you a glass of beer." The voice came from behind him, and he turned to discover David Freeman striding toward the counter.

Surprised, Luke didn't know what to say at first, so he stood staring at Freeman for a few seconds before finally coming out with a thank-you. This was the first time he had seen the man up close. Every time before, David had been up on his wagon seat. "Much obliged," Luke said, "but I'm afraid I can't stand good for the second round."

"Don't matter," Freeman quickly commented. "Let's take 'em over to the table and sit down. There's something I wanna talk to you about."

Luke had a pretty good notion as to what Freeman wanted to talk about, but he hated to tell him no before he had a chance to say it. He at least owed him an ear since he bought him a glass of beer, so he picked up the glass before him and followed Freeman to the table.

"I saw you ride up from the river just now," David started, "so I thought I'd catch you before you rode off somewhere. Let me be honest with you, Mr. Sunday. When I was talking to Ben Clarke yesterday, he told me that he didn't think you'd be scouting for the army anymore." He paused to gauge any reaction from Luke, but there was none, so he continued. "Ben said you know the country between here and the Yellowstone as well as anyone riding scout for the army—maybe better." He went on to tell Luke what Luke already knew, that he was looking for a guide who might lead him away from potential danger while taking him to a little town named

Coulson. "I don't have a lot of money, but I've got a little saved back for our new start up there, and I'll pay you for your time. Ben Clarke said the going rate for scouts was a hundred dollars a month. I'd be willing to pay you a month's pay to take us to Coulson."

Not the slightest bit interested moments before, Luke was forced to give David's offer serious consideration. One hundred dollars could take him a long way, and he had to admit that he was sorely tempted. He took a long look at the slender young man, trying to judge the steel in his spine, wondering how much help he would be in the event of an encounter with a Sioux war party. He found it a tough decision to make. Finally he responded, "I don't know where it is you're lookin' to go on the Yellowstone," he said. "I ain't ever heard of a town called Coulson."

"I'm not surprised," David said. "I guess it's not really even a town yet, but there are some people who have already planned it, and it's gonna be one in a short time."

"Like I said," Luke repeated, "even if I was to take you up through the Powder River country, I don't have any idea where you're tryin' to go on the Yellowstone."

"I can tell you that it's not very far east of the Gallatin Valley. Will that help?"

"Well, yeah, some," Luke conceded. "I know where that is."

"Whaddaya say, then?"

Luke still hesitated, reluctant to be pushed too rapidly into an agreement. He had no concerns about traveling through that country alone, for he was totally confident of his ability to remain invisible to the eye of a Sioux hunting party. But a wagon traveling alone through the volatile Powder Valley was damn hard to hide, therefore calling for increased caution and a good portion of luck. He told David as much. "You sure you wouldn't be better off just turnin' around and headin' back where you came from? It ain't really the best time for white folks to be riding up through the Powder River country, especially just one wagon by itself."

David shook his head, a fatalistic gleam in his eye. "My wife and I have made up our minds to go on, even if we can't get someone to guide us. We've talked it over, and decided that the best chance we have for a future is to find good land in Montana with my brother's family. There's nothing for us back in Cheyenne, and we think it's worth the risk to finish what we started."

That's about the dumbest thing I've ever heard, Luke thought, but his emotionless expression never changed as he studied the impassioned young man's eyes. He decided that David was sincere in his determination. The question in his mind now was whether he wanted to be a part of the couple's risky endeavor, and he pictured their bodies lying dead and mutilated beside their burning wagon in the middle of the frozen prairie. It was not easy to count them as fools and say it was of no concern to him. In addition, there was the prospect of earning a hundred dollars, which he could surely use. In the end, he decided that it wouldn't be right to send them off across that expanse of prairie on their own. In his decision-making process, he never considered danger to himself. "All right," he finally said, "one hundred dollars when we find this place on the Yellowstone."

"Agreed," David replied eagerly, and extended his hand.

"All right," Luke repeated. "If you and your missus are hell-bound to go to Montana, I reckon I can take you, but you've got to understand you're riskin' your hair endin' up on a Lakota lance—if you don't get buried by a spring snow-storm."

"Understood," David said, and they shook hands on it. "We can be ready to roll first thing in the morning if that's all right with you."

"That suits me," Luke said. "I'll bring my stuff over after a while, and bed down near your wagon. You bring any extra grain for your horses? It'll be a spell before the grass starts to green up good, and your horses probably ain't used to scratchin' around in the snow to find somethin' to eat."

"I've got a pretty good supply of grain," David replied. "I hope it'll be enough."

"Don't worry about havin' to have some for my horse," Luke said. "He's an Injun pony. He ain't used to grain. He's et it before, but he ain't used to it."

Luke remained seated at the table for a few minutes while David hurried out to give Mary Beth the news. Having given his word, he had no thoughts toward changing his mind, but he continued to consider the potential for trouble on the journey. He knew that reports from a Lakota man who had recently come from Sitting Bull's camp placed the Sioux leader on the Rosebud. The man had said that the war chief would likely move back to the Powder. Luke doubted this because it made no sense to him. He would expect Sitting Bull to move farther away, toward the Bighorns, in hopes of discouraging the soldiers from following him. He reasoned that Sitting Bull would fight if the army pressed him, but if given a choice, he would avoid a confrontation. If he was right in this assumption, it should lessen the danger the three of them might face in their journey north, with the necessity only of avoiding stray parties of Sioux and Cheyenne who might be on their way to join Sitting Bull and Crazy Horse. *I reckon we'll see,* he thought as he got up from the table.

CHAPTER 5

"I hope we're doing the right thing," Mary Beth wondered aloud when she saw Luke Sunday approaching their wagon.

David paused to look accusingly at his wife. "Don't tell me you're having second thoughts now," he said. "We talked this thing over a hundred times, and you said you wanted to push on to Montana. I wouldn't have said anything to the man if I thought you were gonna change your mind."

"I haven't changed my mind," she replied quickly. "I was just wondering, that's all. I hope we've put our trust in a dependable man. He just looks so wild, he scares me a little."

"I don't think Ben Clarke would have recommended him if he wasn't trustworthy," David said. "At any rate, I'll be keeping an eye on him." His comments were intended to assure his wife. In reality, he was a little intimidated himself by the solemn-looking scout.

"Still, if he's so trustworthy, a person has to wonder why he isn't scouting for the soldiers anymore," Mary Beth said.

"We don't know the whole story on that," David replied. "Could be any number of reasons. Like I said, Ben Clarke said he was a good scout, and it's lucky for us that he's available to help us. That's the main thing." There was no more time for comment, for the object of their discussion was approaching to within earshot. David put the piece of harness he had been mending on the tailgate of his wagon and walked out to meet Luke.

"You ain't changed your mind yet?" Luke asked in greeting.

"No, sir!" David replied with enthusiasm. "We're ready to go to Montana." He waited for Luke to dismount before introducing Mary Beth. "I know we talked briefly on the trip from Medicine Bow when you led us across that river, but we never introduced ourselves. This is my wife, Mary Beth. Honey, shake hands with our partner, Mr. Sunday."

"It's just plain Luke," he said, embarrassed by David's formal introduction. He took the hand offered to him as if afraid he might break it, then quickly released it. Pointing toward the river then, he said, "I'll make my camp down below the bluff a ways, and we'll start out in the mornin'."

"You can camp here with us," David said. "I thought you might want to make your bed under the wagon, in case we get a little snow shower during the night."

" 'Preciate it, but I'll be all right," Luke said, glancing up at the sky. "It don't look much like snow tonight."

"Well, suit yourself, but you're welcome to share our fire," David said. "What about supper?"

"I've got somethin' to eat. I'll be fine," Luke assured them, then stepped back up in the saddle to discourage David's offering more. "See you folks in the mornin'."

"Well, that's a relief," Mary Beth said when Luke had ridden out of earshot. "I don't know about you, but I'm just as happy not to have him sleeping under me. I almost kicked you in the shins when you suggested it." She followed their strange new partner with her eyes until he dropped out of sight below the bluff. "Come on, supper's almost ready. You'd best wash up." She glanced again at the bluffs. "I expect he just eats his meat raw, like a caveman." For a few moments she paused to consider the situation in which she found herself. Minnesota seemed an eternity away. Even Cheyenne seemed a hundred years ago. She and David had been so young when they decided to buy a wagon and accompany a group of people starting out for Wyoming Territory. Thinking back, she realized it had really been only a little over a year and a half, and they had been filled with the optimism of youth. They had their health and ambition; what could go wrong? It didn't take long before the harsh reality of trying to build a home on the bleak Wyoming prairie killed the bloom on their dream, and she realized that David lacked the skills and drive of his older brother, John. But she placed no blame for that on David. He tried as hard as any man, and he loved her. As long as the two of them kept trying, she felt sure they would eventually establish a home somewhere in this vast country of wild Indians and men like Luke Sunday. The latter caused her to think, *If he doesn't decide to kill us and steal all our possessions.*

The next morning Luke waited until he saw David's fire freshen up before he led his horse over to the wagon. Sounds of an army preparing to move out had awakened David and Mary Beth, even though General Crook's column would not actually get under way before twelve or one o'clock that afternoon. Glancing up to see their guide approaching, David called out, "Good morning," loud enough to alert Mary Beth, who was still inside the wagon. "We can have a little breakfast here in a few minutes," David offered.

" 'Preciate it," Luke responded, "but I already ate." His breakfast had consisted of nothing more than a few strips of deer jerky, and the only thing he needed now was a cup of coffee. He had just bought a supply of coffee beans from the sutler's store the day before, but he was gambling on the strong possibility that the Freemans would offer theirs. He was not to be disappointed.

"You can at least have a cup of coffee," Mary Beth said as she stepped down from the wagon.

"Yes, ma'am," Luke replied. "That'd be mighty kind of you." He dropped the paint's reins to the ground, got his cup from the parfleche secured behind his saddle, and moved up to kneel by the fire while David filled the cup.

David poured a cup for himself, then sat down to drink it while Mary Beth cut strips of bacon to fry. Feeling somewhat awkward and at a loss for conversation with the solemn man he had hired to take him to Coulson, he made a show of concentrating on sipping his coffee. Sitting across the fire from Luke, he couldn't help making a judgment on the strange man's earthly possessions. Obviously, everything Luke Sunday owned was on that one paint pony—or the man himself. Dressed in animal skins, like an Indian, he carried a skinning knife on his belt and a bow on his back. In addition to the parfleche, his horse carried a buffalo robe behind the saddle, rolled to possibly contain a blanket and maybe some cooking utensils. The parfleche, with a hatchet strapped to it, was balanced by an ammunition bag and a quiver of arrows on the other side of the saddle. This, then, was the sum total of the man's wealth—no home base, no family, nothing stored for the future, probably no thoughts beyond finding food for himself and his horse each day. *It's a strange partnership you've made, David Freeman,* he told himself. *I hope to hell it was a wise one.*

When Mary Beth could stand the awkward silence no longer, she questioned Luke, "How long do you think it will take us to get to Coulson, Mr. Sunday?"

"Luke, ma'am. My name's Luke. There ain't no Mr. Sunday. I can't say exactly. It'll depend on how far you can drive your team in a day without wearin' 'em out. I figure it's best for us to head straight north from here for most of the way, before cuttin' over to strike the Powder. If what I hear is true, that big bunch of Sioux and Cheyenne the army's goin' after is on the Rosebud, so we need to steer plenty wide of 'em. It's longer than headin' straight across the Tongue and the Bighorn, but I figured you folks wanted to get there with your scalps still on. I expect it'll take us eleven or twelve days to get to the Yellowstone, then maybe another five to seven days from there to this town you're lookin' for, dependin' on how far west it is."

Mary Beth cast an uncertain glance in her husband's direction. Luke's estimate seemed much longer than they had speculated on. "We didn't think it was that far," she said, wondering if David was going to question Luke, but David remained silent.

Reading the doubt in their eyes, Luke said, "Well, like I said, I'd have to see how your wagon travels. This time of year you can't count on the weather. I figure we can make twenty miles a day if we don't run into any trouble. You might wanna ask Ben Clarke, or one of the other scouts, how far they think it is—give you a little peace of mind."

David was quick to respond, afraid that Mary Beth might have offended him. "Oh no, we don't have to do that. We don't doubt your word on it. It's just that it's farther than we thought it was."

"It ain't too late to change your mind if you're havin' doubts about goin'," Luke said. "I couldn't say I blamed you."

David looked to Mary Beth for confirmation before stating, "No, we've made up our minds. We're going."

Luke nodded in reply, then looked at Mary Beth. She looked as if still uncertain, but made no comment. He could not read complete trust in either of their eyes, but he figured that it was their problem, not his. "Well, if we've still got a deal, then I reckon you'd best hitch up your horses, and we'll get a start before we burn any more daylight." He got up to rinse out his cup, and David went to fetch his horses.

It was half an hour past sunup when they finally broke camp and headed north across a treeless landscape of rolling prairie that stretched ahead of them in a patchwork of brown grass and scattered patches of snow. In the beginning, Mary Beth rode on the wagon seat beside her husband, the uncertainty of their decision still fresh in her mind. "What's to stop him from leading us off in this wilderness and murdering us for our money?" she whispered in spite of the fact that Luke was some fifty yards out in front of them.

"Well, I guess that would be my responsibility," David answered.

"I didn't mean to imply that you couldn't take care of me," she quickly assured him, fearing she had hurt his feelings. "I know you will always protect me. I guess I'm just saying that we had better always be on our guard around him and give him no opportunity to take advantage of us." She would not for the world belittle her husband's protective potential, but she would not care to see him in a confrontation with a man who moved with the lethal grace of a puma, whose very demeanor spoke of a capacity for violence. "I'm just saying that it would be a good idea for you to wear your pistol belt. You never know when you might need it." She didn't voice it, but she also intended to get her father's old pistol from the trunk and keep it by her bed at night. "Don't forget, Ben Clarke told you that man was raised by Indians."

Behind them, General Crook's column of cavalry, infantry, and supply wagons moved out of Fort Fetterman at approximately one o'clock. Near the head of the column, Lieutenant James Findley rode with two of his scouts, Bill Bogart and George Wylie. "What happened to that feller and his wife that came with you from Medicine Bow?" Bogart asked. "They turn around and head back?" His interest in the couple was inspired solely by the glimpse he had gotten of David Freeman's comely young wife and the wishful thinking it had created.

"No," Findley replied. "They're bound and determined to make it to someplace on the Yellowstone River. I heard his brother struck it rich up in Helena and they're planning to join him." He paused, then continued with a faint grin. "Your friend Luke Sunday went with them as a guide."

"That son of a bitch," Bogart blurted. "Well, I feel sorry for them folks, 'cause I wouldn't give 'em much chance to make the Yellowstone." He allowed himself to fume for a few moments over the mention of Luke's name, and then another thought entered his mind. "You say they had folks that struck it rich?"

"That's what I heard."

"Mighty interestin'," Bogart muttered to Wylie, "and Luke Sunday's gone with 'em. I wouldn't mind headin' out through Powder River country with that pretty little woman. There's a lot of things could happen on a trip like that—some of 'em bad." He winked at Wylie and grinned. "And some of 'em damn good." The grin remained on his face as he brought to mind the trim figure of Mary Beth Freeman.

• • •

As the afternoon wore on, Mary Beth became tired of riding in the wagon, and got off to walk beside it. At the rate of about two miles an hour, it wasn't difficult for her to keep up. She had always prided herself in her stamina and her capacity for physical activity. As she walked, she became aware of the endless sameness of the prairie. In all directions, the scene was identical, with no trees other than a lone pine here and there that caused her to wonder how even that happened to be. The most prominent growth seemed to be scattered clumps of sagebrush. *I surely hope this is not what the country around Coulson looks like,* she thought. Noticing an increase in the number of clouds, she was struck by the thought that a person could easily lose her sense of direction if the sky was overcast. She concentrated her gaze on the broad back of their guide then, while thinking of the discussion she had had with David earlier. Maybe her fears about the man were unfounded, she allowed. She had to admit that he had seemed genuinely indifferent to their commitment to make the journey, and had not pressed them to go.

Unaware of the state of uneasiness he had caused, Luke rode on ahead of the wagon, alert for anything in their path that might cause a problem. There was no road to follow, not even a trail, but the terrain was not so difficult as to cause delay. While he rocked gently with the paint's easy motion, his mind wandered back to the couple behind him. There was no doubt that the woman was the decision maker in that union, and Luke was not convinced that her husband really knew it. This country would eat up a man like David Freeman. He needed a woman as spunky and determined as Mary Beth appeared to be.

By early afternoon, Luke estimated they had probably covered more than ten miles, and figured it time to stop to rest the horses, so he signaled David when he came upon a small stream, bordered by sagebrush and one lone cottonwood tree. "I expect this is about as good a place as any to rest the horses," he said to David when he caught up. "Might be the best time to eat somethin' while we're here." Glancing up at the sky, he continued. "We might be in for a little snow, the way those clouds are lookin'. If we're lucky, maybe it won't be much more than a light shower—be a good idea to feed your horses some of that grain, too. They might have to work a little harder—in case we ain't lucky."

Old ashes near the edge of the stream served as evidence that others before them had picked this place to camp. The lack of available firewood was of major concern, but Luke assured them that a small fire, enough to boil a quick pot of coffee, could be built with sagebrush roots and branches. "I've still got plenty of deer jerky to keep you from starvin' till suppertime. I figure we can make it to a little creek about halfway between here and the Cheyenne River. There's firewood there and grass for the horses, if it ain't snowed under by the time we get there."

While David went about the business of unhitching his team, Luke guided his horse under the solitary cottonwood. Standing on his saddle, he was just tall enough to reach the lower limbs of the tree. With his hatchet, he chopped off as many of the branches as he could manage. Watching him, Mary Beth realized that this was the reason the tree was pruned so high up the trunk. Others before him had done the same. She assumed he was after wood for the fire and wondered if the green branches would burn well enough to serve their purpose. She learned that he had other intentions, however, when he took his knife and began skinning the bark from the branches, after which, he fed the shavings to his horse.

They rested there for an hour before hitching up and starting out again. They had driven for a couple of hours when the wind picked up and heavier, dark clouds began to roll in from the northwest, signaling an end to the fair weather. Mary Beth climbed back into the wagon and spread a blanket over her and David's knees. "If this keeps up, I'm going to have to get our heavy coats out again," she said as she pressed close to her husband.

"He doesn't seem to mind it," David said,

nodding toward the lone figure sitting relaxed in the saddle some fifty or sixty yards ahead.

Contrary to their thoughts, Luke was perturbed by the sudden blast of wintry air blowing out of the mountains, but not because it was cold. He was as eager to complete this journey as the couple he was leading, and he was disappointed to see any weather that might lengthen it.

Another hour passed before the first flakes began to fall, so he was confident that they would reach the creek he had planned on with no trouble. By the time he caught sight of the little cluster of trees along the bank of the creek, the snow had begun to accumulate upon the prairie. So it was with a welcome sigh that David wheeled his wagon between the trees to park it as close to cover as he could manage. Mary Beth didn't wait for the men to build a fire, but started gathering dead limbs while David and Luke took care of the horses. She was cold and hungry, so she gathered enough for a large fire. Then a thought entered her mind as she was about to light it. Turning to Luke, who was carrying his saddle back to throw under the wagon, she asked, "Is this too big? Should we be worried about our fire being spotted by Indians?"

Amused by her question, he showed no sign of it, however, when he answered, "No, ma'am. Make it as big as you want. I wouldn't expect to find any Injuns in this part of the country, except maybe a Crow huntin' party, and they'd just wanna get warm. We don't have to worry about runnin' across any hostiles till we get beyond the Cheyenne River and the Belle Fourche."

"What's the name of this creek?" David asked.

"I don't know if it's got a name," Luke replied. "At least I ain't ever heard one. I expect the Crows call it somethin'."

"We'll name it, then," David said, cheered by the news that he had worried about hostile Indians needlessly. "We'll call it Freeman's Creek. Whaddaya think, Mary Beth?" He chuckled playfully.

When Mary Beth replied with only a look of mock impatience for her husband, Luke said, "As good a name as any, I reckon." He started to withdraw then to set up his own camp, but was stopped by Mary Beth.

"There's really no need for you to go off by yourself," she said. "You might as well eat with us. For goodness' sake, we're going to be traveling for quite a long time and I can cook for all of us." She said it because it was the thing to do, although she was still uncomfortable in his presence. Then she chided herself and admitted to being uncomfortable when he was not around as well, and she had to wonder what he might be up to.

As stoic as ever, Luke nodded thoughtfully before replying, "I reckon it makes more sense at that, instead of makin' two fires and two camps every day. If you're offerin' to do the cookin', then I reckon I can volunteer to provide the meat, so we don't cook up all the salt pork you've got. Is that all right with you folks?"

"That's a fair arrangement," David said. So the partnership was struck, although David still wore his pistol belt and Mary Beth kept her late father's revolver close to her, even while cooking the supper. The only one not wearing a weapon while they were camped was the one the other two sought to defend themselves against. It did not go unnoticed by Luke, but it failed to concern him. In fact, he couldn't say that he really blamed them.

After a supper of boiled beans, bacon, and coffee, Mary Beth was relieved to hear Luke turn down David's suggestion that he should sleep under the wagon to give him some protection from the snow, which had shown no sign of stopping. " 'Preciate it," Luke said, "but I think it'd be a good idea if I slept over on the other side of the creek where I can spot anythin' movin' on the prairie behind us. I can make a half shelter with my buffalo robe to keep the snow off." He figured that was as good a reason as any, although it could have occurred to David to point out that something might come upon them from the other direction. His real reason was having no desire to sleep under the young couple. During supper,

David had remarked that he and Mary Beth had only been married for less than two years. Luke didn't want to hear them struggling over his head all night, in case the bloom had not faded in their lovemaking yet. When there was no comment from either of them questioning his reasoning, he finished his coffee and said good night.

Thank you, Mary Beth thought as she watched him depart, for she unknowingly shared similar feelings. David was still inclined to seek intimacy at what she considered inappropriate times, and she did not care to share them with their sinister guide. She never denied her husband's advances, even though her mood might not match his. David was not a confident man, having never really succeeded in any important endeavor, and she was careful not to discourage his ardor, lest he feel rejected. Her mind returned to the circumstances of their marriage. The only daughter, raised in a household with four brothers, she was eager to accept the first decent opportunity to escape the madhouse of her family. Being the eldest, she was more like a second mother to her brothers, and burdened with the responsibility of cooking, washing clothes, and cleaning up after the rowdy boys.

David's family owned the farm next to her father's in Minnesota. The youngest of the Freeman boys, David soon came to call on Mary Beth. She was a little ashamed to admit it, but when he proposed to her, she said yes, primarily to escape her family. The fact that David had dreams of making it on his own in the free country of the West, as his older brother had done, suited her even better. So they bade farewell to family and friends and set out for a plot of land near Cheyenne, Wyoming Territory, a piece of land that David had bought sight unseen. The land turned out to be one hundred and twenty-five acres of arid soil, incapable of sustaining crops. Mary Beth did not complain during the long, hard months they worked to bring life to a land that refused to support it. She worked just as hard to build her marriage and strengthen a love for her husband that she had to admit was not fully there in their beginning. When they received word from David's brother inviting them to join him in Montana, they were both ready to go. Now it appeared that, after some discouraging setbacks, they had found a way to continue their quest—even if it was with a half-civilized guide. She could not consider herself a brave woman, but she was determined as hell at this point.

David and Mary Beth were awakened the next morning by the sound of distant gunfire from the north. Alarmed, they scrambled out of the wagon to discover Luke standing on the opposite bank, his ear to the wind, listening. Seeing that the couple was awake, he crossed over to their side, carrying an armload of dead limbs for the fire.

"Whaddaya think it is?" David asked. "You think we're in trouble?"

"I don't think so," Luke replied calmly. "Sounds to me like somebody's run up on some buffalo, most likely a Crow huntin' party. I was just fixin' to go take a look. I was waitin' for you folks to wake up—didn't want you to think I'd run off and left you. I'll get a fire started." About a four-inch blanket of snow had fallen during the night, ending an hour or so before sunup. Luke raked it away to uncover the charred remains of their fire from the night before. In short order he had a healthy blaze glowing, and when he was sure of its promise, he got to his feet. "I won't be gone long," he said as he started toward his horse.

"How long should we wait here?" David asked.

"You go ahead and fix your breakfast and get ready to break camp. If I ain't back by then, start out without me." Before David could form words to voice the alarm at once reflected in his eyes, Luke turned and pointed toward the northern skyline. "See that line of hills with what looks like a chimney at one end of it? You just start your horses on that line, and I'll meet you before you get there."

"Don't you want to wait and get some coffee before you go?" Mary Beth asked.

"No, ma'am," Luke replied. "You folks ought not take too much time gettin' started. I wanna make camp tonight at the Cheyenne River. That's about twenty miles from here, and this snow ain't gonna make it any easier."

"What if you aren't there by the time we reach that rock?" David asked.

"I'll be there," Luke assured him. "That rock's the best part of ten miles away." He stepped up in the saddle and guided the paint along the north bank of the creek.

Mary Beth moved up to stand beside her husband, and they both watched him until he faded into the early morning mist hovering over the creek. There was no need to express the feeling of emptiness that descended upon them at that moment. Their wagon, a pinpoint in a vast ocean of stark white prairie that extended on all sides to a distant horizon, left them with the realism that without their guide, they were truly lost. "You don't suppose—" Mary Beth started.

"He'll be back," David interrupted her. "He said he'll be back, so don't start worrying your mind about it." Another thought occurred to him then. "He ain't gonna leave before he gets his money, so let's just get some coffee boiling and get ready to go."

Breakfast was a hurried affair on this morning, with no lingering over coffee afterward. Mary Beth was washing her dishes and the frying pan before David had a chance to finish his bacon. Gone for the moment were her feelings of suspicion and discomfort she had harbored for the tall scout whenever he was around. They were replaced by a need for reassurance from his quiet confidence and indifferent manner.

After a ride of approximately five miles, Luke approached a low ridge that appeared to be one side of a wide, grassy draw. The sound of random gunfire from the other side of the ridge, and the rumble of many hooves, told him that what he had suspected was probably true, that someone was killing buffalo. To make sure, however, and to determine if they were friend or foe, he left his horse when almost to the top of the ridge and climbed the rest of the way on foot.

Lying on his belly at the top of the ridge, he watched for only a minute or two before uttering, "Black Feather." He had run up on the Crow scouts he had been sent to find several days before, led by his friend Black Feather. He watched for a few minutes as the small herd of perhaps one hundred buffalo swept through the draw with the Crow hunters darting in and out of the mass of bodies to kill what they needed, their nimble ponies quick to avoid the dangerous horns. With no further need for caution, Luke got to his feet and went back to get his horse.

Riding diagonally down the side of the ridge, he urged the paint to join the hunt. Having done it many times before, the fearless horse charged into the mob of thundering hooves. So intense was the chase that the Crow hunters were not aware of the addition to their hunt until the Henry rifle spoke and a young cow collapsed with a .44 slug placed neatly behind her left front leg to take a tumble in the snow-covered grass. Surprised, for there had been no rider to his left moments before, Black Feather jerked his head around to see Luke bearing down on another cow. "Hi-yi!" he cried out excitedly. "Dead Man!"

Luke raised his rifle overhead in greeting to his friend, then abruptly reined the paint back, veering away from the stampeding herd. The one buffalo cow was enough to supply the Freemans and himself for a good while, so there was no sense in killing more. The Crow hunters, most of whom were still unaware that he had joined them, continued their chase for a short while longer before breaking off to return to butcher the carcasses left behind. Upon seeing Luke, they quickly gathered around him.

"Have you come to join us?" Black Feather asked.

"No," Luke answered in the Crow tongue. "I didn't expect to find you here. I thought you were going to meet General Crook."

"We go to meet him at the Powder River near Dry Fork, where the army fort used to be," Little Bear said.

"The soldiers left Fort Fetterman one sleep

ago," Luke said. "Maybe two more sleeps they'll reach Fort Reno and think you'll be there."

Black Feather shrugged indifferently. "We had big hunt, killed plenty meat for our village. That was important before we left to fight Sioux." He and the others went on to explain that they were on their way to meet General Crook when they happened upon a second herd of buffalo. They were fortunate to be able to take advantage of this smaller herd to make meat for their battle with the Sioux.

"Need strong meat," Little Bear said. "Soldiers fight on coffee, beans, and tree bark. No iron in their food. Absaroka warrior need iron in food."

Luke had to smile at Little Bear's comparison of the army's hardtack to tree bark. He shared the sentiment. "Crook expects to find you at Fort Reno when he gets there," he repeated.

"We go," Black Feather said, "when we butcher the meat." Luke knew there was no use in trying to hurry him. The Indian tended to put things in proper priority, and having decent food was more important than being at a particular point on the Powder because the soldiers would be there at that time. "Soldier Chief send you to find us again?" Black Feather asked.

"No, I'm not goin' with you," Luke replied, switching back to English. "The general fired me. I'm taking a couple of white settlers to the Yellowstone. I thought you were long gone." The

Crows could not understand the reason for not using Luke as a scout, even after he tried to explain the events that led to his dismissal. Luke refrained from telling them that he was also a friend of Two Moons of the Cheyenne. That might have been a little difficult for Black Feather to understand. He went on to tell them about David and Mary Beth, and his promise to lead them to the Yellowstone.

"Maybe we don't go to scout for Soldier Chief," Little Bear said in support of Luke. His comment was followed with grunts of agreement among the warriors gathered around.

"No," Luke insisted. "The general needs you, and he wants you to keep all the Sioux ponies you can capture."

This served to remind the warriors of the main reason for volunteering to scout for the soldiers, the prospect of stealing many ponies, so the focus of their attention was returned to the business of butchering their kill. Luke knew they would be another day or two longer before arriving at Fort Reno. They would feast on the fresh meat today while drying out the rest. As for his cow, he would butcher it right away, using his knife and hatchet, wrap the portions he wanted to take in the buffalo's hide, then ride to intercept David and Mary Beth. The weather was still cold enough to keep the meat until they reached the Cheyenne River, so he planned to camp there long enough to smoke the meat to preserve it. When his butchering was done, and the meat loaded on his horse, he wished his Crow friends good luck and bade them farewell.

Mindful of his pony's heavy load, he slow-walked the paint on a course that would intercept the wagon before it reached the stone pillar he had pointed out to David. Random thoughts played upon his mind as he guided the paint through a series of deep gullies with frequent outcroppings of the unusual dark brown rock, prevalent in this broad prairie. The rock had always struck him as odd. It looked soft and had a lot of little holes in it as if a carpenter had taken an awl and drilled it, and he could think of no practical use for it.

It was well past noon while resting in the shadow of the stone pillar when he spotted the wagon in the distance. Assuming they would be ready to stop to rest the horses and eat something, he placed more sticks on the fire he had built, and cut some strips of fresh meat to roast. Firewood was scarce, since the only source were two dwarf trees that survived on the tiny trickle of water generated by the melting snow on the ridge above. For that reason, he had no thoughts of smoke-curing the buffalo meat until they reached the Cheyenne River.

"Well, looks like we made it to the rock, and where in hell is our guide?" David complained as they approached the tall stone pillar. Already starting to wonder what he would do if Luke failed to show, he was about to voice his concern when Mary Beth interrupted.

"Is that smoke I see?" She pointed to the thin column wafting up from the base of the pillar.

"I think you're right," David said, wary now that they might have encountered some Indians. His fears were alleviated at once, however, by the appearance of Luke Sunday when the rugged scout stepped up on a rock and waved them on. More than ready to stop for a while, David drove his wagon around the rock to discover a fire going and the aroma of roasting meat. It was a welcome sight, and Mary Beth wasted no time in getting out her coffeepot.

"I've got a pretty good supply of meat that I need to smoke before it starts to turn," Luke told them. I need to load it on your wagon, if you've got room. Then if you folks ain't in that big a hurry, we can lay over for a day to dry it out when we get to the Cheyenne."

"We'll make room for that," Mary Beth replied. "It'll save some of our supplies." She glanced at David and he nodded in return.

There was still an invisible wall of caution between the young couple and their somber guide. Luke could sense it, and was becoming tired of it, so he thought it was time to comment on it. "Look, folks, you can stop worryin' about me. I said I'd take you to this little town of yours, and that's what I'll do. I ain't gonna rob you, or kill you, or leave you on your own out here on the prairie."

David blanched, embarrassed by Luke's accurate assessment of the situation. Mary Beth clearly blushed. "Why, Mr. Sunday, we didn't worry about that at all," she started, then paused before continuing. "Well, yes, we were a little worried about that, I'll admit. I guess we owe you an apology, but we didn't know anything about you, and you're so . . ." She didn't finish, unable to find a word that wouldn't offend.

Luke had to smile. "It's Luke, ma'am. There ain't no Mr. Sunday."

Mary Beth returned his smile. "All right, Luke." She emphasized the name. "We won't worry about you anymore, but you should smile more often, so you don't look so fierce." Obviously relieved of a heavy burden, she said, "If we're going to stay an extra day when we get to the river, I might go into my flour barrel and bake us some bread to go with all this meat you've supplied."

CHAPTER 6

After a day spent to prepare the meat Luke had supplied, the travelers moved on with horses rested and bellies filled with meat. A day's travel took them near the headwaters of the Belle Fourche, where they camped overnight before following that river north for the next three days. After camping one last time on the Belle Fourche, Luke left the river and headed in a more westerly direction to strike the Little Powder. In all the time since they'd left Fort Fetterman, there had been no sighting of Indians, although they came upon travois and pony tracks in several spots that indicated parties on their way to join Sitting Bull or Crazy Horse.

Even though still chilly, the weather remained stable with no further snowfall, allowing them to make good progress, averaging almost twenty miles a day. With no sign of hostile Indians, each day became easier on David's and Mary Beth's nerves. Although their guide still presented an image of a creature of the wild, more Indian than white, they no longer harbored the fear that he might have thoughts of murdering them in their sleep. David reasoned that had he possessed any such intentions, it made no sense to wait until this late date to act upon them. Even so, Mary Beth continued to find it uncomfortable at times when his intense gaze followed her movements around the campfire. Still, she could not deny a certain fascination for their tall sandy-haired guide. She wondered how he came to be the mysterious man that he was, and one evening when camped about a mile short of the forks of the Powder and Little Powder, she was given the opportunity to learn more. Thinking he had ridden away from their camp to scout the area around and ahead of them, she went down to the edge of the river to wash her frying pan.

"Oh!" Mary Beth exclaimed when she started down a gully to suddenly find Luke kneeling by the water's edge. "I didn't know you were here." He turned to look at her, a straight razor in his hand. "Oh," she went on, thinking she might have imposed upon his privacy, "you're shaving." It struck her as odd that he would be, since he seemed so much like an Indian that it never occurred to her that he might have whiskers. Feeling somewhat awkward at that point, she made an effort to offer light conversation. "Your razor looks like the one my father used to use. Where did you get it—from your father?"

"Zeb Gaither gave it to me," Luke replied. Offering no further explanation, he turned to rinse the razor in the water.

"Oh," she said again, curious now, and hoping

she could inspire him to talk. "Is he a friend of yours?"

"No, he raised me." He dried the razor on his sleeve and got up to leave.

"I didn't mean to chase you off," she quickly stated. "I can go farther upstream to wash my pan. I didn't mean to interrupt your shaving."

"I was done," he said, and started up the gully.

"You'll have to tell me about your friend Zeb sometime," she called after him, realizing as soon as she said it that it was a stupid thing to say.

"He's dead," Luke replied as he reached the top of the gully and headed toward his horse, left grazing in a stand of trees farther up the riverbank. Behind him, Mary Beth stood perplexed, shaking her head. *The man is incapable of carrying on a casual conversation,* she thought.

Her questions had triggered thoughts in his mind that seldom came to the surface, but now prompted him to think of the circumstances that caused the razor to be in his possession. *Zeb Gaither.* He repeated the name in his mind and pictured the old trapper who had found a white boy-child near a Lakota camp. The child was no more than a toddler; his parents had been killed in a raid on their wagon train by a Sioux war party. The child was the only survivor of the massacre, having hidden under a washtub while the wagons were burned and the bodies of his

130

parents and the others were mutilated. He didn't know how long he had remained hidden under the tub, but Zeb had told him that he was half-starved when he found him.

The old trapper took the boy to raise, although he was not pleased by the prospect of having the responsibility of a child. Knowing it was too much for him to take on alone, he enlisted the help of a Cheyenne woman named Owl Woman to take care of the boy. Zeb had lived with Owl Woman off and on for quite a few years. She was childless, so the gift of a son to raise was welcomed. Zeb insisted on a proper white name for the child, so he sat down and thought about it. He didn't think it fitting to give the boy his own name. *After all,* he thought, *he might not grow up to amount to anything I'd be proud of.* In case he did, however, he decided to give him his father's first name, Luke. Then, as near as he could recall, he had found the child on a Sunday, so he settled on the name Luke Sunday. As far as the boy was concerned, it was as good a name as any, so there were never any thoughts about changing it.

Zeb Gaither died when Luke was about twelve years old, when his horse was startled by a rattlesnake and bucked the old man off, breaking his neck. With Zeb gone, Owl Woman seemed to lose interest in a life without him, so she followed him after a bout with pneumonia when Luke was fourteen. For Luke, it was a sign that it was time for him to leave the Cheyenne village to see for himself something of the white man's world, the world he had been born into. The experience had not been to his liking. He had gone to Fort Laramie with hundreds of Sioux and Cheyenne warriors when some white men had come from Washington to create a great treaty between the red man and the government. There were many soldiers there as well as civilian government people. He went to the sutler's store and looked at the many things offered for sale, and watched the soldiers as they marched by in formation. He even exchanged a few words with some of them, since Zeb Gaither had taught him to speak white man's talk. He did not really understand the treaty talk, but Red Cloud, the Sioux chief, became very angry with what the government proposed and abruptly left the meeting with his people. Luke left with the others, never to visit Fort Laramie again until ten years later.

At that point, he had decided that he was neither Cheyenne nor White and for the next several years he made his home in the Absaroka Mountains where he hunted and trapped, content to live alone. He never spent much time thinking about his solitary existence. It was something he was accustomed to. It had always been that way, even while he was living in the Cheyenne village. He was different from the Cheyenne boys his age, partially because of Zeb's influence, but also because the forest, the rivers, and the mountains spoke to him in a different tongue, one he could not ignore. As a consequence, he had always hunted and trapped alone to the puzzlement of the other boys.

There came a time, however, when he realized that it was necessary to abandon his solitary ways. Because of increased numbers of white settlers moving into the traditional hunting grounds of the Indians, the Sioux, the Cheyenne, and the Arapaho began to seek new hunting grounds, even to the point where he saw more and more signs of them in his mountains. This was added to the fact that he needed some means to buy ammunition for the Henry rifle that had belonged to Zeb Gaither. War had come to the plains as the government insisted that all tribes should move to the reservations, and he knew that he was going to have to choose sides in the conflict. It was difficult to give up his independence, but he decided to cast his lot with the people of his birth, the whites. He left his mountains to join a village of Crows on the North Platte, since they had always been allied with the soldiers. He had lived with them for almost a year, befriended by a young warrior named Black Feather, when the army sent word that they needed scouts. He had at once seen an opportunity to buy the cartridges and supplies he needed, in spite of the fact that he wasn't enthusiastic about working for the army.

Bringing his thoughts back to the present, he paused to take a thoughtful look at the straight razor before returning it to his saddlebag. He pictured Zeb Gaither on the last day of his life. *That horse never bucked a day in its life,* he thought, *until that rattlesnake struck at its legs.* "I reckon that's why Zeb got throwed," he mumbled. "He never expected it." He dropped the razor in the saddlebag and stepped up in the saddle that had also once belonged to Zeb.

A bright three-quarter moon, riding high in the clear night sky, revealed the sharp lines and the many draws and ridges that extended as far as the eye could see. Beyond the ridges, the prairie waited with no relief except for scattered patches of cottonwood trees along the serpentine river. There had been no contact with hostile Indians so far, but the growing number of trails, some from entire villages, was enough to cause Luke to consider traveling at night until reaching the Yellowstone. As long as the weather held, there should be no problem in driving the wagon by moonlight. He nudged his horse gently and the obedient paint started at once, making its way down the backside of the ridge at a comfortable walk.

He had planned to scout the next morning's trail as far as the forks of the river, where the Little Powder flowed into the Powder, before circling back to return to camp. But the flickering light from a campfire below the bluffs caused him to stop. At once alert, he dismounted and led the paint down along the bluffs until he came to a thick stand of berry bushes. Leaving his horse there, he continued on foot until he was close enough to see the camp. It was impossible to get an exact count, but he knew there were at least twenty or more, judging by the several fires. It was not a war party, for there were women and children, but he could not tell whether they were friendly or hostile. Regardless, there should be no trouble with them, he reasoned. They were most likely heading west to join Sitting Bull, like so many others, and would probably be on their way in the morning. *As long as they don't know we're camped just up the river from them,* he thought.

He remained there for a few minutes longer before deciding to withdraw and return to his camp. It struck him then that he could smell the aroma of roasting meat. He paused to sniff it, then suddenly realized that the steady breeze was coming from the south. It was not the Indians' cook fire he smelled, but that of his companions, and less than a mile away! *There's no reason for them to think it isn't their own fire they smell,* he told himself. *Unless they've got somebody scouting around just like I'm doing!* With a sense of urgency then, he stepped up in the saddle and started back to the wagon.

• • •

After watching Luke fade away in the darkness, Mary Beth had returned to the chore of washing her iron skillet. Using a little sand to loosen some of the grease that had baked on the bottom, she wiped the pan out and rinsed it thoroughly. Satisfied that it was as clean as she was likely to get it, she made her way back up the gully to the top of the low bluff. Looking toward the wagon, she saw David coming to meet her, but he suddenly stopped in midstride to stand perfectly still while looking to his left. Puzzled, she followed his gaze toward the cottonwoods that bordered the riverbanks. When she saw what had stopped her husband, her heart fairly threatened to leap into her throat. There in the shadows of the trees stood an Indian warrior, his rifle leveled at David.

With no chance to run, both David and Mary Beth were momentarily paralyzed as they stared fearfully at their unexpected guest. The warrior, equally surprised to find the wagon and the white couple less than a mile from his camp, was uncertain what to do. So with the advantage his, he cocked his rifle and aimed it at David, still hesitating for a moment while he made up his mind.

"There is no reason to spill blood here." The words in the Cheyenne tongue came from the trees behind the warrior, accompanied by the distinct sound of a rifle cocking. The warrior spun around expecting a bullet to come his way, but there was nothing to be seen in the shadows. "These people come in peace." Luke spoke again, his voice calm and without emotion. "They wish you no harm."

The warrior paused, his rifle still at the ready while he strained to see where the voice had come from. Having moved from the spot from which he had originally spoken, Luke stepped from the shadows to face the warrior, both men still holding their weapons prepared to fire. "It is foolish for us to shoot each other," Luke said. "We are not enemies." Although he could now see that the warrior was Sioux, he guessed that he understood the Cheyenne tongue. "We are not soldiers," he continued while the warrior appeared to be undecided. "We are passing through your land. That is all. We take nothing from the land but what we need to eat. Let there be peace between us."

The Sioux warrior lowered his rifle and released the hammer, convinced that the deadly calm white man would kill him if he made any effort to shoot. "What you say is wise," he said. "There is no need to spill blood. Go in peace." He turned then and disappeared into the trees.

Terrified, Mary Beth ran to her husband. Wasting no time, Luke quickly said, "Hitch up your horses and pack up your things. I'll be back in a minute. Be ready to move outta here as soon as I get back." Leaving them to act on his instructions, he slipped into the cottonwoods after the Sioux warrior.

Moving cautiously through the shadows, he came to the edge of the trees in time to see the warrior jump on his pony and gallop away toward the Sioux camp. Knowing that it would only be a matter of minutes before the warrior could get back to his people to report the discovery of the wagon, Luke returned to David and Mary Beth, who were frantically hurrying to follow his orders. He waited a couple of minutes while David closed the tailgate and ran to climb up on the seat beside Mary Beth. When they were set to go, he pointed toward a low bank at the edge of the river. "Take your wagon across to the other side. You oughta be able to cross there all right," he said, hoping he was right, because there was no time to test the river bottom. When David started toward the spot indicated without hesitating, Luke kicked dirt over the campfire and jumped on his horse to follow. Heading them off before they reached the water, he grabbed the bridle of one of the horses and led the team toward a section of the bank that looked firmer to him. The wagon threatened to bog down near the center, but with Luke's and David's urging, his horses hauled it to the other bank.

Relieved that the spot he had picked to ford the river had been a good guess, Luke looked toward a line of ridges to the west. He was acting purely on instinct, because he could not predict what the Sioux party would do when the warrior returned to his camp. One thing he felt strongly about, however: He did not feel comfortable remaining where they were and trusting that the Indians would be content to leave them be. So he continued to lead the wagon toward the treeless ridges, searching for a cut or ravine that afforded sufficient cover to withstand an attack. There was little thought toward finding a place to hide, for the wagon tracks leading out of the river stood out in the bright moonlight as if it were midday. Time was short, so he urged David to hurry. There was bound to be a scouting party visiting their camp within a very short time, even if the Sioux meant them no harm.

Picking a narrow ravine at the base of a high ridge, Luke pulled up and waited for David to drive his wagon between the rocky walls. "Leave the wagon in the openin'," he instructed. "It'll give you a little protection to shoot behind. Unhitch the horses and lead 'em back to the end. We don't wanna take a chance on one of them gettin' hit." David was quick to respond and when he had led the horses to safety, Luke led the paint back to join them. "We might be doin' all this for nothin', but it's better to be ready in case those Sioux decide to pick up a couple of horses and a wagon full of supplies." The frightened couple stood wide-eyed, awaiting his every command.

"David," Luke continued, "get out that shotgun of yours and your pistol, and keep your eyes open." He turned then to Mary Beth, who was busy wringing her hands in anguish. "Get that big ol' pistol you've been totin'. You think you can use it for anythin' besides shootin' me?"

She almost smiled when she recognized the barb for wearing the weapon during the first days of their journey. "I guess I can use it to shoot at Indians if I have to," she answered, and went at once to her trunk to get it.

"You can watch David's back while he's watchin' the mouth of the ravine," Luke said.

"What about you?" David asked. "Where are you gonna be?"

"I'm gonna climb up to the top of this ridge," he replied. "I'll do us more good up there with my rifle, where I can see if they try to circle around behind us." Unwilling to waste any more time, he pulled the Henry from his saddle sling and started climbing the side of the ravine. David and Mary Beth looked at each other anxiously, knowing he was doing what was best for their defense, but still reluctant to be left alone. It was only for a moment, however, and then they moved quickly to their posts, each resigned to do whatever was necessary to ensure the safety of the other.

With pistol in hand, Mary Beth took a position near the front of the wagon as David crawled up on the tailgate. He gave her a reassuring nod and she returned it with a determined smile. At that moment, she was proud of her husband—and proud of herself as well. They would show Luke Sunday that they would stand together against the savages.

Luke's instincts were not wrong, for he had barely had time enough to scale the ridge when he heard excited voices coming from the campsite he had just left. After a few moments more, he spotted the first of several warriors examining the wagon tracks at the edge of the river. After a short discussion, they spread out, joined by several others, and began a stealthy advance upon the ravine. There could be no mistaking it for a friendly visit, so Luke prepared to start picking apart their attack. Standing out in sharp relief on the moonlit prairie, the warriors offered inviting targets as they darted from one small hummock to the next, seeking the scant protection offered between the river and the line of ridges. When they were well within range of his rifle, Luke took aim at the foremost warrior and squeezed the trigger. The warrior threw up his arms and collapsed, causing the man next to him to stop abruptly. It was his mistake, because it gave Luke time to crank in another cartridge, and dispatch him with his partner. Without the advantage of Luke's lofty position, David and Mary Beth could only search frantically back and forth in front of them as Luke's rifle shots snapped over their heads, reducing the number of warriors by four. Expecting the Indians to suddenly appear at the mouth of the ravine, they could only wait and watch. In a few minutes time, however, the rifle fell silent, causing them more concern. There had been but two or three answering shots from their attackers. Could the silence mean that one of those shots had found Luke? A great sense of relief washed over them when they heard his voice.

"Don't shoot, I'm comin' down," Luke said. Moments later, he appeared. "They figured it was costin' them too much to keep comin'. They might have had enough, figured they wouldn't risk anybody else gettin' shot. But you never know what they'll do—might decide they need to revenge the four they lost. Anyway, they ain't gonna be happy about it, so you'd best hitch up again, and we'll try to put some distance between us and them while they're decidin'."

Luke's intention was to swing wide around the Sioux camp. Since the Indians had been traveling east to west, however, it would be necessary to make their circle to the east of the forks of the Powder and Little Powder. Otherwise, the Sioux would cross their wagon tracks as they headed north. So when they left the ravine, he led them south along the river for a mile before crossing back to the other side and circling back north once more.

The moon was riding lower in the sky by the time they made it back to strike the Powder again, some six or seven miles north of its fork with the Little Powder. There had been no sign of pursuit by the Sioux, for which they were all thankful, because David's horses were exhausted after such a short rest. Luke figured that there had not been many fighting men in the village after all, and his rifle had taken a greater toll than he had at first thought. "We couldn't have run any farther, anyway," David declared. "My horses were plumb played out." They made their camp on the Powder and remained there for the balance of the night. Early the following morning, Luke hurried them along. The horses needed more rest than the few hours allowed, but he thought it more important to push them farther. If the warriors decided to follow, they could be easily overtaken.

Angry Bull stood over the body of his brother, his fists clenched tightly, as he looked up at the sky to release his anguish in a low moan. He could not contain his grief and he dropped to his knees beside the body to cry out his vow for vengeance against the people who had killed his young brother. Close around him, others were wailing over the loss of the other three men killed in the ill-fated attack on the white man's wagon. Angry Bull remained on his knees even as the women of his small band took over the preparation of the bodies, as was the custom. Gray Bird, the old chief, came to try to console Angry Bull as the women carried his brother away, but there was nothing he could offer the grieving warrior that could replace his thirst for the white man's blood. "It is but one man," Angry Bull cried out, certain that what he said was true. "It is the man with the rifle that Wind Walker saw in their camp. Wind Walker saw that the man had strong medicine. It must have been him who was shooting from the top of the ridge."

"We must bury our dead," Gray Bird said, "and mourn their loss."

"No one will mourn more than I," Angry Bull declared, "but I must not wait too long and let his killer escape."

"The wagon cannot travel as fast as a man on a horse," Gray Bird said. "And it leaves tracks easy to follow. I cannot tell you what is best for you to do, but I think you would have no trouble over-taking the wagon after the dead are prepared for their journey."

It was not his preference, but Angry Bull deferred to the old chief's wisdom. The women dressed the bodies in their finest clothes, wrapped them in blankets, then sewed them up completely in buffalo hides. Since there were numerous suitable trees near the river, there were many limbs to choose from to build platforms to hold the bodies high enough to be out of the reach of coyotes and wolves. Angry Bull and some of the others slashed their arms and legs with their knives in mourning, and then finally the vengeful warrior could wait no longer. With his Spencer carbine in hand, he climbed on his war pony and asked which of his fellow warriors would ride with him. His friend Broken Glass stepped forward immediately, but there were no others. Insulted, Angry Bird was about to protest and shame them, but Gray Bird interrupted.

"Others wanted to ride with you," he said, "but there are only a few warriors left to protect the women and children. I know this vengeance that eats away inside you must be satisfied, so go and listen to the voice that speaks only to you. The others must stay to protect the village."

"There is wisdom in your words," Angry Bull conceded. "Broken Glass and I are enough to kill one white man." He looked at his friend for confirmation and received a solid nod in reply. Turning back to Gray Bird, he said, "We will be back before another sleep." After taking one last look at the bodies lying in the tree limbs, the two warriors were off, to return to the site of the previous night's battle. As Gray Bird had predicted, the tracks of the wagon were easy to find and follow to the south. *You will be avenged this day, my brother*. The thought turned over and over in Angry Bull's mind as they loped along the west bank of the Little Powder.

• • •

By the time the sun was directly overhead, David's horses were weary to the point of exhaustion. Even Luke's paint was tired and Luke had dismounted and walked beside the horse. "If we keep going, they're gonna fall in their traces," David called out to Luke. "I don't think those Indians are coming after us. We haven't seen hide nor hair of 'em all morning."

"Maybe not," Luke answered, but he could not be sure. He knew an Indian was like any other man. Some would seek revenge, no matter what. Others might yield to the superior firepower that he had demonstrated with his Henry rifle, and figure it wiser to restrict their losses to four. He hoped the latter was the prevailing disposition. There was no choice to be made, however. David was right. If they pushed the horses farther, they might kill them. "Over there," he called out to David, "where the river bends around that stand of trees." David nodded gratefully. "There's a little cover there," Luke said, "and maybe we can see anybody tryin' to sneak up on us if we keep our eyes on our back trail."

After the horses were watered and hobbled to graze, David and Luke sat down to eat the meat that Mary Beth had roasted over the fire. There had been little opportunity for sleep during the last two days, so Luke suggested that the two of them should take advantage of the time while the horses were rested. "I'll keep watch while you sleep." They were too tired to protest after their harrowing experience of the previous night. Their gentle nerves were not toughened to life in the wild of the Powder River country. Like obedient children, the couple made their bed in the wagon and climbed in. Luke took his rifle and walked back up the bank to take a position under a cottonwood where he could see the way they had come.

The afternoon passed slowly by with still no sight of anyone trailing them. Still his exhausted traveling companions slept on. Since there was nothing moving on the expanse of prairie behind them, he decided to let them sleep past dusk. The horses would benefit and it would soon be dark enough so that their camp would be difficult to see.

He was in the process of rekindling the fire when Mary Beth climbed down from the wagon. "Here," she said, "let me do that. Then I'll fix us something to eat." She looked back in the wagon to chastise her husband. "Get up, sleepyhead. You're gonna sleep the night away." Reluctantly, he roused himself out of his warm bed and came to join them. She handed him the coffeepot and said, "Here, fill this with water."

"I've got to go to the bushes first," David replied.

"I'll do it," Luke volunteered, and took the pot from him. He was feeling the need for some sleep himself and wanted the coffee to overcome it.

The thought occurred to Mary Beth then and she voiced it. "You've been standing guard all afternoon while we slept. You must need some sleep, too."

"I'll be all right," he replied, "and we need to keep movin', travel at night until we get outta this part of the valley."

She looked up at the sky and commented, "It looks like it's going to be another clear night. I don't see any clouds. I don't see why we couldn't wait for a couple of hours after supper before we start. You could get a couple of hours' sleep."

He had to admit he was tempted. He was tired, and a short sleep would surely help his sense of vigilance. "Maybe," he said, and left to fill the coffeepot.

The two men arrived back at the campfire at the same time and Mary Beth pointed out to her husband that Luke had had very little sleep in the last two nights. "I told him we could wait a couple of hours before starting out tonight, so he could rest a little."

Her comment served to embarrass the stoic guide. "I don't need no sleep," he protested, "and we need to keep movin' while the horses are rested."

"Yes, but you're not," David said. "Mary Beth is right. We can wait a couple of hours." Seeing Luke's obvious reluctance, he insisted in a joking manner. "We're paying you to guide us to

Coulson, and we need to have you alert enough to do the job." Luke was about to protest again, but David said, "I'll stand guard while you sleep. You don't have to worry about being surprised by Indians."

"There," Mary Beth said, "nothing to worry about. David will stand guard." She turned to give her husband a warm smile.

It was not easy for him to do, but after he had eaten, he gave in to their concern for his health and agreed to a brief rest, insisting that should he fall asleep, he be awakened in one hour, no more than that. He walked with David to position him at a good spot to watch their back trail. With that done, and settled in his blanket several yards beyond the wagon, he realized how much he needed sleep.

Some fifty yards above the camp, David sat propped up against a cottonwood and looked back where the river turned back on itself to form a U-shaped bend, the banks already fading in the approaching darkness. Rising low on the distant horizon, a full moon began its journey across the prairie sky. Mary Beth had been right; it was going to be another clear night to travel. David felt useful at last, knowing that he was standing guard while their invincible guide slept. He didn't even realize that he was still sleepy himself, and he was unaware that he had fallen asleep until he awoke for the fraction of an instant when a hand was suddenly clamped over his mouth and he felt the cold steel blade on his throat.

Roused abruptly from his slumber by the sudden sound of gunshots, Luke was instantly alert. Rolling out of his blanket while cocking his rifle, he discovered Mary Beth standing by the fire, her father's revolver in her hand, aimed at two Sioux warriors bearing down on her. She had missed with both shots, and the heavy pistol was wavering in her hand as she tried to steady herself to fire again. With very little time to react, Luke took dead aim at the foremost warrior. Mary Beth was between him and the savage, so he had to be sure of his aim. He squeezed the trigger when Angry Bull was no more than ten yards away from her. His shot, in the center of the Indian's chest, dropped him at once, his momentum causing him to roll dead at her feet. Broken Glass, running several yards behind Angry Bull, veered from his path, trying to react to the muzzle blast of Luke's rifle in time to return fire. He was too late, for Luke's second shot knocked him over backward, shattering his breastbone.

Mary Beth stood screaming for a long moment before unconsciously firing the pistol one last time, then dropping it on the ground and running to David's side, where she sank to her knees beside his still body. Luke, his rifle cocked, peered into the shadows of the trees, prepared to shoot again. When all was quiet, with no sign of any more than the two Indians, he went to Mary Beth. He didn't have to be told that her husband was dead, for she was sobbing uncontrollably. With no thought as to how he should try to console her, he sat beside her while she cried. After a few minutes with no end to her tears, he spoke in as soft a voice as he could manage. "I'm gonna take you back to the wagon while I take care of your husband." She started to protest, but offered no resistance when he lifted her to her feet. Once on her feet, she started to collapse, so he picked her up in his arms and carried her back to the wagon. "I won't be long," he told her as he placed her gently on her bedding.

He was not concerned about there being more warriors lying in ambush for him. He was pretty sure that, had there been others, he would have known it by now. He was pretty sure why David had been surprised as he stood guard. He must have fallen asleep. Looking at him now, lying beside the tree, his throat gaping open and several deep wounds in his torso, Luke re-created the killing in his mind. It was unfortunate that Mary Beth had to see her husband like that. At least he had not been scalped. The Indians had no doubt planned to collect all three scalps after they had killed everyone. At the moment, Luke gave no thought toward the complications to follow with David's death. His only concern was to do what he could to soften the shock of Mary Beth having seen her husband this way, so he went back to the wagon to get a blanket to wrap him in.

Mary Beth had stopped crying, but she was still curled up on her blankets, rocking gently as if calming a baby. Luke paused to look at the bodies of the two Lakota braves. With evidence still fresh of the many knife slashes on their arms and legs, he knew that the four he had killed before were heavily mourned. There was still some reason to concern himself with future attacks by other members of the village, but he figured the odds were against it. These two must have been close to the deceased. He turned when he heard Mary Beth climb down from the wagon.

"David," she cried, and started to go to her husband.

Luke caught her elbow to restrain her. "Better you don't go back to him just yet," he urged. "Best wait till I can clean him up a little."

"David never did anything to harm those people," she exclaimed. "Why would God let this happen?"

"It'll be better if I wrap him in a blanket before we bury him. I can tell by his wounds that he most likely didn't feel no pain." That was a lie, but he saw no sense in making it worse for her. "Give me a blanket to bury him in." He helped her up in the wagon again and she selected a proper blanket for her husband's burial shroud. "You wait right here, and I'll bring him so you can see him," he said. Too drained to protest, she did as he said. "Have you got somethin' I can use—?"

Knowing what he wanted, she got him a towel before he finished his request. Then she sat down on the tailgate to contemplate the end of her life, staring vacantly at the two Lakota corpses.

He did the best he could to clean most of the blood away from David's face, then wrapped him tightly in the blanket Mary Beth had given him. When he carried the body back, Mary Beth got off the tailgate so he could lay David across it. She could not suppress a gasp of pain when seeing the gaping slit across his throat again. Luke had tried to wrap the blanket up close under David's chin, but it had loosened as he carried the body. "My poor darling," she sobbed, repeating it over and over as she stroked his cold face. Luke left her to say her final farewell in private.

While Mary Beth spent her last moments with her husband, Luke took a rope from the wagon and tied it around the ankles of both Sioux warriors. Then he climbed on his horse and dragged the bodies out of the camp and up through the bluffs, where he left them for the buzzards to find. Returning to the wagon, he took a pick and shovel from the side and turned again to the grieving woman. "Ma,am," he said, "I don't mean to be disrespectful, but it's best to get your husband in the ground. I'm thinkin' about that spot up there under the trees." He pointed to the spot. "Is that to your likin'?" She nodded vacantly. He went to work then, digging David's grave.

The ceremony was brief after Luke lowered the body into the grave. Mary Beth removed a heart on a chain that David had given her on their first anniversary and placed it inside the blanket. "I bury my heart with you forever," she whispered, then turned away while Luke filled in the grave.

When he was finished, he scattered brush and limbs over the grave in an effort to disguise it against predators. He took a moment to lean on the shovel while he speculated on the tragic turn of events, and what he might expect to happen. Looking toward the wagon, he could see Mary Beth trying to busy herself around the fire, trying, he guessed, to keep from collapsing into a paralyzing fit of grief. He supposed it was his fault that David had been killed. He should never have let them talk him into taking a nap. *But, hell,* he thought, it was obvious that David had fallen asleep. "Damn greenhorn settlers," he mumbled under his breath, irritated that he should even share the blame. But he could not help feeling sympathy for the woman. He wished that he could do something to ease her pain, but he was at a loss as to what that might be. *She'll get over it as soon as she cries herself out,* he thought. The next question to be answered was, what would she decide to do now that her husband was gone?

CHAPTER 7

By the time Luke had finished with the burial and taken care of the horses, there were barely a couple of hours left before daylight. He decided to start out as soon as they could break camp, thinking it best to get Mary Beth away from the scene of her husband's death as soon as possible. As they had already planned to travel at night before the attack occurred, most of the camp had been packed away on the wagon. With very little left to do, Mary Beth attempted to occupy her mind with cleaning the coffeepot and washing cups that had already been washed. Try as she might, however, she was unsuccessful in blocking dreadful images of David's face in death. In the beginning, when David first began to woo her, she had not been sure that she loved him enough to marry him, but she was certain now. She had loved him with all her heart. The thought caused her to break down in tears once again, even as she was aware of the half-savage guide standing helpless as to what he should do.

Finally he spoke. "I expect we'd best move away from here. There's a couple of Sioux ponies back yonder in the brush. I'll fetch 'em, and then I'll hook up your horses for you. Can you drive your wagon?" She answered with a nod. He hesitated, reluctant to ask the question, but he figured he needed to know now. "Beggin' your pardon, ma'am, but what are you figurin' on doin'?"

"I don't know," she answered truthfully, for she had been unable to think beyond the fact that David was gone.

"You want me to take you back to Fort Fetterman, or Medicine Bow maybe? Or are you still figurin' on goin' on to the Yellowstone?"

"I don't know," she repeated, then shook her head several times, as if to clear her mind of sorrow. "Can you give me a minute to think?"

"Yes, ma'am," he answered. "I'll go round up those Indian ponies while you decide."

Both ponies submitted peacefully to him as he took their reins in hand and led them back to the wagon. "I guess I smell enough like an Indian to you," he said to the spotted gray. Mary Beth was laying out the harnesses when he brought the ponies back, put them on a lead rope, and tied it to the wagon. "Here, ma'am, I'll do that for you."

"Thank you," she said, and let him take over. "I could do it, though." She watched as he harnessed the team and looped the reins around the side of the seat. "We'll go on to Coulson," she announced, and climbed up to the wagon seat.

"Yes, ma'am," he said, and climbed up on the

paint. "We'll follow the river for a while as long as it's still headin' straight north. The river takes a big swing to the east before it works its way back on the line we've been followin', so we can save a fair amount of time if we cut straight across and strike it again in about a day and a half."

So they started out under a clear sky with the moon settling upon the distant hills as day approached. Behind them, a lonely grave and the bodies of two Lakota warriors lay as testimony to the savagery of the harsh prairie. And a tentative partnership between a grieving widow and an uncertain guide continued on its way. It was not the first time Mary Beth had driven the horses, but they seemed to know it was not David's hands holding the reins and they seemed a bit balkier than usual—so much so, in fact, that Luke came back and took hold of the bridle of one of the horses and led them until they picked up the pace. They seemed better after that, but Mary Beth really wasn't aware of the change. Her mind was laden with guilt and worry, guilt over encouraging David to stand guard when there was a danger of Indians coming after them—and worry over the decision she had made to continue on to Coulson. No matter which choice was for the best, leaving David behind was the hardest thing she had ever had to do. And how could she explain David's death to his brother? John and Doris would certainly take her in, but what would she do for the rest of her life? She couldn't live with them forever.

Then her thoughts centered on the broad back of the man on the paint pony, and her original fears about him came back now to concern her. Would his manner change now that she was a woman alone? It would be so easy for him to murder her and ride off with all her possessions. He had said in the beginning that he would guide them only because he needed the money. With David gone, would he now be thinking about taking all of her money? In the middle of this godforsaken prairie, no one would ever know what had happened to her. Or would he simply rob her and ride off to leave her to the Indians and the lonely prairie? She reached down for David's shotgun and propped it up close beside her.

Up ahead, Luke was turning over concerns of his own in his mind. He was wondering if he would come to regret the decision to lead the couple to the Yellowstone now that he had a grieving widow on his hands. He was now more anxious than ever to find Mary Beth's people as quickly as possible. He had to assume that her late husband's brother would take her in, but what if he found this place they had talked about and the brother was not there? He had agreed to take them to Coulson, and that was all. He had no obligation beyond that. *But, damn it,* he thought, *I can't leave her alone if her in-laws ain't there.*

She seemed to be so vulnerable and helpless since David was killed. It might have been a wiser decision for her to return to the place they started from. Who could say what was best for the woman? *What will be will be,* he decided with a sigh of resignation and gave the paint a nudge with his heels to quicken the pace a little.

Sometime around noon, he reined back to let Mary Beth catch up to him. When she pulled the horses to a stop beside him, he took a moment to study her face. She looked tired and haggard as the sunshine reflected off freshly formed trails left by her tears. He made a decision to stop for the rest of the day to let her rest. "The next little patch of trees we come to, we'll make camp and go on in the morning. We'll most likely leave the Powder after that and figure on strikin' it again in about a day's travel, and maybe we'll be far enough north by then that we won't have to worry about that band of Sioux anymore."

"Whatever you think best," she replied.

Once Luke settled on their campsite, Mary Beth dutifully began gathering wood for a fire while he took care of the horses. He took a few minutes to give the two Indian ponies a closer inspection. Both horses seemed docile enough, considering the new experience of trailing behind a wagon. Neither horse had a saddle; both were haltered with a cord made of woven strands of buffalo hair about the size of Luke's little finger. Of the two, he preferred the spotted gray, although the sorrel appeared to be the younger horse. He hobbled all but his paint and left them by the water to graze. When he returned to the wagon, Mary Beth had her fire started and was filling the coffeepot. He noticed that she was again wearing her father's pistol belt around her waist. He really couldn't blame her for being cautious, and he knew there was no way he could reassure her that she was safe with him.

"I'm gonna ride back to that low ridge we passed a while back and take a look behind us," he told her. "I won't be gone long." She nodded solemnly and continued grinding the coffee beans.

He didn't expect to see anyone along their back trail, but he thought it wouldn't hurt to check. It was difficult to hide a trail left by wagon wheels, but he figured the odds were in their favor. The paint loped along comfortably as he neared the ridge until Luke reined him back to climb up to the top. He paused there for a few moments while he scanned the horizon. Bringing his gaze back to the south along the river, he was startled to detect movement beyond a clump of bushes on the bank. He immediately backed his horse below the crown of the ridge while he scrambled back to determine if he had caught sight of antelope, or deer—or man. Kneeling at the top of the ridge, he waited, staring at the bushes that now blocked his view. If it was a herd of deer that caught his eye, they might have gone down to the water's edge to drink. He waited and watched.

"Damn," he swore when he saw them emerge from the screen of berry bushes. There were six of them—no doubt Lakota; he couldn't tell at that distance. "Damn wagon," he cursed as the Indians followed the obvious tracks of the wagon's wheels. The tracks presented a clear picture to the scouting party following them—a single wagon, settlers probably, and little means to protect themselves from six armed warriors. If the trackers were keen enough, they could determine that it was indeed a farm wagon, and not a heavily loaded freighter, probably meaning a weaker defense. "Damn the luck," he swore for the third time, for he had hoped not to run into any more Sioux parties, even though they had continued to come upon many trails heading west. Judging from the distance, and the evident pace of their pursuit, he figured he had about half an hour before the six warriors would reach the stand of trees and the wagon. He returned to his horse at once and hurried back to Mary Beth.

She paused when she saw him racing back to their camp at a gallop, knowing that the reason for his haste could not be good. Without thinking, she emptied the coffeepot full of water on the fire, anticipating his call to pack up. "No time to waste," he called out as he pulled the paint to a sliding halt. "We've got to get outta here! There's an Indian war party on our trail." He slid off his horse and ran to bring the others up from the river. Mary Beth tossed the coffeepot and her cooking utensils into the wagon, then ran to help him with the horses.

With no thought toward running, he followed the river with his eyes, searching for a better spot to defend. "There," he said, pointing to a deep gully on the other side of the river a few hundred yards distant. "We'll pull your wagon up in the mouth of that gully and park it. It'll give us some protection from the front." He could have hoped for a better place to stand off an Indian attack, but there wasn't time to be choosy. He glanced at Mary Beth as she helped him hitch up the horses. She might have wondered why he had chosen a place out in the open where there was no place to hide and little cover beyond shoulder-high brush along one side of the gully, but she did not question him. In fact, she displayed little emotion of any kind, going about fastening the harness as if in a trance. Misinterpreting her expression, he hoped she wasn't about to go loco on him.

In truth, Mary Beth had resigned herself to the same destiny that had befallen her husband. Friends back in Minnesota had advised against her and David's decision to strike out for a future in the undeveloped West. Now David was gone, and she was convinced that she would soon be joining him. She had cried herself out over David's death. There were no tears left in her, certainly none for herself. She was now resigned to wait patiently for her fate, and possibly making it costly for the Indians bent upon killing her. As for Luke Sunday, there might no longer be a reason to fear what his ultimate designs might be on her meager possessions, or her body. They would never make it to the Yellowstone. The Indians would see to that.

When the three Indian ponies had been tied to the tailgate, Luke climbed up on the wagon beside Mary Beth and took the reins. Giving the team a sharp pop of the lines, he started them off at a fast walk, heading out through the cotton-woods toward the bend in the river. Once across the river, he drove the wagon as far up into the mouth of the gully as the horses could pull it, causing Mary Beth to wonder how they would be able to pull it out again. Wasting no time, he looked back inside the wagon. "Pile everything you can up against the side of the wagon," he instructed. "That mattress and the beddin', stuff it against the sideboards—and that trunk." She responded immediately, preparing their fortifications while he jumped down to unhitch the horses and lead them, along with the others, to the back of the gully. When he saw her start to move their store of smoked meat out of harm's way, he said, "Leave it. It'll stop a bullet."

When the horses were safe and they had done all they could to prepare their battlements, there was nothing to do but wait. Luke picked up David's shotgun and checked it to make sure both barrels were loaded. "You might have better luck usin' this shotgun instead of one of these carbines those two Sioux had back at the forks." He placed the box of shells next to the trunk she had pushed against the side of the wagon. "This is a good spot for you to sit and shoot from." He paused and looked her in the eye. "I didn't ask you if you know how to shoot that thing."

"I know how," she replied calmly.

"Good," he said, for he remembered that she was none too accurate with a pistol. "Might be a good idea to eat a little somethin' while we've got a chance, 'cause we're liable to be a little busy before long. Matter of fact, a cup of coffee would go a long way." He looked around at the shrubs beyond the wagon. "I believe I can find enough branches in those bushes to make a fire."

Having said no more than a few words since leaving their previous camping spot, she picked up her coffeepot and started toward the water's edge to fill it. "I'd better get water before they show up," she said. "We're so out in the open, we might not be able to get to the water when they find us."

"I know it ain't shady in this gully," Luke replied. "But we've got a helluva lot better chance of keepin' our scalps here where we can see 'em comin' after us. They can hide back there in the trees, but they're gonna have to cross a wide space of open bluffs, or swim across the river, if they're plannin' on attackin' us. And if they do, I hope I can make it so hot for 'em that they'll change their minds about jumpin' us." He didn't say it, but he also knew there was the possibility of a long siege, depending on what the Indians had in mind and how patient they were. If they mounted an all-out attack, he hoped he could inflict enough damage to discourage them, and possibly cause them to give up before incurring too many casualties. On the other hand, if they were patient, they could wait him out, hanging back far enough to minimize the range of his rifle until he and Mary Beth had to make an attempt to run.

He didn't have long to wait, for in the next few minutes, the six warriors appeared at the edge of the trees, talking among themselves and pointing to the wagon tracks just recently left on the bank. In the next instant, one of them looked up and spotted the wagon in the gully several hundred yards away and began talking excitedly as he pointed to it. "Lakota," Luke pronounced dryly. They were still too far for him to recognize the markings on their ponies as a symbol of that tribe, but he had a gut feeling. He could also feel Mary Beth tense as he said it and pull the shotgun up to her shoulder. "Let's wait and see what they're gonna do," he told her. "They're a little out of range right now."

The warriors took only a few minutes to decide their plan of attack. It was the option Luke had hoped for, because he could use his rifle most effectively that way. Screaming out their war cries, they spread out in a fan and charged across the bluffs. "Wait," Luke cautioned Mary Beth. "Let 'em get a little closer." He climbed up behind the seat where he could steady his rifle.

Forgetting her earlier morbid thoughts of doom, Mary Beth drew the hammers back on both barrels of her shotgun and braced herself, her fear having been replaced by a thirst for vengeance for David's death. Anxious now to make someone pay for it, she could wait no longer, and pulled the trigger when they were still a hundred and fifty yards away. Her shot, ineffective, was followed by one from the other barrel with the same results. With little choice, Luke took his first shot at the lead warrior, knocking him from his pony's back. The Sioux were well within the Henry's effective range, but Luke had planned to let them get within fifty yards, figuring that he would have time to eliminate two or three before they could retreat out of range. As it was, the five remaining warriors scattered to draw back out of range. In hopes of a lucky shot, he threw another round after them, but missed.

Thanks to Mary Beth's premature shot, Luke's

plan to deliver a devastating blow to the war party was rendered ineffective. It would do little good to admonish her for it, or complain that her impatient action would probably serve to lengthen their siege. So instead, he patiently advised her that her shotgun would be of little use at that range.

"We got one of the bastards, though," she said as she loaded two fresh shells into her shotgun.

"I reckon," he replied, and resisted the temptation to tell her that if she had waited just one or two minutes longer, he would most likely have eliminated three of the warriors, and the rest might have gone home. In considering their present situation, however, he had to lay some of the blame at his feet. Thinking that most of the hostile Sioux were already in Sitting Bull's and Crazy Horse's villages, he had underestimated the number of small bands of warriors still leaving the reservations to join them. Already, they had been discovered by two different parties while traveling the Powder River Valley, and his thoughts returned to curse the wagon once more. *Damn wagon,* he thought, *like dangling bait in front of a wolf.* It was at this point that he decided to abandon it, although he had to admit that he had probably subconsciously made the decision when he had driven the wagon so far up the gully. His thoughts were interrupted then by a question from Mary Beth.

"What do you think they're gonna do?"

"Don't know," Luke replied, although he had a pretty strong idea. "They pulled back to talk about it. We'll know soon enough." He climbed down from the wagon. "I've got some things to do while they're makin' up their minds. You keep your eyes peeled on that riverbank and sing out if you see any of 'em movin' toward us again."

While she watched for any signs of another attack, he gathered up David's extra rope and, using straps cut from the traces, began to fashion some packsaddles for the horses. He was convinced that the only chance they had of eluding this and any other war party was to abandon the wagon. It was going to be a hard decision for Mary Beth, but it was impossible to run from any hostiles that spotted their tracks in this open country, so it was now a matter of survival. For this reason, he didn't tell her yet. He still had another decision to make. There was no doubt that she would want to take more than they would be able to carry on the horses. But with five horses, three of which to use as packhorses, she could take a fair amount as long as it could be carried on a horse's back. The thing that troubled him was the fact that the two horses pulling the wagon were shod, while the other three were not. This fact meant they would still leave a white man's trail, even though they were traveling faster. David had the tools on the wagon to remove the shoes, but then they would be confronted with the probability of horses with sore feet slowing them down. It was a simple fact, the two of them on horseback, leading one packhorse, would move faster and more easily hide their trail.

"They're coming back!" Mary Beth called over her shoulder.

Luke dropped the pack he was working on and moved up beside her in the wagon. He saw at once what had caught her attention. The five warriors were spread out again, moving cautiously among the bluffs of the river in an attempt to get within range of their weapons. Without knowing how well they were armed, Luke had to wait to see what they considered an effective range. He was answered soon enough when one of the hostiles popped up from behind a tree at the edge of the riverbank and fired a shot that knocked a hole in the wagon's sideboards. Both Luke and Mary Beth ducked behind her trunk. "That ain't good," Luke muttered. "One of 'em's got a rifle—sounds like an army Springfield." The news was not good because it told him that the hostiles had a longer-range weapon than his Henry, and judging from the hole in the wagon's sideboard, they knew how to shoot it. To confirm it, a second shot rang out, sending another chunk of wood flying from the wagon.

Before scrambling around the end of the trunk

toward the wagon seat, he had a pretty good idea what was going on. And when he eased his head up so he could see, it was confirmed, as a third shot punched a hole in the mattress propped up against the side. As he guessed, the warrior with the rifle intended to keep Luke down while his brothers made their way closer to the gully, probably carrying weapons of shorter range than the Springfield. *Come on, then,* he thought, *let them get a little bit closer and we'll see.* "Stay down behind that trunk," he told Mary Beth. It was an unnecessary command. He crawled back to the tailgate and dropped to the bottom of the gully. Crouched behind the gully wall, he ran past the wagon tongue to a notch in the sandy soil. Laying his rifle in the notch, he eased up high enough to see the riverbank before him. After a few moments' search, he spotted the other four hostiles working their way in closer to him. Patiently, he waited for the shot. Finally one of the Indians broke from the bluffs about one hundred yards downriver and started to cross. Luke took careful aim and squeezed the trigger. The warrior collapsed and floated slowly down the river with the gentle tide. As soon as he fired, Luke moved a half-dozen yards to a new spot. Moments later, the Springfield spoke again, kicking up gravel in the spot he had just vacated.

"Keep your head down," he called to caution Mary Beth again as shots from less powerful weapons opened up. From the popping sound of them, he guessed they were carbines similar to the Spencers he had taken from the first party. Searching back and forth along the bluffs, he waited for a glimpse of one of the warriors. When their assault offered no signs of success, the hostiles became impatient. It was what Luke was counting on. Anxious to be the first to kill the white man, one of the hostiles leaped up from his hiding place and bolted toward a high hummock near the water's edge. Luke took aim, leading him a little less than he would have a deer, and patiently shot him in midstride, causing him to tumble and roll a few times before remaining still.

Luke had barely withdrawn from the spot before two quick shots from the Springfield tore into the rim of the gully. "That damn Injun's pretty good with that rifle," he muttered as he shifted to a new location. Crawling up beneath the branches of a clump of sagebrush, he found a better place to scan the terrain between the gully and the cotton-woods on the opposite bank. For a while, there were no more opportunities for a clear shot, for the two remaining hostiles, who had moved in closer, had evidently seen enough of Luke's accuracy with his Henry rifle to discourage them from continuing to advance upon the gully. All was quiet for quite some time before the two suddenly sprang from their hiding places and fled back to the cover of the trees as fast as they could run. Luke was not quick enough to hit either one. He cursed the missed opportunity.

"I think that'll most likely be it for the afternoon," Luke said when he moved back to the wagon.

"Do you think they'll give up and leave us alone now?" Mary Beth asked, still huddled behind the trunk and clutching the shotgun.

"Don't know," Luke replied. "Maybe. There's three of 'em dead. That might be enough for 'em. On the other hand, they might just be waitin' for dark and try to sneak in on us. They probably figure one of 'em can get around behind us and we can't cover all three of 'em. That's more likely what they're plannin' on." He looked up at the afternoon sun. "It ain't gonna be much longer before dark, and they know we can't drive this wagon outta here with them sittin' there watchin' us."

His assessment of their situation did very little to comfort Mary Beth's fears. From what she could see, they could not leave the gully without great odds of getting shot, and it was impossible to drive the wagon up the back of the gully. It was already wedged fairly snug in the mouth of it. "What are we going to do?" she asked, not at all comfortable with the idea of sitting in this grave they had dug for themselves and waiting for their executioners to close in on them.

"We're leavin' here as soon as it gets dark," he answered. Before she could question him further, he laid it out for her. "We're leavin' your wagon right where it is. We can't outrun anybody with that wagon, and it leaves a trail that a blind Injun can follow, so we're ridin' outta here on horseback." He paused to comment, "I hope to hell you can ride. Even if you can't, that's the way we're goin'." She at once looked alarmed, and began to glance around in the wagon, concerned for all her possessions. Guessing her thoughts, he continued. "You're gonna have to leave most of this stuff. I rigged up a packsaddle for that sorrel, so we'll take the most important stuff, whatever we can get on the packhorse and behind us on the other two ponies." Without waiting to hear her protests, he asked, "Can you ride a horse?"

"Well, I have ridden one," she answered, still struggling with the notion that she might lose all her earthly goods.

"Good," he replied curtly. "I expect you'll do better in the saddle, so I'll put you on my horse and I'll ride the spotted gray pony."

"We didn't bring much furniture because David's brother said we could build most of what we needed out there," she said. "But we have the bedstead and my trunk and some personal things that I can't leave. We can't carry all that on the horses." She frowned her distress. "My mother's china, I can't leave that, our grandmother clock—"

That was as far as she got before he interrupted.

"Ma'am," he said sternly, "you ain't got no choice. If we're gonna get to your brother's house alive, you're gonna have to leave all that stuff. Take some clothes, some food, somethin' to cook it with, and whatever money you've got—guns and cartridges—that's all we have to have. We ain't takin' but one packhorse." He went on to explain his reasons for setting her two horses free. "I know it's a hard thing for you to part with your things, but that's the way it's gotta be if you're gonna save your scalp. I'm ridin' out of here as soon as it's dark—with you or without you." He knew he was putting it to her pretty harshly, but he didn't want to give her any room to argue the point. In truth, he would never leave without her, but if it became necessary, he would take her forcefully, convinced as he was that it was their best chance for escape. He felt now, since their recent Indian encounters, that it was too dangerous to try to continue pulling a wagon through the Powder Valley.

On her knees in the back of the wagon, she stared at him, stunned by the realization that she must discard possessions that had belonged to her mother and father, and desperate in the knowledge that her immediate fate depended on the rugged sandy-haired scout. The feelings of distrust she had felt in the beginning came back to frighten her now, but what choice did she have? He had threatened to leave without her if she balked. "All right," she said finally, "I'll get my things ready to go." She couldn't help adding "I guess you want to make sure I take all our money, money we saved up for our new home."

"Only a hundred dollars of it," he answered. "The rest is up to you." He turned his attention back to the expanse of sand and gravel between the gully and the trees on the opposite bank of the river. Without turning to look at her again, he said, "Put everythin' you wanna take on the tailgate and I'll pack it on the horses."

When the sun began to drop low on the hills to the west of them, he slid back down from the perch he had taken on the rim of the gully. "Crawl up there and keep your eyes open while I load the horses," he instructed her. "Be mindful of the river both ways in case one of 'em tries to swim across and get in behind us."

She dutifully did his bidding, although greatly disturbed that her situation had been so drastically changed. She no longer held any authority over a man she had originally hired. The fact that she was in no position to challenge his decisions added to her dismay, all the while knowing that if she was to escape this siege with her life, it would be him that saved her. These were the thoughts that crowded her mind while she strained to detect movement of any kind in the long shadows of twilight. They were not helped by the underlying basic fear that, at any moment, a screaming savage might suddenly spring up to take her scalp. So intensely was she watching the river and the bluffs beyond that she didn't hear his question. "What?" she asked.

"I said, is there anythin' else you wanna take?" he repeated. " 'Cause this horse can carry a little more than what you pulled out here." He took another look at the items she had selected. "Maybe you don't need some of these things. You could leave 'em and take some more of your personal things." He nudged a heavy large gunnysack with his toe. "What's in this?"

"Corn," she replied.

"Well, like I said, maybe you'd wanna leave it and take somethin' else instead."

"No," she quickly said, "I want to take it. I can't leave it."

He was confused by her insistence. "What is it, seed corn?" She nodded. He shrugged and reached down to heft the sack up on the horse. "Damn!" he involuntarily blurted, for the sack was a good deal heavier than he expected. "This must be some special kind of corn. I'm gonna have to repack this stuff to balance the load. You got somethin' else you wanna pack on here?"

Surprised, she turned to look at the horse, for she thought she would be told that she had chosen too much. She hurried back to the wagon to select some of the personal items that she had thought to sacrifice, amazed by the efficient way in which he had fashioned the pack. While waiting for her, he took over her post as lookout. "Be quick," he called back softly as the sun sank out of sight and the shadows faded into evening. "We've got to get outta here right now." The river valley that had been bathed in twilight only moments before was now cloaked in darkness as if someone had suddenly blown out a lantern. He wanted to move out of the gully before the moon came up, knowing that the Sioux warriors would probably try to sneak in close to them while it was darkest. And he intended to be gone when that happened.

When all was packed and tied securely, Luke saddled the paint and helped Mary Beth up in the saddle. He saw at once that he had to adjust the stirrups for her shorter legs, which he did while she sat quietly as the Indian pony shifted nervously. "He'll be all right," Luke assured her, "once he gets used to you." Knowing that the horse was accustomed to more weight than that of the slender woman, he packed a good portion of their dried meat behind the saddle. Satisfied that they were ready, he said, "Wait here. I'll be right back."

With his rifle in hand, he climbed up the back of the gully on foot. Near the end, where it reached the top of the bluff, he dropped to his hands and knees to search the darkness, upstream and downstream. He saw no one in the deepening night. About to rise to his feet, he stopped suddenly when a slight movement near a clump of berry bushes caught his eye. Unconsciously lowering his body close to the ground, he then remained motionless while locking his eyes on the bushes. In a few seconds, his suspicions proved to be accurate as a shadowy form emerged from the clump and moved stealthily toward him. Judging by his movements, he figured the Indian had not spotted him, so he very carefully backed away from the edge of the gully and drew his skinning knife, hoping to do what he had to quietly. He continued to edge his way back down the gully until he came to a spot that formed a little bit of a step that created a darker hole below it. Deciding he was not going to find a better spot, he crouched there against the sandy side of the gully and waited.

Behind him, he heard one of the horses snort at the bottom of the gully. It served to hurry the warrior, who was now at the top. Anxious to surprise the occupants of the camp, he stepped down in the rough trench, his carbine at the ready. Unaware of the demon awaiting him until it sprang up from the darkness to plunge the skinning knife deep into his gut, the Sioux warrior expelled a sharp grunt, as much a reaction of surprise as a cry of pain. Down they went, in a tumble, to land at the feet of the waiting horses, causing them to fidget nervously to get out of the way. Like an enraged puma, Luke withdrew his knife from the hostile's gut and drew it across the warrior's throat while the hostile struggled helplessly in his grasp.

A witness to the violent execution, Mary Beth sat rigidly in the saddle, terrified by the savage exhibition of hand-to-hand combat. She grabbed the saddle horn with both hands to keep from coming off the horse when it became excited by the two bodies rolling near its hooves. When the Sioux warrior was finally subdued, Luke dragged his body to the side, then freed Mary Beth and David's team of horses. He tossed their bridles in the wagon and glanced at Mary Beth. "Come," he said, and jumped deftly on his pony's back. She did not follow at once when he started up the gully, still stunned by the horrible scene. "Come!" he repeated sharply, and she followed immediately, afraid not to. With the lead rope in hand, he started up the back of the gully, his rifle ready, in case the other two hostiles had moved faster than he figured. Once he was clear of the gully, he quickly scanned the bluffs, and when he was certain no one else had headed them off, he motioned for Mary Beth to follow. Much to her relief, the paint responded obediently to her urging.

Even though it was dark there in the bluffs, she felt as if she was exposed to anyone in the valley, and expected to hear gunshots ring out at any minute. A few yards ahead, Luke looked back briefly at her before walking his pony along the bank until entering the water at a low spot about twenty yards above the gully. Walking the horses slowly to minimize their splashing in the knee-deep water, he led Mary Beth down the river. After they had made their way about a hundred yards downstream, Luke felt they were clear of any ambush by the other two warriors. He rested the heavy Henry rifle across the gray's withers since he had no saddle, and consequently, no scabbard for the rifle. What happened next was dependent on the disposition of the remaining Sioux warriors, he decided. He could not guess what they would do when they found the body in the gully. He had taken a toll on their small scouting party, reducing it to two warriors. He hoped they would consider their medicine bad on this scout, pick up their dead, and break off their pursuit, but there was also the possibility they would follow, determined to avenge their dead. For this reason, he remained in the river, hoping to disguise their trail.

Mary Beth finally relaxed to let her body adapt to the gentle motion of the paint pony. She had been rigid for so many tense moments that she now ached in her legs and back. It was going to take some time, however, before the picture of the killing just witnessed would leave her mind. It was stronger even than that of David's gaping throat, and she wondered how many of these brutal scenes she could live through before she was driven out of her mind. Then she thought of the many things left behind in the wagon to be stolen or destroyed by savages. And the horses, what would become of them? She had seen both of them follow the Indian ponies out of the gully and down to the river's edge, but they had stopped there, content to drink and graze. She would never see them again, and she hoped that they could survive on their own. There was very little left of her and David's life, a few sentimental trinkets, some dishes, some clothes, a few other things. She suddenly felt tears inching down her cheeks as she found herself in hopeless despair, and though fearful of the man leading her down the river, she was more afraid to be without him.

Luke continued down the river for almost a mile before coming to a low bank covered with short grass. Figuring this to be as good a place as he was likely to find to leave the river, he turned the gray toward the west bank and climbed up out of the river. He dismounted and waited for Mary Beth to catch up. "You doin' all right?" he asked. "Just got your feet wet a little, I reckon." She only nodded in reply. He took a minute to check the packs on the sorrel. "Looks like nothin' got too wet. I ain't sure those other two ain't found out we're gone yet, but if they were of a mind to come after us, we shoulda heard somethin' from 'em by now." She remained silent, nodding only to acknowledge understanding. He went on. "We'd best make as good a time as we can while we've got a clear night. I don't know how much longer this weather is gonna favor us. It's mighty unusual for this time of year. We're gonna leave the Powder now and head on a more straight line for where we're goin'. If we head west and a little north, we can strike the Pumpkin by daybreak, now that we ain't slowed down by a wagon."

It didn't occur to her that he had said more words at one time than he had ever spoken before, so she was unable to recognize his clumsy attempt to set her mind at ease after the shock of their narrow escape. "If we still ain't seen any sign of 'em after a couple more hours, we'll stop and rest the horses—and get you a little somethin' to eat." He felt reasonably sure that, if there was no sign of the two Sioux warriors by the time they reached Pumpkin Creek, he could stop worrying about them. Hopefully, they would see fewer trails left by other hostile parties since that should place them about three or four days northwest of the big Sioux camp. If he could believe reports the Crow and Shoshoni had told General Crook, Sitting Bull was camped somewhere along Rosebud Creek, and would probably move toward the Big Horn. The mental image of General Crook led him to thoughts of the scout who had caused him to lose his job. *It should have been Bill Bogart in that saloon back at Fort Fetterman instead of Sonny Pickens,* he thought. But he had not been given a choice when Pickens took a shot at him. He had not given Bill Bogart any thought for quite some time, and he wondered why he came to mind now. *I've got a strong dislike for that son of a bitch,* he thought. *It's a good thing I'm done with him, else one of us would wind up dead for certain.*

CHAPTER 8

Maybe by coincidence, the man Luke Sunday had brought to mind a hundred miles away was at that moment sitting by a campfire at Goose Creek, grousing with his partner, George Wylie, after receiving a brutal dressing-down by Major Potter. "By God," Bill Bogart complained, "that pompous little banty-rooster ain't got no call to blame me for none of that whuppin' them hostiles put on the soldiers. I ain't the only one that thought the Injuns would run instead of fightin'."

Wylie only shrugged and made a face in response. He figured it would profit him little to point out that Bogart had been the one who assured Major Potter that the Sioux and Cheyenne were running like scared rabbits. It had only enforced a general belief most of the army officers already held, and it led to a major portion of General Crook's forces getting caught with their pants down while they stopped to rest and let their horses graze beside Rosebud Creek. Had it not been for the vigilance of the two hundred and sixty Crow and Shoshoni warriors that had come to fight with Crook's forces, and their firm belief that Crazy Horse would stand and fight, Crook's army might have been massacred. The Crows' and Shoshonis' counterattack gave Crook time to collect his forces to stop Crazy Horse's advance. And now Crazy Horse and Sitting Bull had moved on toward the Big Horn, while the soldiers had withdrawn to Goose Creek to await reinforcements. "I reckon he jumped on your ass pretty hard at that," Wylie finally commented.

"Threatened to fire me, he did," Bogart fumed. "The son of a bitch, he better not be standin' anywhere close to me the next time we get caught in a hot battle with them Injuns. He just might get unlucky enough to catch a stray bullet." He started to say more, but realized that it might not be the kind of talk to bandy about casually. It wouldn't do for the wrong person to overhear him, so he changed his tune. "I expect he needn't worry 'bout firin' me. I just might quit." It was no more than boastful talk, for he would hang on as long as the army would pay him. "Hell, I'm tired of talkin' about the bastard. I'm gonna turn in," he told Wylie, and got up to leave.

With a bladder filled with coffee, he walked down toward the officers' latrine to relieve himself. Enlisted men and scouts were not permitted to use the latrine, but Bogart customarily did his business in the bushes behind the tent. Ordinarily, he would relieve himself wherever he happened to be standing, but he was warned against that practice, and instructed to retreat a respectable distance from the common camp. It irritated him to do so, but he complied reluctantly. It was just one more thing that added to his dislike for officers. There they were, camped out along Goose Creek, and they dug a hole in the ground and built a wooden seat over it, so the officers wouldn't have to stand out in the open to answer nature's call.

He encountered one officer on his way to the latrine. By unfortunate coincidence, it happened to be Major Potter. "Son of a bitch," Bogart muttered under his breath. Then with an attempt to remove the scowl from his face, said, "Evenin', Major," and paused to let the major pass in front of him.

Potter halted abruptly when he saw who it was. "Oh, Bogart," he said. "I was going to send for you in the morning. This will save us both the trouble. Your services as a scout will no longer be required. You can pick up any pay you've got coming at the end of the month."

"Fired!" Bogart sputtered. "You're firin' me?"

"You're not the only one," Potter replied unemotionally. "We're letting a few other scouts go as well. That partner of yours, George Wylie, is one of them."

"You can't fire me," Bogart stormed. "I'm the best damn scout you've got!"

"No use to make it hard on yourself," Potter said, his voice still calm. "It's already done."

"Why, you prissy-ass son of a bitch, I oughta

stomp your ass in the ground. You got no call to fire me."

"Now you've gone too far," Potter threatened, heating up and drawing his frail statue up in indignation. "You're going to find yourself in irons if you don't close your mouth and get out of my way."

With fists clenched and every muscle in his body tensed to the breaking point, Bogart could barely restrain himself. The urge to strike out at the major was overwhelming, and the knowledge that there were too many people around for him to get away with it left the oversized bully sputtering helplessly while Potter continued on his way to the latrine. Still fuming, Bogart walked after the major, but went around behind the tent as was his original intention. But instead of relieving his bladder, he edged up to the back corner of the tent to listen for voices inside. When he heard none, he drew his bowie knife and slit the corner of the canvas, large enough for him to peek inside. Potter was alone. The picture of the diminutive officer seated on the wooden structure was sufficient inducement to squash him like a bug. His desire to take out his anger on the unsuspecting officer was too strong to ignore, and the time was right. He didn't expect to be presented with another opportunity to catch Potter alone and vulnerable. He would worry about the consequences later.

Leaving the back corner of the tent, Bogart inched his way to the front while watching the open space between the latrine and the cavalry encampment. It was dark enough at this point that even his bulky figure would hardly be noticed, but he knew he had to hurry before one of the other privileged few authorized to use the facility might feel the urge. With his knife still in hand, he pushed the tent flap aside and entered.

"What in hell are you doing in here?" Potter demanded, trying to maintain his indignant aplomb while his trousers were still down around his ankles.

"I came to see if you needed anybody to wipe your scrawny little ass for you," Bogart snarled, his face a mask of evil delight, his knife concealed behind his leg. "And I wanted to see if there was anythin' between your legs that proved you was a man."

Only half-finished with the business he had come to do, Potter leaped up from his wooden throne, while frantically trying to pull his trousers up. In the process, he did not take notice of the bowie knife in Bogart's hand. "By God, I'll have you hanged for this intrusion," he managed to spit out before Bogart stepped up close and thrust his knife to the hilt up under his breastbone. The force of the blow was so powerful that the slender officer was lifted off his feet to drop back across the toilet, gasping for breath.

Far too lost in the moment of triumph to be concerned with being caught, Bogart took his time to enjoy the execution. "Who you gonna hang now, you little bastard?" he taunted the dying man. "I'm fixin' to scalp you, and when they find you, they'll think an Injun done it." Then ignoring the futile efforts of the stricken officer to protect himself, Bogart clamped both hands over Potter's face, shutting off air to his nose and mouth, muffling his screams of agony, while the dying man flailed frantically for his life. After a couple of minutes, Potter's body relaxed into death. The bug was squashed. To make sure, Bogart continued to hold his hands over his face until positively certain his victim was dead. Then he yanked the knife out of Potter's body and proceeded to lift the scalp from his head.

Once the savage ritual was accomplished, a sense of urgency returned, and he went at once to the tent flap to see if anyone was approaching. There was still no one close by, so he returned to stand over the pitiful remains of the major who had cost him his job, and he favored the body with a grin of satisfaction. He glanced down at his knife as he was about to replace it in its sheath. Seeing the blood on the blade, he wiped it on Potter's shirt before putting it away. He turned then to leave before anyone showed up to use the latrine. It was at that moment that a sense of urgency of another kind came to remind him that he had never rid himself of the coffee he had consumed, and the reason he had happened to bump into Potter in the first place. Now that his body was no longer locked in a sense of passion, the urgency to empty his bladder took preference once more. Hurrying to the tent flap again for another quick look just to make sure, he then returned to empty the complaining bladder on the still corpse lying across the rough toilet seat. Content with himself, he slipped out of the tent and disappeared into the night.

"Where you been so long?" George Wylie asked when Bogart joined him at the makeshift camp they shared close to the horse herd.

"I told you I had to take a leak," Bogart replied.

"Musta been a helluva one," Wylie said with a chuckle.

"Yep, it was mighty satisfyin'. I ran into our favorite officer, Major Potter, and we had a little talk." He looked down at Wylie and grinned. "Now, this oughta tickle you real good. Me and you ain't got no jobs no more." This captured Wylie's attention immediately.

"What are you talkin' about?" Wylie asked, not understanding. "Startin' when?"

"Startin' right now," Bogart said. "He told me we wasn't needed no more."

"Damn!" Wylie swore. "Just you and me? Any of the other scouts cut loose?"

"Well, he said there was some of the others let go, but he didn't say who or how many, but I figure there ain't no use to hang around here. Hell, I'm ready to head outta here right now."

"Damn," Wylie swore again softly. He hadn't expected anything this drastic to happen. He knew Bogart wasn't on the major's list of favorites, but he figured Potter was just riding him. He wasn't really planning to fire him. And he sure didn't think *he* was in any trouble. "You know, that ain't right. I'm thinkin' we oughta go talk to Ben Clarke about this . . ." He paused. "Or Potter."

"You might could talk to Ben about it, but Potter ain't gonna be talkin' to nobody about nothin' no more. And like I said, I'm figurin' on ridin' outta here tonight. You goin' with me?"

"Damn," Wylie swore once more. He knew Bogart well enough to recognize a hint of mischief in his tone. "I was just fixin' to crawl under my blanket. Can't you wait till mornin'?"

"I reckon I could, but I ain't," Bogart replied, already in the process of packing up his gear. "I ain't fond of hangin' around where I ain't appreciated. You goin' or not?"

"What'd you do?" Wylie pressed, certain now that his big friend had somehow gotten into trouble. "You didn't step on ol' Potter's toes, did you?"

"I did worse than that, so that's why I'm leavin'

tonight," Bogart said. "I don't plan to be around here when they start askin' questions in the mornin'."

"Anybody see you jump on him?" Wylie wanted to know. He was trying to make up his mind whether to go with Bogart or not. If it was true that he no longer had a job, there was no use in remaining there at Goose Creek. If Bogart was set on getting away from there right away, he must have done some serious work on the major, and there might be an army detachment on his tail by morning. On the other hand, if nobody saw him do whatever he did to Potter, then they might think they just left camp to get a start somewhere else. Wylie knew that he needed a strong friend like Bogart, and that's why he had jumped right up to take Sonny Pickens's place when Luke Sunday shot Sonny. He wasn't confident on his own, and Bogart had taken to him right away.

"Ain't nobody seen me," Bogart answered him.

Wylie hoped that was true. "Well, I reckon I'd best be gettin' my things together, if we're gonna get outta here tonight," he said, and started rolling up his blanket. He paused while tying the rawhide cords and asked, "How bad did you hurt ol' Potter?"

Without saying a word, Bogart grinned, reached into his pocket, and pulled out an object rolled up in a bandana. He unrolled the bandana and held the gruesome object up for Wylie to see. It took a moment, but then Wylie suddenly realized it was a scalp. In that moment he was aware that he had no choice but to go with Bogart. He now knew too much.

Bogart picked up his saddle and rifle. "Let's get our horses saddled and cut outta here before somebody finds that little bastard," he said. "We need to put a little territory between us and Goose Creek."

"Right," Wylie replied, and picked up his saddle. "Where are we goin'?"

"Let's just get away from here first. Then we'll decide what part of the territory suits us best— somewhere we can make a helluva lot more money than what the army pays scouts."

No one seemed to notice, or care, that the two scouts were saddling their horses and riding out of camp in the early evening. Not even the picket they passed as they headed across the open prairie was interested enough to question them. Bogart smiled to himself as the campfires faded away in the darkness behind them, knowing he had gotten away with the brutal murder. *They'll play hell trying to track me down,* he thought, confident in his ability to hide his tracks. It was not the first murder he had gotten away with, and as he rode on into the night, he was reminded of the time a deputy marshal had attempted to question him about a bank holdup in Oklahoma Territory six years before. He actually had nothing to do with the holdup. He just didn't like the deputy marshal. He despised lawmen as much as he hated army officers. He had to chuckle when he thought about it, because they never knew for sure who shot that deputy in the back, although they had a pretty good idea. Didn't make any difference, anyway, 'cause he was long gone when that posse came after him.

They continued on until the horses began showing signs of tiring, so when they came upon a creek that emptied into the Tongue River, they camped there for the rest of the night. Secure in the belief that no one was on their tail, they slept past sunup the next morning until Wylie rolled out of his blanket and rekindled the fire. Owing to their hasty departure the night before, there had been no opportunity to acquire any extra supplies, but between them they had some coffee and a small amount of salt pork, which Wylie soon had over the fire. "One of the first things we got to do is go huntin'," Bogart commented when Wylie offered him a couple of strips of bacon. "I'm a big man and I need a helluva lot more than this to eat."

"This oughta hold us till we run up on some deer or antelope, though," Wylie said. "Where you figure we oughta head? Back toward Cheyenne?" When they had left the army encampment, they had ridden out to the north, for no particular reason other than it seemed the quickest way to put the various battalion and company camps behind them.

"Don't seem like the smartest thing to do, does it? Goin' back to Cheyenne? There's liable to be some questions asked about us leavin' right after they found that little bastard's body." He took a long look at the simple man who had taken Sonny Pickens's place as his partner. So far Wylie had proven to be little more than a toady, striving to make himself useful in Bogart's eyes. *Well, I've got a use for someone like that,* he thought. But all the same, he missed Sonny's fearlessness when it came to a barroom brawl, or a throat that needed slitting. His musing brought another to mind, the man who had killed Sonny. The thought caused him to grunt irritably, "Huh." He reached over and speared another slice of bacon on the tip of his bowie knife. "I've been thinkin' about where I wanna go, and the more I think about it, the more I'm satisfied that we need to head out for the Yellowstone."

"Why?" Wylie wondered. "What's up there?"

"Well," Bogart replied with a devilish grin, "there's a couple of things. You remember that wagon that came up from Medicine Bow with them folks that was hurtin' so bad to get to some new town on the Yellowstone? I expect you remember that fine-lookin' wife that feller had." Wylie nodded. "Captain Findley said them folks

195

was tryin' to get up there 'cause some of their family had struck it rich and was lookin' to buy up a whole lotta land up on the Yellowstone." He paused to wipe the bacon grease on the sleeve of his shirt. "You know who they took to guide 'em?"

Again, Wylie nodded, then said, "Luke Sunday."

"That's right, Luke Sunday. And that murderin' Injun lover ain't the kind to do nobody no favors unless there's somethin' in it for him. So that says to me that he knows somethin' he don't feel like talkin' about, and I don't think he's got a right to whatever it is any more than we do. If somebody's got some gold they're lookin' to spend, then we need to be up there and see if we can help 'em get rid of it."

"Well, that sounds all right to me," Wylie said. "Whatever you think is best."

Bogart was silent for a long moment, a deep furrow etched across his brow. He held his knife up before his face and tested the sharpness of the blade with his thumb. "I've got somethin' to settle with Mr. Luke Sunday, and the sooner, the better."

CHAPTER 9

A chilling rain had set in right after they left Pumpkin Creek and Luke unrolled the canvas he had removed from Mary Beth's wagon. Half of it was used as a tent for her when they camped. The other half he had cut into two pieces. With one, he fashioned a raincoat to drape over her head and shoulders. The other was secured over the packs on the extra horse. For his own protection against the rain, he always carried a cloak made out of deer hide. The rain never let up throughout the morning as they continued on a northwest course, and it was close to noon before it began to taper off. By the time they reached the east bank of the Tongue River, horses and riders were both ready to stop and rest.

After Luke took a good look around them, he picked a spot on the west bank, and they crossed over. Mary Beth was bone-weary, but after Luke got a fire going, she rallied to take on the chore of fixing something for them to eat while he removed the packs and the saddle from their horses. "We'll stop here for a spell and give you a chance to rest up," he told her. His demeanor also told her that he was no longer worried about being followed by the two Sioux warriors. Enough time had passed since their flight from the Powder to suggest that they had left that danger behind them. Added to that was the possibility that the morning rain had helped to obliterate their tracks. In spite of the improvement in their situation, Mary Beth was still unable to discard the feeling of tension that had remained with her ever since David's death—for she was still a woman alone with a man as close to a wild savage as she had ever met in her entire life. Now that imminent danger was no longer upon them, would he attempt to take advantage of her as a savage might? As if intercepting her thoughts, he turned at that moment to gaze at her. After a lengthy pause, he said, "You look like you need some extra time to rest. We'll stay an extra night here."

"All right," she replied hesitantly, "if you think that's best, but I'm not too tired to go on right now."

He continued to gaze intensely at her for a few moments longer, then said, "It's best we stay here and rest. Then we'll head for the Yellowstone."

He seemed forceful in his tone. She wasn't sure she liked it, for it might be a sign that he had things on his mind now other than their escape from the Sioux. Suddenly she felt exhausted. If what she feared was true, there was very little she could do to stop him. Sooner or later she was going to find out what was on his mind. It might as well be sooner. Weary from carrying such thoughts of fear of the man, she poured them out on the ground between them. "I'm afraid of you," she blurted. "Do I need to be?"

Her blunt statement caught him completely by surprise and his eyes opened wide. "Why, no, ma'am," he replied, baffled by the question. "Why'd you think you did?"

She stared at him, half expecting him to fly into a rage, but the genuine astonishment she read in his eyes was enough to finally convince her that she had made a gross misjudgment of the man. "I swear . . . ," she started to apologize, realizing she had let her fears and imagination create a ridiculous picture. Suddenly she found the situation hilarious and started to laugh uncontrollably, unable to finish her remark. His bewildered reaction to her laughing fit almost convinced her that, contrary to the fears she had harbored, he might be more afraid of her. Her nerves, strained to the point of exhaustion by the harrowing events of the last several days, seemed to release their tension with her laughter. He stood, perplexed, watching and wondering if the woman really had gone mad, accustomed as he was to the resolute reaction of Crow or Cheyenne women when faced with danger. Although he was born a white man, he had always lived with one Indian tribe or another. This was his first exposure to a white woman and he had wondered if they were different. Maybe she was not really mad. Maybe she was just white.

When finally she was able to recover from the massive release of the fear she had built up, she dropped to the ground, feeling very much like a rag, but with a great sense of relief, for she felt safe with her wild man for the first time. She wiped her eyes with her sleeves, and released a long sigh that signaled the end of her attack. "Mr. Sunday," she stated in straightforward words, "I apologize for not trusting you completely, for thinking you might rob me or harm me. I promise I won't misjudge you again."

"Luke," he reminded her again. "There ain't no Mr. Sunday."

His reply brought yet another smile to her face. "Luke," she repeated. "Thank you for all you have done for David and me."

"I ain't got you there yet," he reminded her.

Her smile broadened. "Even so," she said, "I thank you." She realized that he didn't really know how to accept thanks for doing something he was being paid to do. "Now, let's see if I can cook up some more of that meat we're packing, and if the flour stayed dry, maybe I can come up with something to go with it."

Things went better for both of them after that. Mary Beth no longer tried to keep one eye on Luke, secure in the belief that her welfare was his main concern. As for Luke, he couldn't help noticing the change in her manner, and that made it more comfortable for him. After spending an extra day at the camp on the Tongue River, they started out on a course that led them to the northwest, leaving the river. One day's ride brought them close to the Yellowstone at the point where Rosebud Creek emptied into it. There had been no sign of Indian travel between the Tongue and the Yellowstone except for one trail heading west where unshod ponies, some pulling travois, had passed. Luke determined that the trail was several days old. They continued through a line of low hills until he figured they could be no farther than a mile or two from the river, so he turned the gray toward the slope of the highest ridge and climbed to the top. From there, they could see the wide, peaceful river as it flowed snakelike through the high plains of Montana Territory.

While Luke was intent upon searching the river for as far as he could see, east and west, for any sign of Indian camps, Mary Beth was struck by the beauty of it. "I didn't know it was so big," she said. "It's so wide and peaceful."

"I reckon it is peaceful on this part of it," Luke allowed, "but it ain't that peaceful back up in the mountains where it starts out."

She turned to look at him then. "You've seen where it originates?"

"Yes, ma'am, up in the Absarokas. It's pretty country up that way."

She smiled and slowly nodded with a slight

feeling of envy. "You really are a child of the wilderness, aren't you?"

He shrugged, not knowing how to answer the question. It seemed that since she had decided she had nothing to fear from him, she tended to talk to him more. And much of what she said confused him. "Well," he said, "I can't see any sign of trouble, so I reckon we best get movin'."

Having reached the Yellowstone, Luke was now as much in the dark as she, for he had never heard of a town called Coulson until he met David and Mary Beth. The Crow people had frequented the area for many years, but Luke had not been back for quite some time. Based on what David had told him, Coulson was on the river, some distance east of the Gallatin Valley. That could be anywhere within a large area, so the only thing they could do was to travel west along the river until they eventually found it.

Late in the afternoon of their first day following the winding river, they came upon a trading post. Little more than a shack perched on the edge of a high bank, the store looked in danger of tumbling down the bluffs to land in the water at the first gust from a north wind. The owner apparently lived in an old army squad tent beside the store. Luke pulled the gray to a halt to study the shack. " 'Pears to be a tradin' post," he said to Mary Beth.

His remark caused her to pull the paint up closer to the trail leading down to the store to get a look for herself. "It doesn't look like much," she said.

"I expect he mostly trades with the Indians," Luke replied.

"Do you suppose there's any chance he might have coffee beans?" Mary Beth asked. "We're almost out, and we don't know how far it is to Coulson."

"Don't know," Luke answered. "He might."

Mary Beth looked doubtful. "Where on earth would he get them?"

"Riverboat," Luke replied. "I expect that's where he gets most anything he sells."

She was still skeptical. "Why would a riverboat stop at that little shack?"

Luke pointed to several stacks of logs, cut into even lengths, down near the water's edge. "Wood," he answered. "Those riverboat captains will pay for wood for their engines."

"Oh," she exclaimed softly, then gave him a smile. "Let's go see if he has any coffee beans, because in about two more days we're going to be out."

Luke glanced at the packhorse, then back at her. "I ain't got no pelts or nothin' to trade," he said apologetically.

She laughed. "I've got a little bit of money," she said. "Remember?"

"I forgot," he replied, truthfully. Nudging the

gray gently, he guided the horse down the path to the trading post.

Lem Sloat frowned and squinted in an effort to identify the two riders descending the path to his store. As they came closer, he reached up and thoughtfully stroked his beard, curious as to what they might be carrying in the packs on the extra horse. "Pearl," he called. His Crow wife, Walks-With-A-Stick, whom he called Pearl, came from the tent to stand beside him. "You ever see them folks before?" Lem asked. She shook her head. "One of 'em's a woman. T'other's an Injun or a trapper. I ain't sure which, but it don't look like a load of pelts on that horse." He got up from the stool he had been seated on by the fire, and then set his plate on it. "Seems like somebody always has to come when I'm eatin' my supper." He rubbed his ample belly with one hand, wiping the grease from his fingers, and started toward the front of his store to greet the strangers.

"How do?" Lem called out when Luke and Mary Beth pulled their horses to a stop before the door. "Ain't seen you folks around here before. Where you headed?"

"Coulson," Mary Beth volunteered cheerfully as she stepped down from the saddle, her spirits lifted by the mere sight of another white man. "Maybe you know where that is."

"Yes, ma'am, I surely do, and a right lively little town is what I hear. It's about three days west of here, dependin' on how fast you're traveling." Sloat smiled pleasantly for the lady while his eyes never left the sandy-haired scout holding a rifle in one hand with a bow strapped on his back. "My name's Lem Sloat," he said. "This here's my place of business. What can I do for you folks?" He stepped back cautiously when Luke threw a leg over and slid off the spotted gray pony. The couple was not a common sight on the trail along the Yellowstone, and Lem's mind was already turning over the different explanations for the seemingly odd pairing.

"We were wondering if you might have some coffee beans we could buy," Mary Beth spoke up as they followed him inside. If anything else came to mind, she decided it would have to wait, for Lem Sloat's shelves were sparsely stocked.

"I do," Lem replied. "You're in luck. I've got some come fresh up the river last month, and we got two forty-pound sacks of 'em already roasted. My wife is the one who roasts 'em, and there ain't nobody does 'em better."

"I reckon she'd be the woman standin' at the back of the cabin with that rifle stickin' through the knothole," Luke commented dryly.

Lem Sloat had close to a full face of dingy gray whiskers, but even so, the sudden flush was clearly evident in the small parts of his face not covered by hair. "No offense, mister, but with what just happened southwest of here on the Little

Big Horn, ever'body's kinda jumpy." He hesitated before adding, "And you did look a helluva lot like an Injun when you came ridin' up, even if you was with him, ma'am." He favored Mary Beth with another smile, then called to his wife, "It's all right, Pearl. Come on in." Turning to Luke again, he said, "You got pretty sharp eyes, mister. Most folks don't spot that rifle barrel stickin' through them pelts hangin' on the back wall."

Astonished by the words just exchanged between Luke and Sloat, Mary Beth was at a loss for words, but soon recovered. "I guess we'll take one of those forty-pound bags if the price is not too high." She looked at Luke then for approval. "Is that all right? Can I put forty more pounds on the horse?"

"Yes, ma'am," Luke replied. "It ain't too much." Without pause, he then turned back to Sloat and asked, "What trouble on the Little Big Horn?"

"You ain't heard?" Sloat responded with surprise. "Some army troops under General Custer attacked a big camp of Sioux and Cheyenne on the Little Big Horn. Only problem, I reckon, is them soldiers didn't know there was so many Injuns in that camp. What I heard was ol' Sittin' Bull and Crazy Horse's people were there, Cheyenne, Arapaho, thousands of Injuns, and Custer jumped 'em. They wiped out ever' last one of them soldiers, includin' Custer himself. Don't know how many was killed, maybe five hundred or more, maybe a thousand. The word I got was that that big Injun camp broke up after they whipped the soldiers and scattered, so folks along the Yellowstone has been seein' Injuns behind ever' outhouse, expectin' to get scalped ever' time they go to do their business."

"Have you seen any Sioux war parties up this far?" Luke asked.

"Nah, I ain't seen none, but there's a lot of settlers movin' into this part of the valley, and they're scared them Injuns might take a notion to start raidin' up through here."

Sloat's story had a chilling effect on Mary Beth, just when she was beginning to believe she was soon going to find her brother-in-law. She had visions of a giant red horde overrunning the countryside, plundering and killing innocent white settlers. Luke noticed her trembling and sought to set her mind at ease. "But you ain't seen no Indians hereabouts yourself?" he repeated.

"No, I ain't," Sloat replied.

"Well, I reckon you'd best pay him for the coffee," Luke said to Mary Beth, "and we'll be goin' along. Not much daylight left before we'll have to make us a camp for the night." He paused to nod a greeting to Pearl when she walked in to join them, then said to Sloat, "We'll be right back."

Outside the store, he led the packhorse to the side where it could not be seen through the open door. "You want me to untie that knot on your sack of corn, or can you reach it all right?"

His question caught her quite by surprise, for she realized that he had obviously known all along that she had hidden all her money, eight hundred dollars in gold and silver coins, in the sack of corn. She should have guessed that he knew a sack of corn didn't weigh that much, but he had made no further comment on it after his initial statement. Embarrassed now that she had assumed he was too dumb to question it, she made no comment on the matter. Instead she proceeded to untie the sack and dig around in the kernels until coming up with the required amount. "I'll tie it back," he said.

"Thank you," she replied politely, her face still slightly flushed with embarrassment, and turned at once to return to the store.

Inside, Lem Sloat, moved quickly back from the wall, where he had witnessed her search through a crack between the boards on the side of the building. "Yes, ma'am," he offered jovially when she placed the coins on his small counter. "Hard cash, I was hopin' you weren't gonna try to pay with paper. I'da rather had pelts than paper money." He watched while Luke took the sack of coffee beans and rearranged his packs to make a place for it. "You folks oughta stick around for a while," Lem suggested. "You could camp right here and Pearl can cook you up some supper—

plenty of wood, plenty of grass for your horses, easy to get to the water."

"Thank you kindly," Luke replied at once, "but we've got a piece to go before we call it a day, so I expect we'd best move along." He walked over to stand by Mary Beth's stirrup, waiting to help her up in the saddle.

"Stop by and see us if you're back this way again," Sloat called after them as they ascended the path to the main trail. He stood there watching until they disappeared near the bend of the river, then beckoned to Pearl. When the stoic Crow woman came to him, he said, "Go find Ben Kirby. Tell him I need to see him." She nodded and turned to do his bidding.

It was rapidly approaching dark by the time Luke found a campsite to his liking. Mary Beth was beginning to wonder if he planned to continue on into the night before he finally came to a lively creek that emptied into the river where the bluffs were some six feet high. "This'll do," he stated simply, and turned the gray to head up the tree-lined creek. After a ride of about a hundred yards, he pulled up and looked around a small clearing in the cottonwoods where the creek made a U-shaped bend. "Here," he said, and slid off his horse. "We'll build a fire in the crook of that creek."

She looked at the spot he pointed out. "I'll make

the fire while you take care of the horses." She smiled as she walked past him. "We've got plenty of coffee now. I'll grind some of the new beans."

He tried to answer her smile with one of his own, but his mind was occupied with the layout of his camp. He had a gut feeling about Lem Sloat that told him the man was not to be trusted. That was his reason for keeping Mary Beth in the saddle for a longer day than usual and also the reason for selecting a campsite far enough removed from the main trail along the river. He decided not to tell Mary Beth of his concerns until after they had eaten. She had already been troubled earlier that day with reports of Sioux and Cheyenne war parties, so he wanted her to be comfortable for a while until bedtime. Then he would tell her of his concerns.

With supper finished, Luke got more wood and built up the fire as he usually did, but when she started to lay out her bedding, he stopped her and led her to another spot farther up in the trees. "I want you to sleep back from the fire a ways tonight," he told her. "I've got a feelin' that we ain't seen the last of Lem Sloat. Take that big ol' pistol of your daddy's to bed with you, just in case." He pointed to a willow thicket on the other side of the creek. "I'll be right yonder in those willows, and I'll be keepin' an eye on things. Maybe my hunch is wrong, might not be nothin' at all, but it won't hurt to be sure. If we do get any visitors tonight, you just lie low right here, and I'll take care of it. That pistol is just in case I'm not as smart as I think I am. All right?"

"All right," she answered after a hesitation that reflected her uncertainty.

"I'm just gettin' spooked a little," he said, trying to reassure her. "Probably nothin' at all."

"All silver," Lem said, "she paid me in silver coins, had 'em hid in a sack of somethin'. It looked like a sack of grain, or corn, or somethin' like that. She went diggin' around in that sack and pulled out a handful of money."

"I swear," Ben Kirby exclaimed. "And there wasn't but the two of 'em, a man and a woman?" A lean, lanky man of average height, clean-shaven except for a drooping mustache that formed almost a full circle around his chin, he pursed his lips to shoot a stream of tobacco juice toward the porch post.

"That's right," Lem replied, "just the two of 'em."

Kirby grinned and worked his chew around to the other side of his mouth. "Sounds to me like me and ol' Gopher here oughta go see what the lady has in that sack. Whaddaya think, Gopher?" He shot a stream of tobacco juice in the direction of his partner's foot, but the simpleminded brute's reactions were quick enough to jerk it out of the way, causing Kirby to chuckle. Gopher simply grinned in response to his partner's question, his swift reactions being confined to physical, rather than mental, agility. Kirby turned back to Sloat then. "Hell, if there wasn't but two of 'em, and one of them a woman, how come you didn't just do the job yourself?"

"There wasn't but one man," Sloat explained, "but he looked like he mighta been half mountain lion." He shook his head at the thought. "He held a Henry rifle in his hand the whole time he was here, and his eyes never missed nothin'. If he'da ever turned his back on me, I mighta thought about it, but he never did." He tilted his head back and scratched under his beard while he recalled the broad-shouldered scout. "Besides, that's your job. I'm just supposed to spot 'em for you."

"Might do you some good to get out from behind that counter once in a while," Kirby needled. "Work some of that fat offa ya."

"If I did, then you and Gopher would be out of a job, wouldn't you? Now, I expect if any of us is gonna get any of that woman's money, you two better start doin' some trailin'. They've already got an hour's start on you, and mind you don't take my warnin' lightly 'bout that feller with the rifle. He was wearin' a bow on his back—didn't look like one of the usual pilgrims that come by here."

"I reckon we can handle him," Kirby said. He

grinned at his oversized partner, and said, "I'll let ol' Gopher tie his ass in a knot. Then I'll slit his throat and scalp him." Gopher beamed and nodded in response.

"Sometime they gonna cheat you," Pearl said when she came to stand beside Sloat as they watched Kirby and Gopher ride up the path.

"Maybe," Sloat replied, "but those two ain't got brains enough between 'em to pour piss out of a boot. They need somebody to tell 'em which way to go. They'll be back with the money." He was truthful when he said he wasn't worried about them, for he figured they needed him more than he needed them.

"It's gettin' so dark I can't hardly see the damn tracks no more," Kirby complained.

"There ain't no tracks on this side," Gopher said from the other bank of the creek.

"You mean you can't see no more?"

"I can see good enough," Gopher answered. "There ain't no tracks to see over here."

"They rode up the creek," Kirby said, while Gopher continued to puzzle over the disappearance of tracks. "We'd best take it real slow now, till we find out where they made camp. Come on back on this side, and we'll follow it till we catch sight of 'em."

They had gone no farther than about twenty yards when Kirby caught the movement of their intended victims' horses in the trees up ahead. He signaled Gopher to dismount and be quiet, then dismounted himself. "They ain't very far up this creek," Kirby whispered. "Let's go back a little and wait till it gets darker."

It was not a long wait until a hard dark set in the cottonwoods bordering the narrow creek. The conscienceless assassins sat on the ground, each with his back against a tree, impatiently waiting for the proper time to strike the unsuspecting camp. Gopher was eager to get on with it, but Kirby convinced him that it would be far easier if they waited until the man and woman were asleep. "Then all we'll have to do is walk in and shoot 'em while they're still in their blankets," he said.

"Maybe we'll catch 'em goin' at it in the same blanket," Gopher said, his perverted mind conjuring an image that appealed to him. "That'd be somethin', wouldn't it?" His voice trailed off as he pictured it. "I'd like to see that."

"I wanna see what's in that damn sack Lem saw," Kirby said. "We need to wait till they've had time to fall asleep. Don't make no sense to go in there earlier and take a chance on gettin' shot. Lem says this feller looks like some kinda stud hoss."

"I reckon," Gopher conceded, unable to rid his mind of the picture he had formed, "but I'd like to see 'em goin' at it." Kirby shook his head in disbelief, but he said nothing and Gopher could not see his gesture in the darkness.

An hour passed and finally Kirby thought it was time. "All right," he said, "let's get movin'." He got to his feet and looked down at his simple-minded partner, who had fallen asleep. Taking him by the shoulder, he shook him awake. "Come on, you big dummy. You was so damn anxious to go a while back. You wanna stay here and sleep while I go do the job?" Gopher scrambled up quickly, his grin wide in anticipation of the pleasure he always enjoyed when falling upon innocent victims.

Leaving their horses tied in the trees, they drew their rifles and advanced upon the camp on foot. In a short distance, they spotted the flames of the campfire. A gentle breeze rustled the branches of the low bushes that grew between the cotton-woods, causing the flames to flicker nervously. Inching a few yards closer, they stopped to look over the camp before walking in. As they had planned, there was no activity in the camp. All was quiet except for a few inquiring whinnies from the horses. To make sure this was not enough to wake the sleeping couple, they continued to wait a few minutes more before advancing once again. Still there was no sign of movement.

"Where the hell are they?" Kirby whispered, for he had expected to see two sleeping forms close to the fire. "You see 'em?"

"Nope," Gopher replied.

"Well, they gotta be here somewhere," Kirby

said, and proceeded to make his way to a closer position. "You step across the creek and head toward them willows. They musta figured to bed down outta sight. I'll go up this side. One of us is bound to spot 'em."

"All right," Gopher said, and stepped into the waist-deep water, causing a soft splash as he did so. Kirby grimaced at the sound, but still there was no evidence of alarm in the camp. Gopher grinned sheepishly for his clumsy step while he continued across to the other bank. Pulling his heavy body out of the water was not without a slight sound, but not as loud as his entry had been. In silence now, save for the singing of frogs along the creek bank, he moved toward the willow thicket. Suddenly he spotted what he searched for, a form rolled in a blanket. He did not wait. Pulling his rifle up to his shoulder, he fired, cocked it, and fired again to be sure. At that distance, he did not miss. "I got one, Kirby!" Eager to see which of the couple he had shot, he ran into the willows.

Kirby did not answer. The only sound he could make was a choking gurgle as his throat was cut from ear to ear. When released from the powerful grasp that had held him, his body dropped lifeless to the creek bank. Luke wiped his knife blade clean and returned it to its scabbard. He reached over his shoulder and drew an arrow from the quiver. Notching it, he stepped up in the shadow of the trees and waited. In a few seconds, Gopher lumbered out into the clearing after finding he had killed an empty blanket. "Kirby!" he yelled. "They ain't here." With no answer from his partner, he started to yell again, but was stopped abruptly by a solid blow to his chest. Confused by the sudden pain, he looked down to discover the arrow shaft protruding from his body. He staggered backward, still on his feet when the second arrow struck, piercing his abdomen. Like a wounded buffalo, he snorted, dazed, unable to defend against an antagonist he could not see. There were no muzzle flashes to tell him from whence his assailant struck, only the silent missiles from somewhere in the darkness of the trees. Helpless against the assault, he tried to escape and turned around to go back to the creek, but found that his steps were uneven and awkward, causing him to drop his rifle and clutch a willow trunk to keep from going down on his knees. The final arrow, shot from a much shorter distance than the first two, struck him in the back, piercing his lung, and the simple brute collapsed face forward in the creek.

Luke walked slowly to the creek to make sure of the kill. He reached for Gopher's foot and pulled the heavy body to the bank of the creek, where he stripped it of its gun belt. He took a good look at the man, just as he had done with his partner. Neither of the two was Lem Sloat, which surprised him. Even so, he felt that Sloat had a hand in it, but there was no way he could know for sure. Thoughts of vengeance filled his mind as he tried to pull his arrows out of Gopher's corpse, but there was the possibility that Lem Sloat had nothing to do with the attempt on their lives, that it was just coincidence.

He was able to recover only one of his three arrows. The other two broke when he tried to extract them, having been driven too deeply into the carcass. He heard Mary Beth call behind him. "Luke," came the cautious cry, "are you all right?"

"Yes, ma'am," he replied.

"I heard the shots and then there was nothing," she said, her voice trembling. "I didn't know who did the shooting. I was afraid you might have been shot."

"I reckon that was the plan," Luke said. "It might be best if you go on over closer to the fire while I take care of these two. I'll take a look back down the creek just in case, but I don't think there was anybody else with 'em." He had thought to keep her from seeing the bodies of their assailants, but it was too late.

"Oh my dear Lord," she gasped when she saw the huge body lying on the creek bank. "Oh my Lord," she said again. "Why would they come to kill us?"

"I expect they found out what was in that sack of corn of yours," he replied.

"But why kill us for it? Why not just rob us and be on their way?"

He was surprised by her naïveté, especially in light of the suspicions that she had harbored for him in the beginning, but he chose not to remind her. "That's just their way of makin' sure nobody comes after them," he said. "You go over by the fire now, and I'll be back when I'm done with this one and his partner over in the trees."

She did as he said, suddenly feeling a chill about her shoulders that was not totally a result of the night air. There was no doubt in her mind that sleeping was out of the question for the rest of that night. And even though he had said there were no others to fear, she knew that she would be afraid until he returned. *What a fool I was,* she scolded herself. *I should never have agreed to go to Montana.* The few friends she had made in Cheyenne had told her of the harsh reality of trying to carve out a life in that wild territory, but David's brother had told them that it was no rougher than life in Wyoming Territory. *Well,* she decided, *my friends were right, and now look at me. David's gone and there's been nothing but murder and savagery at every turn.* She was suddenly struck by the stillness of the dark trees along the banks of the creek, and she could not help feeling that someone, or something, was watching her every move. She shivered once again and thought, *I wish Luke would hurry back here.*

When Luke had found the horses tied in the trees, after a short walk back down the creek, he was positive that the two men he killed were the only assailants he had to worry about. Having pulled Gopher's body halfway up the bank, he had decided that hauling the hulking carcass away from the clearing was work better suited to a horse. He got on one of the horses and led the other back to the camp, where he tied a rope around Gopher's ankles and looped the other end around the saddle horn. He dragged the body well out of the way past the edge of the trees, then repeated the chore with Kirby's corpse. "Well, boys," he said upon completion of the chore, "I expect the buzzards will be right glad to see you in the mornin'." He paused again to consider whether or not he should pay Lem Sloat a visit. It bothered him to think the grubby little man might have set these two upon them, but there was no way he could know for sure. *I reckon I'd best just forget about it and worry about getting Mary Beth to her folks,* he told himself. He wondered now if he could believe Sloat when he had told him that Coulson was three days west of his store.

When he returned to the clearing, he found Mary Beth making a pot of coffee. When she saw the look of surprise on his face, she informed him that she was positive that she could no longer sleep, although it was in the wee hours of the morning. "This place is just too creepy," she said. "I just want to get away from here as fast as we can, and I can tell by the expression on your face that you're thinking about waiting until morning. So it's a good thing I made some coffee. It'll help me keep my eyes open, because I have no intention of closing them again in this place."

Astonished by her long and frank statement, Luke paused, still holding the reins of the horses that had belonged to the men just killed. He guessed that she must have really been frightened by her rude awakening to gunshots only a few dozen steps from her bed. But he could not understand why she was still afraid now that the danger was past. "Both of them fellers are dead," he reminded her, hoping that would ease her fear. She looked at him as if she thought he was insane.

"Yes," she exclaimed, as she would have if trying to explain something to a child. "They're dead! They came to kill us, but you killed them instead!" Her voice became louder and louder as she released her emotions. "The Indians tried to kill us, but you killed them. Everyone in this territory is trying to kill everyone else! My God! What's wrong with you people?" In an attempt to vent her frustration, she began kicking dirt on the fire. Luke could only stand and watch while she threw her tantrum. He had never seen a woman behave in such fashion, and he had no idea what was wrong with her, but she was going to put out the fire if she kept kicking dirt on it. So he realized something must be done to settle her down. He dropped the reins he had been holding, moved quickly toward her, and in one swift motion, he swept her up in his arms. While she fought helplessly against him, he calmly walked to the edge of the creek and dropped her in the middle of it. Then he stepped back and watched as she thrashed about furiously in the cold current, gasping for air while spitting blasphemous oaths. Still straining to catch her breath, she struggled to climb out of the creek, only to slip and tumble back to sit down once again in the chilly water.

He waded part of the way out to her and extended his hand. "Here, take hold and I'll pull you outta there." She eagerly grasped his hand.

"I'm freezing," she exclaimed when she gained her footing on the grassy crest of the creek bank. Drained of her anger and frustration, she shivered uncontrollably.

"You'd best get outta them wet clothes," he said. "You've got some dry things to put on, ain't you?"

"In the packs," she replied, and hurried to find them. She paused for just a moment to ask, "Why did you do that?"

"I saw a dog throw a fit one time in a Crow village. It was kinda like the one you just threw, only the dog didn't say all them things you did. The Indian the dog belonged to grabbed him by the hind legs and threw him in the river. He came out of the river and slinked off in the woods—seemed to be calmed down. I thought maybe the same thing might work on you."

She shook her head in exasperation as she gazed at him, finding it hard to believe what had just happened. "Well, I'm calm now," she said, "freezing, but I'm calm. I've just got to get out of these wet clothes before I catch pneumonia."

"I'm glad you're calm, but I'll still be keepin' my eye on you for a while."

"Why?" she asked.

" 'Cause a couple of hours after that Crow threw his dog in the river, that dog came outta the woods growling and foamin' at the mouth. He came after one of them Indians and they had to shoot him." A slight smile threatened to appear on Luke's face. "I was hopin' it wouldn't come to that with you."

Shocked, by his casual manner, she didn't know how to react for a few moments until it struck her. "You're joking, aren't you?"

"Yes, ma'am," he replied, the smile expanding to a grin. "I wouldn't have shot you. Fact is, I was afraid you mighta shot me after I threw you in the creek."

She found that she could not be angry with him, and she realized that this was the first time he had ever joked since she had known him—about anything. She could not help uttering it. "You actually joked with me. I can't believe it, *Dead Man*."

It was his turn to be surprised. "How did you know my Crow name?"

"Oh, I know a lot of things," she teased as she pulled some dry clothes from the pack. "Women know a lot more things than men suspect."

"I wouldn't know about that," he said. "I'd have to take your word for it. You'd better get outta them wet clothes, though. I'll take a walk back down the creek if you wanna stay by the fire."

"No," she said. "I'll go back in the trees to change. You stay by the fire." *Where I can see you,* she thought. She was willing to trust him with her life, but she didn't rule out the natural curiosity that men seemed to be born with.

While she changed, he took a more thorough look at the horses they had just acquired. Fairly sturdy, he decided, but nothing special; both were sorrels. At least he could use one of the saddles and would no longer have to ride bareback. His first thought was that he would get his horse back now, with two saddled horses to choose from for Mary Beth. But after thinking about it for a moment, he decided that he had better leave her on the paint. She had become accustomed to the horse, and with possibly only about three days left to Coulson, maybe it was a good idea to let her be. Next, he considered the possibility of putting a saddle on the spotted gray pony he had been riding. It was a good horse, but had obviously never had a saddle strapped on its back.

A spirited pony, the gray might not be willing to accept the saddle without a lively protest, and he wasn't willing to take the time at this point to saddle-break a horse. *I reckon I'll just ride the one with the best saddle,* he thought, *and worry about breaking the gray when we get to wherever we're going.* His decision made, he yanked the saddles off both horses and let them rest with his three Indian ponies, for in spite of Mary Beth's tirade, he did not intend to leave until daylight.

Mary Beth came back to hang her wet clothes up to dry on some small limbs Luke had driven into the ground by the fire. She glanced at the saddles on the ground, then looked at Luke with a question in her eyes. He answered it before she had a chance to put it in words. "There might be some rough places along the river trail, and I'd rather see 'em in the daylight," he said. "And I'm plannin' on gettin' a couple hours' sleep. It's gonna be a long day tomorrow. I expect you oughta do the same."

She looked at him, amazed that he could even think about going to sleep after what had taken place on this night. He gave no indication that he was preparing to sleep as he poured a cup of coffee from the pot she had put on the fire, and gnawed on a strip of dried venison. "Well, I'm not closing my eyes," she reminded him. "So I guess I'll act as lookout while you're sleeping." She could not help adding a little barb. "Maybe I will see them if somebody else comes sneaking in to kill us."

"I hope so," Luke replied rather casually. He finished his coffee in silence, then held his blanket up to inspect the two bullet holes. "They didn't do my blanket any good," he commented. Settling himself a few feet from the fire, he soon was asleep. Mary Beth was left to her thoughts of frustration and astonishment. That he could simply roll up in his blanket and go to sleep was beyond her understanding. She poured herself a cup of coffee and sat down near the fire, clutching her father's old revolver in one hand.

He awoke with the first rays of the sun that filtered through the cottonwood branches. Before going into the trees to relieve himself of the coffee he had drunk the night before, he paused to look at the woman sleeping peacefully by the dying fire. Her empty coffee cup lay on one side of her and her pistol lay on the other, and as she slept, she had hugged herself in an effort to keep warm. He took the blanket she had spread to sit on and folded it gently across her shoulders, then proceeded to the woods to take care of nature's call.

By that afternoon they came upon signs of civilization. Passing fields being cleared of trees, even some that had been cultivated, they assumed they were nearing Coulson. The task now was to find the land claimed by John Freeman. Finally they overtook a man driving a wagon loaded with cordwood, a wood-hawk, Luke guessed. When Mary Beth asked, he explained that it was a term for men who stacked firewood by the river to sell to steamboat captains. "Like Lem Sloat. Remember?" When aware of the riders coming up behind him, the man pulled his horses over and positioned himself behind his load of firewood with his rifle in hand, relaxing only after he saw that one of the riders was a woman.

"Howdy," Luke called, and held both hands up in the air. "We're lookin' for Coulson."

Still using his firewood as protection, the man said, "Well, you're almost there—another five miles, about."

"Much obliged," Luke said.

"Do you happen to know John Freeman?" Mary Beth asked when it appeared that Luke was not going to.

"Why, yes, ma'am, I do. He staked out a tract that runs right down to the river, not more'n a mile from here—right on the road you're ridin'. You'll see where the road passes a corner of a field he's been clearin'. There's a lane runnin' down to his place right at that corner."

Mary Beth thanked the wood-hawk, then nudged her pony forward, unable to resist giving Luke a knowing smile as she passed him. "I'll be your guide the rest of the way," she teased. "Just follow me." He nodded soberly, then grinned. His reaction was so rare that she had to take a second look.

Chapter 10

"Pa, somebody's coming!"

John Freeman looked up to see where his young son, Jack, was pointing. There appeared to be two riders leading three horses behind them. They were still too far distant to see in any detail, but John laid his axe aside and walked over to a tree to pick up the shotgun propped against the trunk. He remained in the shadow of the tree as Jack came running to stand beside him. After the news of Little Big Horn had reached the valley, every one of the recent settlers kept his firearms close at hand. John was not naïve to the point of thinking one shotgun could protect against a Sioux war party, but he was determined to make it as costly as he possibly could if his family was attacked.

"Looks like an Indian!" Jack said as he strained to make out the figures, now approaching the corner of the field where the lane to his home forked off from the road. "But there ain't but two of 'em," he said. A moment later, he commented, "The other one's a woman, but she don't look like an Indian."

John did not reply. His concentration was focused on the strangers who were now turning off the road and heading down the path that led to his barn and partially finished house. Jack was right; the man did look like an Indian because he was dressed in animal skins, but John wasn't sure. He shifted his gaze to the woman riding a paint pony. He had started to turn his attention back to her companion when he suddenly recognized her. "Mary Beth?" he gasped, hardly believing his eyes. Forgetting he held his shotgun, he dropped it to the ground and stared at his sister-in-law until he was certain it was Mary Beth. "They made it!" he exclaimed, but then turned his attention back once again to the man with her. "But who's she riding with? Where's David?" He ran out from the shade of the tree to meet them while calling back to Jack, "Run get your mother. Tell her your aunt Mary Beth is here."

"Is that him?" Luke asked when he saw John coming toward them. He need not have asked, for upon glancing at Mary Beth, he read the answer in her joyful face. He reined his horse back when Mary Beth gave the paint a kick to hurry it along.

Unaware that Luke had asked the question, Mary Beth rushed to meet John, her emotions boiling over inside her with the joy of finally reaching John and Doris contrasted with the grievous news she must now tell them. Sliding down from the paint pony, she ran to hug her surprised brother-in-law, unable to stop the tears now streaming down her face.

"Lord in heaven!" John exclaimed. "We'd given

you folks up." He stood back then, and held her at arm's length. "Where's David?" Just noticing her tears, he glanced at the solemn figure still seated in the saddle, dressed in animal skins and a bow strapped on his back, watching the reunion with eyes devoid of expression. "Where's David?" John repeated, looking back at Mary Beth in distress.

"David's gone," Mary Beth answered, her voice choking on the words.

"Gone? What do you mean, gone?" He looked at Luke, then back at Mary Beth. "Who's he?"

"He's gone," Mary Beth cried out, almost hysterical as the full impact of her husband's loss returned once again upon seeing his brother. "David's gone," she repeated, and began to sob uncontrollably.

Seeing that Mary Beth had lost control of her emotions, Luke stepped down from the saddle. "Your brother's dead, Mr. Freeman. He was killed by a Sioux warrior," he said.

"Oh my God," John gasped, almost sinking to his knees.

Running from the house, Doris Freeman arrived in time to see her husband's knees threatening to fail him. A few yards behind her, a large woman wearing a faded sunbonnet followed. "John, what is it?" Doris asked. Then turning to her sister-in-law, she exclaimed, "Mary Beth," and went to embrace her. "Where's David? Did something happen to David?" She turned to stare at Luke for a moment before questioning her husband.

John told her that his brother was dead, and then he and the others listened while Mary Beth told them of the hostile attack that took his life. She went on to tell them how the solemn man in buckskins happened to be with her. She saw no need to tell them that David lost his life while acting as a lookout. She felt that Luke suspected, as she did, that David had fallen asleep, but they would never know for sure. It was a sad reunion, indeed, and Luke stood back silently watching the two women crying while trying to comfort David's brother, who was also crying. He felt sorry for them, but to him, death was as much a part of living as life. Then he took a longer look at the large woman in the sunbonnet who was standing a bit apart, just as he. She seemed to be more intent upon studying him than watching the mourners. Big, but not fat, she wore a faded cotton dress that testified to more hours spent in the field than in the kitchen. Beneath the full skirt, heavy boots verified this assumption. She nodded when Luke's gaze met hers. When John and the two women appeared to be under control again, she stepped forward to greet Mary Beth.

"I'm Vienna Pitts," the matronly woman said. "I'm real sorry to hear about your husband, honey, but I reckon that's the kinda thing you learn to expect out here. I lost my husband, Vern, a couple of years back, so I know how bad that hurts." She extended her hand and shook with Mary Beth. "You let me know if I can help you. All right? Us widows have to stick together."

Mary Beth accepted the firm, calloused hand she offered and said, "Thank you. You're most kind, but I don't want to be a bother."

"Bother?" Vienna replied. "Hell, it ain't no bother. You can help me run my place. I ain't got no man. You ain't got no man. We can help each other. How 'bout that stud cougar?" she asked, nodding toward Luke.

Mary Beth explained again that Luke was being paid to bring her and David here. "Had it not been for his knowledge of the territory and his expertise with a rifle, I would never have made it."

"He looks like he ain't been housebroke yet, but he looks strong as an ox," Vienna said, openly appraising Luke's potential. "I could use a man like that. I've got my own place on the other side of the garden patch. We dug a good well, so I don't have to draw water from the river. You could move in with me, and with a man like him, we could make a go of it."

Mary Beth was at a loss for words. She had not been prepared for such a frank proposition. She was not sure what her situation would be since David was dead. It had been her assumption that John and Doris would gladly take her in, but there had been no mention of it so far. She looked beyond them at the house. It was small. They might not have been planning for her and David to move in with them after all. Maybe they thought she and David would live in their wagon until a cabin was built for them.

Vienna turned abruptly to face Luke. "What are you gonna do now that you've got Mary Beth here?"

"I reckon I'll be leavin' as soon as I get my money," he stated flatly. "But right now I'd like to get these horses unloaded and set to graze."

"Leaving?" Vienna responded. "What's your hurry? Where are you going?"

Somewhat nonplussed by the woman's aggressive manner, he paused to consider his response. John stepped in at that moment to save him from having to answer. "Of course," he said. "Jack will help you take 'em down to the corral, and you can throw the saddles in the barn along with the packs."

"Much obliged," Luke said, grateful for the opportunity to escape Vienna's interrogation. Jack scrambled up on the paint while Luke climbed back on his horse and they led the horses down to the corral next to the barn. The thirteen-year-old boy proved to be a capable hand with horses, and he and Luke had the saddles and packs off and stowed in the barn in no time at all. "I 'preciate it," Luke said when they were walking out of the barn. "I'll let 'em out to graze and water in a little bit." He had not decided what he was going to do with the extra horses he had picked up. Maybe he should leave one of the Indian ponies for Mary Beth to use as a saddle horse, but he felt he should definitely leave the two shod horses, since he had set her team of horses free.

"Don't pay too much attention to Aunt Vienna," Jack told him as they walked back to meet the others. "She doesn't waste time being polite—says pretty much what's on her mind. Pa says she has to act like a man, since she ain't got one to rely on anymore. She's got a heart as good as gold, though. That's what Ma says."

Mildly surprised by the boy's maturity, Luke asked, "What happened to her husband?"

"Uncle Vern? Him and Aunt Vienna had a place upriver about eighty miles from here. He was snaking logs out of the woods to build some fellow's cabin, and ain't nobody really sure what happened, whether the log rolled up on his leg or what. When they found him down near the river, they said the log was on top of him, and it looked like he had been dragged to death."

"That ain't a good way to go," Luke allowed.

"No, sir," Jack replied. "But Aunt Vienna decided to come on over to Coulson with my folks. She ain't really my aunt. We just call her that. I think she likes it."

Luke decided he liked the boy.

• • •

Supper that night was a little more than the fare of buffalo meat and coffee that Luke and Mary Beth had become accustomed to. Doris went into her cache of dried beans and flour to bake biscuits to go along with the salt pork and dried apples they had brought from Bozeman. It was Luke's first exposure to biscuits baked in an oven. And there was plenty of coffee to wash them down with. That alone was enough to make Luke happy, and while he drank it and consumed another biscuit, he listened with interest as John and Doris told Mary Beth the circumstances that caused them to come to this valley.

"After our strike ran out in Helena," John said, "that's when we went to the Gallatin Valley— figured we'd stake out some land to farm—but we were too late to get anything you'd wanna turn a plow to. Too much of that land was cattle country already, and there was some bad blood running between the farmers and the ranchers. So when we heard about Coulson springing up, we didn't wait around, and we ain't sorry we didn't. The land here is good for farming and Coulson is handy to the river and the steamboats. It can't miss." He looked at his wife and grinned. "And next year, we won't have to be eating food we brought with us. We'll be eating off our own land, and shipping the rest back east on the steamboats." Doris smiled in return, and John went on. "Right now the little town of Coulson is kinda rough. Seems like the saloons and bawdy houses that moved right in with the first stick drove in the ground have attracted a rather wild bunch of drifters. But the town will grow and those undesirables will be weeded out soon enough." He paused to pull a tough string of pork rind from his mouth, then directed his attention to his silent guest in buckskins. "What about you, Mr. Sunday? What are you aiming to do now that you've seen Mary Beth safely here?"

"It's Luke," he said, causing Mary Beth to smile. "There ain't no Mr. Sunday."

"All right, Luke, then," John said. "You thinking on staying around Coulson? There's still some land available."

"Ah, no, sir," Luke replied. "I'm afraid I don't know much about farmin'. I might just head back down the Yellowstone, or ride on west to the mountains. I ain't been up that way for a spell."

"I doubt you could ever get Luke to settle down on a farm," Mary Beth said.

"Maybe he ain't ever heard the right proposition," Vienna commented. "If I was as young as you, I'd show him some things he might ain't considered." Her remark was aimed at Mary Beth, but caused both of the younger women to blush with embarrassment for her. Doris was the first to speak.

"I suppose Mr. Sunday knows what he wants to

do and probably has other business to attend to," she said.

"It's just Luke, ma'am—" Luke started, but was interrupted by Mary Beth.

"You might as well talk to a Cheyenne warrior about becoming a farmer," she said, having noticed the discomfort the line of conversation had caused in her guide. Unlike the others seated at the long table, she had gathered enough information about the man to know that he was more Indian than white. Ben Clarke had told David that Luke was reared in an Indian village by a Cheyenne woman. At least that's what the chief scout had been told. He admitted to David that he had no firsthand knowledge about Luke's background, but he believed that story to be true. She was, however, unaware how much she, personally, cared that he might be uncomfortable with the conversation. Her speculation was proven to be accurate when, seconds later, the solemn scout excused himself from the table, saying he had to take care of the horses.

The conversation took a decidedly different turn after Luke went outside. Doris was the first to reprimand. "My goodness, Vienna, you might as well have asked him if he wanted to marry Mary Beth, and right after David's passing, too. What if he wasn't interested in Mary Beth? Were you gonna ask him to marry you?"

"Well, Vern never had any complaints," Vienna

replied. "I don't know why you wanna pussyfoot around it so much. He looks like a good man to me, and we sure need some good men around here. With shoulders like that, we could hitch him to the plow. We wouldn't need no horses. Besides, the right woman could take some of that Indian out of him real quick."

"My stars!" Doris exclaimed. "The way you talk!" She shot an accusing glance at her son, who had a wide grin on his face. "Jack, go on outside and help Mr. Sunday with the horses." The boy got up immediately, grabbed a biscuit, and headed for the door. "And don't you repeat a word of what we said," she called after him.

"Maybe we ought to talk about what you intend to do, now that David is gone," John said. When Mary Beth admitted that she wasn't really sure, he continued. "Well, I hope you know that Doris and I are hoping you'll stay on here with us. The cabin is small, but we can add onto it and build you some space of your own."

"Move in with me," Vienna said. "I've already got room enough in my cabin, and I'd enjoy the company."

"Thank you so much, both of you," Mary Beth said. "I really didn't know where I could go after David was killed. I was hoping I could stay here, but I was afraid I'd be a burden without David." She took a long look at Vienna Pitts before she was sure she wanted to make a decision that might come back to haunt her. "Maybe Vienna's right. She's got room for me and she could use the help, and that way I wouldn't be in the way of your family."

Vienna didn't give Doris or John time to respond before she interrupted. "Well, there you go. That's the most sensible way to do it. I need help and you folks need room. It's all settled, then. I'm pleased as punch that we worked it all out." She leaned close to Mary Beth and whispered, "But we still got room for Luke Sunday if you were of a notion." She winked and gave her a playful punch on the shoulder for emphasis.

John and Doris exchanged glances of astonishment. "Wait a minute," John protested. "Is this what you want, Mary Beth? I feel an obligation to take care of my brother's widow."

His remark, though clearly not meant as a negative, was the final piece in Mary Beth's decision puzzle, because she clearly did not want her presence in John's house the result of a feeling of obligation. "If Vienna can stand it, I can stand it. I think it'll be the perfect answer to the problem."

Shaking her head as if exasperated by the whole thing, Vienna reminded them, "Hell, she'll just be across the garden. She ain't goin' to Bozeman or somewhere."

Mary Beth's spirits were immediately lifted with the knowledge that she had a home that welcomed her. "I know Luke is probably getting anxious to get settled up with me," she announced. "So I'm gonna go out to the barn and pay him what David and I promised." She got up to leave.

"You want me to call him in here?" John asked.

"No," Mary Beth replied. "I have to pay him out in the barn. That's where my sack of corn is." With that, she left them to wonder.

"Dang!" Vienna muttered. "If I'da known he'd work that cheap, I wouldn't have given up so easy."

Mary Beth found Luke and Jack about to lead the horses down to the river to drink. They stopped and waited when they saw her approaching from the house. "Go ahead and take 'em to water," Luke told Jack, "and I'll be along directly." The boy did as he was told, while mumbling under his breath that everybody was afraid he was going to hear something he shouldn't. "Is there somethin' you need me to do, ma'am?" Luke asked when Mary Beth came to him.

"I thought you might be wondering about your pay for bringing me here," Mary Beth said, "so I came out to get it for you."

"Well, I've been studyin' on that," Luke said. "I'm thinkin' that your husband said he'd pay me one hundred dollars to get you two out here on the Yellowstone. But seein' as how I only got one of you out here, maybe the price oughta be half that."

She couldn't help smiling in the face of his simple honesty. "No, Luke, we agreed on one hundred, and I think you surely earned your fee, so a hundred it is." She started for the barn. "Come on, you know where it is."

He followed her into the barn, talking as they walked. "I'm gonna leave you those two horses we picked up from those two bushwhackers. That'll replace the horses you lost back on the Powder. I was thinkin' I'd leave you that little mare we used as a packhorse if you want her. She'd be a better ridin' horse for you than either of those other two. I'd like to take the paint and the gray with me. Is that all right?"

"Why, yes, that'll be fine," she replied, surprised that he would not be planning to take all the horses he had captured. The two shod horses might be a welcome addition to Vienna's stock, if she had any. "I'm going to be staying with Vienna in that cabin on the other side of the garden."

He nodded, then said, "I'll tote those packs over there for you." Then he stood and waited while she dug into the sack of corn.

After a few moments, she found what she was groping for and pulled out a small cloth sack, tied with a drawstring. She opened it and took out five twenty-dollar gold pieces and placed them in Luke's open palm. He stared down at the money as if he had not expected to be paid with double eagles, although he knew there was hard cash in the sack. "Seems like a lot, now," he said. "Maybe you should keep some of it."

"I want you to have it," she said, smiling as she placed the empty bag on top of the coins. "It's not your fault that David was killed. You took good care of us, and you're a good friend. David and I were lucky to find you, Luke Sunday." She rose on her tiptoes and placed a quick kiss on his cheek. "Now you're free to go back to your prairies or mountains, or wherever you're bound, and good luck to you."

He was speechless for a few moments, his cheek still burning with the imprint of her kiss. He wanted to tell her that he cared about her, and that he wanted her to always be safe, but he was afraid words would fail him, and she would think him a fool. So he finally said, "Thank you, ma'am."

"You don't have to call me ma'am, Luke. My name's Mary Beth." Then she couldn't resist adding, "There ain't no Mary Beth Ma'am."

"Yes, ma'am," he replied before he caught himself. "I'll tote your things over to your new house now."

She remained there a few minutes longer, watching him as he left to get one of the horses to carry the packs. *A stud cougar,* she thought, recalling Vienna's words, *a truly wild thing. It would be a sin to break a beautiful animal like that to walk behind a plow.* Then she thought about the first time she saw him and recalled that she did not see the natural animal grace of the Indian. All she could see at that time were the cold gray eyes of a lethal predator. Suddenly she felt a chill as if she had lost her protector. She tied her corn sack and returned to the house.

Luke slept that night in the barn, and shared one last meal with the Freemans. Mary Beth and Vienna Pitts were in attendance as well. It was a cheerful affair with invitations to Luke to stop by if he found himself in the vicinity again. Of the participants, Mary Beth was the only one to feel a real sense of regret for seeing him go. When she thought of the many times before she really knew him, she had simply wished to reach her destination and be done with the fierce-looking man, it amazed her that now she felt a deep loss with the departure of her guardian angel. *If David were alive,* she thought, *he'd be telling me, "I told you so."* It was only natural, she supposed, that she should feel the loss of her protection, but it was time for everyone to move on. After her first look at her new home with Vienna, she saw that there was a lot of work to be done to make the rough cabin a fitting home for two ladies. She would be much too busy to let her mind dwell on the unfettered hawk that was Luke Sunday.

His horses already packed with his meager belongings, Luke wasted little time in good-byes. He lingered only a moment to wish Mary Beth well; then he was crossing the yard at a comfortable lope, heading for the little settlement of Coulson. An interested observer, Vienna Pitts studied Mary Beth's face as she gazed after the broad back with the single twist of sandy hair bobbing gently between his shoulder blades. The young widow seemed to be wrestling with her feelings regarding this untamed spirit. *That's something you might come to regret, honey,* Vienna thought.

As John had reported, Coulson was a lively little settlement. Perched right on the side of the river, it seemed to be an ideal steamboat landing, as well as a prime location for a station when the railroad got around to pushing their tracks that far. Already there were stores, saloons, a sawmill, and several other businesses. Luke had no need for anything the town offered other than supplies and ammunition, so he guided his horses toward a newly constructed building with a rough sign that proclaimed it to be a general store.

The proprietor, a grizzled old man with a gray beard streaked with brown from tobacco stains, got up from an armchair next to the stove when Luke walked in. "How do?" he greeted Luke, and spat at the stove. He paused a moment to watch the tobacco juice sizzle right next to a coffeepot on the hot stove. "Don't recollect seein' you around here before," he said.

"How do?" Luke returned. "Ain't never been around here before." He paused to look around him at the merchandise on the shelves. "At least since this town was here," he finished.

Having dealt with many trappers who looked a lot like this stranger, the storekeeper walked over to the door and took a quick look at Luke's horses, expecting to see a load of pelts he was hoping to trade. When he saw the lightly packed horses, he asked, "What can I do for you, neighbor?"

Luke, still looking about him to see if there was anything he needed beyond basic supplies, replied, "I need some forty-four cartridges, three boxes, a sack of salt, one of those sacks of roasted coffee beans, a sack of dried beans." He paused to look around the shelves again until one item caught his eye. "And give me that coffeepot there. I reckon that's about all right now."

The merchant pulled each item from the shelves and placed it on the counter as Luke called it off. When the last item was on the counter, he peered at Luke over the top of his spectacles. "Think that'll do it?" he asked. "That's a right smart list of supplies. Whaddaya plannin' on using for money?"

"Money," Luke answered. "Add it up."

Not without suspicion that he might be the victim of a holdup, the man took a pencil from behind his ear, wet the lead with his tongue, and started listing each item on a piece of brown wrapping paper. "This might add up to more'n you figured," he cautioned. When he had finished, he checked his list to make sure he hadn't forgotten anything, tapping each item with his pencil as he checked it against the list. Sliding down the counter a couple of feet until he felt the butt of his shotgun with his hand, he said, "Mister, all this stuff you got here is gonna come to forty-three dollars and fifty cents. You know, those cartridges ain't cheap."

Luke appeared to think that over for a few seconds while not speaking another word. The storekeeper watched him carefully, his hand tightening around the stock of the shotgun just under the counter. Luke reached inside his shirt and pulled out the bandana that held his money. Carefully untying the knot, he picked two double eagles out, retied the bandana, and stuffed it back inside his shirt. Then he laid the two coins on the counter, still without saying a word.

The storekeeper relaxed at once, spreading his whiskers with his smile. "Well, you're three dollars and fifty cents short," he said, and paused. When Luke said nothing, but continued to fix him with the gaze that earned him his Cheyenne name, the merchant relented. "But, hell, you're payin' with gold. That's worth a discount, I reckon. I'll help you carry it out." He quickly raked the gold pieces off the counter and put them in his pocket.

With help from the merchant, Luke carried his

purchases out and loaded them on his packhorse. It was not the first time he had earned a discount for himself, a practice he had learned from the Indians. It was hard to bargain with someone who would not bargain in return, responding only with looks and one-word answers. "What's your name, young feller?" the storekeeper asked.

"Luke Sunday," was the reply.

"Glad to know you, and appreciate your business. My name's Floyd Garner. You plannin' on stayin' around Coulson for a while?"

"Nope," Luke answered, and finished tightening the straps on his packs. When he was satisfied that they were secure, he climbed on the paint and turned the horse away from the hitching rail.

Floyd lingered for a few minutes to watch his tight-lipped customer ride toward the saloon at the end of the short street. He idly wagered with himself that Luke would pull up to the hitching post in front of the saloon, but had to admit he would have lost that bet when Luke rode on past. Those two double eagles were not the only ones in that bandana, and Floyd was accustomed to seeing any drifter with money in his pocket spend most of it, if not all of it, in a saloon. *As wild a man as any critter in the woods,* he thought. *Ain't no telling how he came by that money, and who got shot in the process.* Unfortunately, that was the type of men who had been drawn to the fledgling little town. He and some of the other businessmen were gambling on the hope that the recent arrival of a few solid farming families in the valley would in time help build a proper town. However, he could not help wondering sometimes if he had made a mistake in thinking there would come a day when a man could walk down the street in Coulson without wearing a gun. Reprimanding himself for the negative thought, he reminded himself that John Freeman, one of the recent settlers, had been in his store a week ago. Freeman was building a house, and he said his brother was on his way to join him. *That's the kind of folks we need to build Coulson,* he thought.

Passing the saloon at the end of the street, Luke only glanced at the two drunks sitting out front on the short wooden stoop. He considered stopping in for one quick drink, but decided against it, thinking it a bad idea to waste his money on something that would gain him no more than a few moments of pleasure. Sixty dollars would not last forever and he would be back looking for work as a scout, or trading for pelts with people like Floyd Garner. The thing he had to decide now was where he was going from here. He could return to find Black Feather's village. They had probably moved from the North Platte, and maybe Black Feather and Little Bear had returned to join them. He had to admit that he felt no enthusiasm for that option. *Maybe it's time I started collecting pelts again,* he thought. *I need the meat, anyway, and it's been a long time since I've hunted in this territory.* That option suited his mood better than going to look for the Crow village. That settled, he nudged the paint with his heels and headed for Clark's Fork of the Yellowstone. A few years back, he had found deer and antelope in plenty along that river.

CHAPTER 11

"Well, I'll be go to hell—Lem Sloat," the huge man with the reddish-brown whiskers exclaimed. "I thought you was dead."

"Bill Kunze," Sloat returned, equally surprised. "I thought they hanged your big ass back in Oklahoma Territory. I know they was lookin' for you for shootin' that deputy in the back." He shifted his gaze to scrutinize the weasel-faced man at Bogart's elbow, who was looking at Bill with a confused expression. "Who's this you got with you?"

"Shake hands with George Wylie," Bogart said, grinning broadly. "Course you're gonna have to take your hand off that shotgun you're holdin' on to under that counter."

Sloat's hand came up at once. "Howdy, George," he said, then cocking a mischievous eye toward Bogart, added, "It ain't a shotgun. It's a forty-four Colt." They both laughed. "Hell," Sloat confessed, "I didn't know who you was, ridin' up to my porch. I shoulda known it was you when you filled up the whole door when you walked in." He turned his head toward the back of the store and yelled, "Come on in, Pearl. They's friends of mine."

"Kunze ain't my name no more," the big man said. "It's Bill Bogart now." He grinned again. " 'Cause of that little matter with the deputy marshal."

"Bogart, huh?" Sloat remarked. "Well, I ain't surprised." Wylie nodded his understanding, no longer confused.

In a few minutes, the stoic Crow woman came in the front door carrying a rifle, causing Bogart to chuckle once more. "I swear, Lem, you don't take no chances, do ya?"

"This here's Pearl. She's been with me for a few years now." Turning to her, he said, "Go see if you can rustle up some grub for these fellers. I expect they're hungry."

"I could eat the south end outta a north-bound mule, and that's a fact," Bogart allowed. "How 'bout you, Wylie?" Wylie just grinned in reply.

Sloat chuckled. "Will beans and bacon do? We're fresh outta mule—maybe Pearl can make up some corn cakes to go with it."

"Anythin' will do right now, long as there's plenty of it," Bogart said.

"Come on, we'll go in the house," Sloat said, referring to the tent beside his store. "I might have a little drink of somethin' to cut the dust while Pearl's cookin'." He led them to a table with two chairs and a three-legged stool. Being the proper host, he took the stool for himself, although he claimed it was because Bogart's big ass might break the legs on his stool.

Pearl placed a bottle of whiskey on the table with three cups, and Sloat poured. "Does she ever talk?" Bogart asked, eyeing the Indian woman.

" 'Bout as much as your friend there," Sloat countered.

His remark brought a foolish grin to Wylie's face. "I can talk," he said. "Bogart can tell you that. I just ain't got nothin' to say right now."

The three of them killed more than half of the bottle before the silent Crow woman removed it from the table and filled the cups with coffee. She had no intention of preparing food that the three men were too drunk to eat. When Wylie started to protest, she declared, "No more whiskey, eat now."

"There you go, Wylie," Bogart roared. "She can talk when she's got somethin' to say."

"You never said what brung you to this neck of the woods," Sloat commented when Bogart quit laughing.

The big man became serious for a few moments when he answered. "I'm lookin' for somebody," he said, "and I'm thinkin' he had to come this way."

"Judging by that look on your face, I'd guess this somebody ain't gonna be glad to see you."

"I s'pose not," Bogart went on, " 'cause when I catch up with him, I'm fixin' to hang his guts up on a fence post."

"What did he do to get your dander up like that?" Sloat asked.

"That damn light-haired Injun crossed me too many times, and he's carrying somethin' that I figure belongs to me." The mere thought of Luke Sunday caused the scar in Bogart's side to sting.

The description struck a chord in Sloat's mind. "He wouldn't by any chance be travelin' with a woman, would he?"

Bogart looked surprised. "As a matter of fact, he was—a woman and her husband, drivin' a wagon. Tall feller with light-colored hair, tied Injun-style, ridin' a paint Injun pony."

Sloat nodded knowingly. "Yep, that's the feller, only they didn't have no wagon, and there wasn't anybody else but the two of 'em. Ain't that right, Pearl?" The woman nodded.

"That son of a bitch," Bogart growled. "He's already got rid of the husband." He gave his partner a quick glance. "What'd I tell you, Wylie?"

"You had it right, Bill," Wylie dutifully replied.

Sloat studied his two guests with a sly gleam in his eye while Pearl set plates of food on the table, amused that Bogart was hesitant about mentioning anything relating to money. "And this poor recently widowed woman was carryin' a feed sack full of money on a packhorse," he stated matter-of-factly, confident now that there had to be more incentive for Bogart's search than the mere satisfaction of a killing. That sack must have carried a great deal of money, more than he had figured, to give Bogart a reason to come this far looking for it. He wondered if that was the reason Kirby and Gopher never came back.

"A sack full of money?" Bogart asked. "She had a sack full of money?"

"Well, I reckon she did," Sloat said. "I saw her get some money out of it." Noticing the expression on Bogart's face, he guessed that this news must have just increased his desire to find the woman. "I'll tell you a little story that might be bad news for you," Sloat continued. "I had a couple of fellers in business with me. We had a nice little arrangement, but I reckon they got greedy on me. I sent 'em after your man and the woman, and I ain't seen 'em since. They mighta beat you to that grain sack, and there was too much in it to wanna give me my cut."

"That mighta been the way it was," Bogart said, "or they mighta got shot. This feller's not an easy man to get the jump on. Hell, he's half Injun. Ain't that right, Wylie?"

"That's a fact," Wylie answered.

Back to Sloat then, Bogart asked, "So, they stopped here, did they?"

"They did," Sloat replied. "Bought a sack of coffee beans."

"Did they say where it was they was headed?"

"They asked where Coulson was." When Bogart

responded with a blank expression, Sloat said, "That's a new town some folks just set up a few months back."

"Coulson, huh? How far is that?" Bogart asked, thoroughly pleased to learn that the woman's relatives on the Yellowstone weren't the only ones with money.

"Two and a half, three days, dependin' on how bad you wanna get there," Sloat said. He could almost see the wheels turning in Bogart's brain as the big man thought about the man he hunted. "You know, there's a chance this feller has got what you're lookin' for and long gone," he suggested. "And like I said, I had a nice little arrangement with Kirby and Gopher. We could work the same arrangement together, the three of us."

Bogart fixed him with a contemptuous stare. "Shit, if you're thinkin' about robbin' and killin' folks, why don't you just do it yourself? I ain't lookin' to split with anybody." He paused then to reassure Wylie, "Except you, partner."

"I'm gettin' too old for that kind of work," Sloat complained. "Besides, I couldn't just start killin' folks right here at the store. It wouldn't be long before somebody caught on. I just thought you might be interested if you was in need of some extra money."

"Hell," Bogart swore, and nodded toward Pearl. "Why don't you just let that Injun take care of it?

She looks like she would just as soon scalp you as look at you." Pearl gave no indication that she had heard the remark. "How long ago was it when they passed through here?"

"Three or four days ago, I reckon," Sloat replied.

"Well, I reckon me and Wylie will be gettin' along," Bogart said, and pushed his chair back from the table, but was apparently in no hurry to leave. "That was mighty fine grub, Mrs. Sloat," he said, and winked at Wylie.

Wylie, thinking it a cue for him to duplicate, said, "That's a fact."

Bogart stretched his arms out, then patted his belly contentedly. "Maybe me and Wylie oughta think about your offer to go partners with you. The thing that bothers me, though, is how many folks stop in here that has enough to go after. It don't sound like much money or goods to split three ways."

"You'd be surprised," Sloat replied. "There's a lot more folks headin' this way every month to start up places like Coulson, and they're carryin' every cent and everything else they own. And the sweet thing about it is there ain't nobody looking for 'em when they don't show up at wherever it was they was headed, so there ain't nobody to miss 'em."

"So you're fixed up pretty good here?"

"I sure as hell wouldn't be here if I had to get by on whatever I was sellin' legit."

"Well, now, that's right interestin'," Bogart said, and casually reached over to scratch under his left arm. It was a simple move from there to drop his hand on the butt of the pistol riding below, butt-forward. Lem Sloat carried the stunned look of surprise on his face to wherever his next stop was destined to be, most likely hell. The sudden pop of Bogart's pistol startled Wylie as well, and he went over backward while trying to disentangle himself from his chair. The next moments were an explosion of chaos as the sullen Crow woman attacked Bogart, diving headlong across the table. Not expecting a violent reaction from the woman, he was caught by surprise. The collision of their bodies knocked the pistol from his hand and it was all he could do to pry her fingers from his throat. Walks-With-A-Stick was a big woman and a natural fighter, giving Bogart all he could handle, and strong enough to make his fight a defensive one. While Bogart fought to keep her from scratching his eyes out, Wylie finally freed himself from the chair. Pulling his revolver, he tried to get a shot at the frenzied woman, but could not take a chance on hitting Bogart by mistake. Finally Bogart was able to get both his hands on her throat and force her away to arm's length. "Shoot her!" he yelled. "Dammit, Wylie, shoot her!" No longer afraid of hitting Bogart, Wylie pulled the trigger, sending two .44 slugs into Pearl's abdomen. Even though mortally wounded, she continued to struggle against Bogart's frantic efforts to free himself. Fascinated by the enraged woman's refusal to die, Wylie stared in disbelief for a few moments more before holding his pistol to her head and firing a bullet into the back of her skull, causing her to finally slump to the floor.

"Damn!" Bogart exhaled, pushing the corpse away from him. He had not escaped the fight without damage, for there were numerous scratches on his face and neck from the clawing Pearl had administered. In addition, he experienced a close call when Wylie's bullet exited the woman's skull and zipped by his shoulder, leaving bits of bone and brain on his shirt. Disgusted, he looked around frantically for something with which to clean it off. Pearl's skirt was the most convenient, so he used that. Still furious at the way a simple killing had mushroomed into such a disgusting mess, he picked up his pistol from the floor and proceeded to pump a couple more slugs into the corpse, just to vent his rage. When that didn't totally satisfy his anger, he considered shooting Wylie for the mess on his shirt, but managed to restrain himself from taking further retaliation. "Let's take this place apart," he ordered. "He's bound to have somethin' hid somewhere—in the walls, under the floor—somewhere."

Not much time was wasted in the tent, since there appeared to be few places to hide anything, so the major portion of their search was in the store. By the time they were ready to give up, they had found very little money, but they helped themselves to basic supplies and ammunition, blankets, tobacco, and several bottles of whiskey, all of which they could surely use. They loaded all their plunder on the two horses in the rough corral behind the tent.

When the horses were fully loaded, Wylie stepped back to gaze upon them. "I swear, Bogart, we got enough possibles to last us six months."

"Maybe," Bogart answered as he dabbed the scratches on his neck with some lard he had found in the tent. "The way he was talkin' about goin' partners with us, I thought there had to be some money hid somewhere. It was all talk. Hell, he was always all talk. I shoulda known better. You can't trust a man like that."

"He sure looked surprised, didn't he?" Wylie remarked.

"I expect he was," Bogart replied, and went to the stove in the middle of the room. "See anythin' else you want, you'd better get it, 'cause I'm fixin' to burn this place down."

"Ain't you gonna take this Injun's scalp?" Wylie asked.

"No," Bogart replied. "Take it if you want it." He raised his boot and gave the stove a solid kick, knocking it over to spill hot coals on the earthen floor. Then the two of them gathered up anything that looked as if it would burn and threw it on the coals. Before very long the shack was too hot to remain inside. "That oughta do it," Bogart said. "Now let's get on down to . . ." He paused. "What was the name of it?"

"Coulson," Wylie replied as he gazed at the long clump of hair he had removed from Pearl's head.

"Right, let's go to Coulson. I got a yellow-headed Injun I'm needin' to see. I might take *that* scalp." The recent bloodletting of one who was supposed to be a friend had served to nourish his feeling of power. The sensation was tempered slightly by the stinging scratches on his neck and face.

With their newly acquired packhorses, they headed up the path to the river road as black clouds of smoke billowed out of the two small windows of Lem Sloat's trading post. After about an hour's ride from the burning store, they approached a wide creek. Wylie called ahead to his partner, "Bogart, look yonder." When Bogart looked back at him, Wylie pointed toward the treetops farther up the creek and a small circle of three buzzards overhead.

"Somethin's dead up that creek," Bogart commented, and studied the birds a few seconds before suggesting, "Let's go see what it is." They turned off the trail and advanced no more than one hundred yards before coming upon the remains of two men, their bones picked almost clean. "I expect that's ol' Sloat's two partners," Bogart said. "I ain't surprised. I told him Luke Sunday mighta got them instead of the other way around."

Gazing thoughtfully at the three buzzards now picking away at the bones, Wylie remarked, "Looks like them three has got to the party late. I bet there was a helluva lot more of them birds when the meat was fresh."

"Let's go," Bogart said. "We got plenty of daylight left." The image of the sandy-haired devil that had twice humiliated him came back to his mind to taunt him and he realized that he wanted to kill Luke Sunday worse than any amount of gold and silver the woman with him might have in that sack of grain.

The yellow-haired man that bedeviled Bogart's mind was, at that particular time, kneeling in the midst of a clump of large service berry shrubs on the bank of the river. His attention was captured by a party of perhaps twenty lodges of Indians crossing the river some fifty yards farther upstream. From that closeness, he was able to identify the party as Cheyenne. He would have preferred to remain hidden until the Indians had passed through, but there was a problem that might effectively prohibit that choice. His camp was on the other side of the river, only a few dozen yards from where the Cheyenne were now crossing. Behind him, in the trees, his paint pony waited quietly. However, he had left the spotted gray and his packs in his camp. Watching now, he could see the Cheyenne scouts riding close in to their people as the women guided the packhorses and travois across to the west bank. If luck was with him, his camp would not be discovered and they would never know he was there. *Unless,* he thought, *the gray decides to say hello.* So far, the horse had not done so.

Approximately thirty-five miles up Clark's Fork of the Yellowstone, Luke had come upon a sizable herd of deer, which was now two short of its original number. Both animals were shot at close range with his bow, a practice he always adhered to whenever possible to save precious cartridges. On this day he was glad that he had been faithful to that practice, for the Cheyenne party had appeared at the river no more than half an hour after he had shot the second deer and followed it into the berry bushes he was kneeling in at present. Now, as he watched the last of the Indians leaving the water and ascending the west bank, it appeared that he might escape detection, and he thought about the choices he would have had to choose between. He had been raised in a Cheyenne camp, by a Cheyenne woman, but he had scouted for the army with a group of Crow warriors. He had thought to be a friend to the

Cheyenne people, but they had joined with the Sioux in a war against the army. He considered the Sioux his enemy, because they had killed his white parents. He might have had to fight these Cheyenne, or lose his supplies and the gray pony if he had chosen to run. He was thankful that the Indians had not been aware of his presence.

A moment later, he realized that he had given thanks too soon, for suddenly there appeared to be a disturbance at the peaceful river crossing, and the Cheyenne outriders wheeled their ponies to respond to the outcry. Raising himself a little to see more clearly between the branches of the bushes, he saw the cause for the village's sudden display of alarm. One of the scouts had circled wide to the left of the others and had discovered Luke's horse and his camp. There was no time to spend on his decision. He could simply withdraw from the berry bushes, return to his horse, and ride away, but he was not willing to lose the packhorse and everything he had just bought in Coulson.

As quickly as he could, he backed out of the clump of service berries, dragging the deer's carcass with him. As soon as he reached a place in the bank where he could step down, he knelt and pulled the carcass to a point where he could get his shoulder under it, then stood up with the deer across his shoulders. Hurrying to his horse, he hefted the carcass across the paint's withers in front of his saddle, then climbed up himself.

Warriors searched the trees and bushes cautiously around the campsite, alert for any attack, while others examined the horse and supplies they found near the remains of a recent fire. Above the buzz of curious conversation, one of the Indians exclaimed suddenly, and when the others turned to see why he had shouted an alarm, they saw him pointing toward the river. To their surprise, a man dressed in animal skins forded the river, riding a paint pony, with the carcass of a deer draped across in front of the saddle. As he came closer, they realized that he was a white man, and the warriors quickly readied their weapons.

Luke held up his hands in a sign of peace, and called out to them in their native tongue, "You look like you have traveled hard and fast. I think you might want to stop at my camp and eat this fresh-killed deer to give you strength to continue your journey." He continued to approach the astonished village with no sign of caution. "There is enough. I have killed another deer on the other side of the river, in the trees. You can send some of the younger boys to get it."

While the others simply stood staring at the unexpected visitor, one warrior spoke out. "This white man is a fool. We will kill him and take his horses and his deer." His remarks were followed by a general scattering of grunts of support.

"No, wait," one of the Indians said. An elderly

man who had come with them from the Little Big Horn after being separated from his village in the fighting there. "This man is not our enemy. His name is Dead Man, and he came to warn us when the soldiers attacked Two Moons's village on the Powder River." Old Bear made his way through the people crowded around Luke's camp to greet him. "Welcome, Dead Man," he called out. "Your gift is most welcome, too, for we have seen very little game in the last two days."

Luke wondered if his immediate sigh of relief could be heard by the mob of Indians staring at him. His expression, however, conveyed no uncertainty. "Good to see you, Old Bear," he said. "I was not there, but I have heard about the fight with the soldiers at Little Big Horn. I am glad to see that you are still well."

The general tone of the people gathered around changed at once with the thought of roasting a couple of deer when seconds before they were preparing to fight. Luke slid the carcass off into the waiting hands of several women. Then he dismounted and led the paint over to his pack-horse. A young man, who had been holding the gray's reins, handed them to Luke, smiling as he stepped away. Luke nodded in return, thinking that his gamble had saved his belongings as well as his scalp, but he was not sure it would have worked if Old Bear had not been there.

The carcass of Luke's other kill was retrieved,

and they were both prepared for roasting. The Cheyenne party decided to make camp there for the night to enjoy the feast, and Luke talked long into the night with Old Bear and some of the other men. He learned of the battle at the Little Big Horn. Old Bear told him that they had been in a big camp with the Lakota villages of Sitting Bull and Crazy Horse. The soldiers were foolish to attack them, he said, for they were heavily outnumbered. "Where do you go now?" Luke asked.

"We know that the soldiers will come now in great numbers, too many for us to fight. Too many of our people, both Lakota and Cheyenne, have gone to the reservations to live on the white man's scraps instead of joining us in this fight. So we left the camp on the Little Big Horn and scattered so the soldiers can't chase us all." To answer Luke's question, Old Bear told him they were heading north to Canada, planning to cross the Yellowstone at a place Luke knew as Canyon Creek. "We do not wish to fight any white men," Old Bear said. "We will pass in peace if they will let us."

The next morning as the Cheyenne were preparing to leave, two of the women came to Luke with the two deer hides rolled into a bundle. "You keep them," he told them. "You will need them." They thanked him and returned to their packing.

Old Bear came then to say good-bye. "The day of the Cheyenne is over," he said. "The land that was ours since Man Above gave it to us is no longer ours to hunt in as He intended. You must decide which world you would belong to, the white man's or your Cheyenne brothers'. But if you choose to live with the people who raised you, Owl Woman's people, then you cannot stay here, for the white man will not let you."

"You may be right," Luke said, "but I must think about this some more. Maybe I'll see a sign that will tell me what I must do."

It was obvious to Old Bear that Luke was not ready to join his party at this time. "Well," he said in parting, "I wish you well, Dead Man. I hope you find your medicine soon."

Luke remained by the campfire, watching until the last of the Indians had disappeared from his view. There was a feeling of sadness left with him after Old Bear had gone, for he could not help thinking about the plight of the Indian now that the white man had discovered the wealth of the plains and the mountains. Already the buffalo were all but wiped out, replaced on the Montana plains by cattle. The fertile river flats were staked out for farming. *So where does that leave you?* He couldn't say. He had lived like an Indian all his life, with the Cheyenne and the Crows, but he was born a white man, and the little bit of a white man's life he had seen during the last month had caused him to wonder. Suddenly he felt a strong desire to see Mary Beth again. He could not explain it. He just knew that it was important to him to make sure she was safe. He shrugged the feeling off, thinking it would pass, and began to prepare to move on to another part of the river, hoping to find the herd of deer again. When his packhorse was loaded and he had saddled the paint, he rode out of the camp, but instead of heading south, which was his original intention, he headed north, back the way he had come. "I guess I made a decision," he told the paint.

Even as he rode back toward the Yellowstone, he was still trying to make up his mind if he was just being a fool. He didn't dare to imagine himself as anything more than a friend to her. After all, he surmised, she might be terrified to know he was even thinking about her, for he remembered how afraid of him she had been when they had first started out for the Yellowstone. He unconsciously reached up and felt his cheek with his fingertips. Why had she felt a compulsion to kiss him? Was it any more than a simple good-bye? *So, what am I going to do if I go back to that farm? What am I going to say is my reason for returning?* Still he rode on, lost in a feeling of helplessness, for he had never experienced these emotions before, emotions that most men had dealt with at a much younger age.

CHAPTER 12

"I declare," Vienna Pitts proclaimed when she walked into the barn, "I believe you've got some kind of magic touch. That cow is givin' more milk than she ever has, ever since you've been doin' the milkin'."

Mary Beth laughed. She did have a gentle touch that the cow seemed to appreciate, and consequently gave more milk. "I think she must be afraid of you," Mary Beth suggested. She didn't go further with the thought, but she suspected it might be because the poor cow was in fear that the big woman with the rough hands might jerk one of her tits off.

"I don't know why she'd be afraid of me," Vienna replied. "I ain't ever done nothin' to cause her to be."

Mary Beth shrugged and changed the subject. "I'm about finished with the milking. As soon as I skim the cream, I'll fill the pan and go over to the house to churn it."

"I wonder if Jack could make us a churn," Vienna said. "His daddy keeps promisin' to make us one, but he doesn't ever get around to doin' it."

"Too bad," Mary Beth said. "I had a good one, but it got left behind with the wagon." A brief reminder of that terrifying night flashed through her mind when Luke had instructed her to leave all that was unnecessary to their immediate survival with the wagon. It was only for an instant, however, and she said cheerfully, "We could probably make one ourselves."

Vienna smiled broadly. "I reckon we could at that," she said. "Hell, between the two of us, we can do most anything that John and the boy can do. You go on up to the house. I'll put that jug of blue-john in the spring box for you."

Mary Beth skimmed the cream from the big pan of fresh milk and poured it into a smaller pan. She covered it with a cloth to keep the bugs out of it while she walked it across the garden to John and Doris's house. Both dwellings were built of logs, but they referred to John and Doris's as *the house* to distinguish it from their cabin. As she made her way across the rows in the garden, she smiled to herself. It had been a good thing to move in with Vienna. Both women thought so, for they were both hard workers and confident in their independence from men. Occasionally, Luke Sunday came to mind, usually when Vienna brought up his name, and she would pause to wonder where he was and what he was doing. Vienna insisted that he would one day return to see her, but she was not sure that was what she wanted. She had been widowed far too recently to think about life with another man. *It would be interesting, though,* she thought, then scolded herself for thinking it and offered a silent apology to her late husband. Even if it was merely idle speculation, she was afraid it would be impossible to break Luke to the matrimonial harness, if that was her objective. She would most likely have to head for the mountains every time she needed him, so she put it out of her mind as she came to the last rows of the garden. It was idle thinking, anyway. She was happy in her new role as a partner to Vienna.

Mary Beth walked in the kitchen door to find Doris soaking some beans for supper that night. "I came to borrow the churn," she said, and set her pan on the kitchen table.

"Help yourself," Doris replied cheerfully. "You know where it is."

While Mary Beth was preparing her cream to be churned, young Jack came into the house, looking for a cold biscuit to carry him until suppertime. "Between you and your pa," Doris commented casually, "it's a wonder there's ever anything like a cold biscuit around here."

"It's your fault, Ma," Jack responded. "You bake 'em too good." He started to say more, but was stopped by something he saw through the open front door. "Who's that up at the road talkin' to Pa?"

His question got an immediate response from both women, for visitors were rare on their farm.

All three went to the front door to see. "Nobody I've ever seen before," Doris said as she squinted, trying to identify the two riders, leading two packhorses. "Probably somebody trying to find town and took the wrong road." She continued to stare at the strangers, wondering if John was going to invite them to stop for a cool drink of water, or a cup of coffee. She hoped not, because she would have to hop pretty quickly to fix something. "They sure seem to be talking about something."

Curious as well, Mary Beth was trying to decide if she had seen one of the men before. The large one with the full reddish-brown beard looked slightly familiar, and she wondered if he might have been one of the scouts that rode with General Crook. Probably not, she decided, for what would he be doing here? As they continued to watch, Jack decided to go out to join his father. He had started for the door when they were startled by a sudden discharge of a pistol. Before their horrified eyes, John Freeman doubled over and fell to the ground. The big man with the reddish beard pointed his pistol down at the body and fired another bullet into the mortally wounded man. Then both strangers turned to look toward the house.

"Pa!" Jack cried out, unable to believe what he had just witnessed. His mother screamed out her husband's name and sank down on her knees in horrified shock. Her son, distraught and confused, yelled out for his father again and started to run to help him.

"No! Jack, no!" Mary Beth screamed, and grabbed the boy by his arm. "They'll kill you, too!" Although as terrified as they were, she was sane enough to know that they were all going to lose their lives if they didn't do something to defend themselves. "It's too late to help your father now," she told the boy. "We've got to save ourselves." She looked around her frantically, searching desperately for something that would tell her what to do. "Guns!" she exclaimed. "Get John's guns! We have to keep them from coming after us."

Jack ran to the front room and got the shotgun from over the fireplace, pausing only a second to look toward the road again to see if the two men were coming. When they did not immediately charge toward the house, taking their horses to the barn instead, he ran into the bedroom and got the sack of shotgun shells from the bottom drawer of the dresser. Then he loaded the gun and crouched at the front window, ready to shoot.

Mary Beth looked around at the doors and windows while trying to calm Doris, who was sobbing hysterically. She knew they could not defend themselves against the two men with only one shotgun. "Doris," she pleaded, "we've got to get out of here." She tried to lift the bereaved woman to her feet, but she was not strong enough to do it.

"They're comin'!" Jack called out from the front room when he saw them come out of the barn.

"Jack!" Mary Beth shouted. "Come help me with your mother!" When he ran to assist her, she said, "We can't stay here! Help me get her on her feet. We'll go out the back door and run to the cabin. We've got a better chance there. Vienna's got a rifle, and I have a pistol. We can defend ourselves there."

Together, they got Doris on her feet and headed her toward the back door. Mary Beth took one last quick look out the front door to discover the two men cautiously approaching the house, no farther away than thirty or forty yards. "Run!" she told Jack and Doris, and they went out the back door. She was right behind them.

They were met almost in the middle of the garden by Vienna Pitts, who had heard the shots fired. "What is it?" Vienna cried, alarmed by the three fleeing for their lives. Gasping for breath, Mary Beth told her what had happened and urged her to run as well. "They shot John?" Vienna asked, scarcely able to believe it. She put her arm around Doris's waist to help support the devastated woman. "Come on," she yelled to Mary Beth and Jack. "Get in the cabin and bar the doors! We can stand 'em off there." Once back inside, she gave orders for their defense. "Mary

Beth, take that window in the front room; Jack, take that shotgun and watch the side window. Doris, if I give you a pistol, can you sit by the window on the other side and sing out if they try to come in that way? With tears streaming down her cheeks, but no longer sobbing uncontrollably, she nodded and said that she could. "Good girl," Vienna said. "I'll be watchin' the back door." She stood firm for a moment, watching to see that everyone got in their places. "All right, good!" she said. "Let the bastards come." She picked up her Winchester rifle and positioned herself by the door. They settled in for the siege they knew had to come. However, it did not come as soon as they expected.

Back at the house, Bogart and Wylie approached the front door, mindful of the windows and the potential for a rifle or shotgun to suddenly appear over the sill. Cautioning Wylie to be ready, Bogart prepared to kick the front door open. One sharp thrust from his heavy boot sent the door flying open. When there was no response from inside, he peeked around the doorframe. "There ain't nobody in there," he called to Wylie. "I'm goin' in." Wylie hesitated for a few moments, just in case Bogart missed someone hiding in a corner, and then followed him inside.

Like two bears at a campsite, the two killers ransacked the house, looking for anything of value, but hoping to find the treasure that Bogart had created in his mind. There was no fear of an ambush by Luke Sunday, for they had seen no sign of the paint pony that he always rode. In the corral behind the barn, they had discovered three horses, and the man out by the road had told them that Sunday had been there, but left several days before, and there was nothing of value inside his house. Convinced that the man was lying, Bogart had shot him. But now, after nearly destroying the cabin, Bogart was nearing a frenzy of frustration. "Where the hell is the rest of the family?" he wondered aloud. "That bastard didn't live here by hisself."

"I expect they might be yonder," Wylie said, peering out the back door. "Looks like another cabin down below that garden patch."

The comment caught Bogart's immediate attention and he shoved past Wylie to see for himself. "By God, you might be right." He stepped off the back stoop and walked to the edge of the garden. "Yes, sir," he said with a malevolent grin, "that's where they are, all right. It looks like they ran a herd of cattle across them corn rows," he said, looking at the obvious signs of their hurried escape. "Little footprints, too, like women leave." He gave Wylie another grin. "Like that pretty little woman ridin' in that wagon that Luke Sunday ran off with. But Sunday ain't around, so they ain't got nobody to protect 'em from the bogeyman." He laughed at his attempt at humor.

"Let's go see if they ain't hidin' somethin' down there."

They hadn't reached the halfway point in the garden when suddenly the blast of a shotgun came toward them, raining birdshot that clipped the young corn around them. Both men dived for protection behind a corn row. "Damn!" Bogart swore. "You hit, Wylie?"

"No," Wylie answered. "Nowhere except on my arms." He paused a minute to further examine himself. "Ain't nothin' bad. Wasn't nothin' but birdshot, and I reckon they's too far away. Stings like hell, though."

Inside the cabin, Vienna was quick to tell Jack that he would have to let the men get closer before his shotgun would be effective. "I shoulda fetched the buckshot," he said. "I was in too big a hurry."

"That's all right," Vienna told him. "It gave 'em somethin' to think about. They'll know better'n to come walkin' in this house.

Vienna was right. Flat on their bellies in the garden, Bogart and Wylie were rethinking their plan. It would seem to be no more than an inconvenience if the only weapon they had to worry about was a shotgun, and it firing birdshot to boot. Bogart, irritated to be held at bay by a bunch of women, decided to see if he could talk them out. "Hey, you in the cabin," he yelled, "come on outside where we can see you, and won't nobody get hurt."

"Hey, you in the corn patch," Vienna yelled back, "go straight to hell."

Further irritated with the response, Bogart roared, "You got a smart mouth on you, lady, and it might just get you in trouble. If you know what's good for you, you'll get yourself, and whoever else is in there, out where we can see you. We don't mean you no harm. We just want what we came for. You got money hid here, and the sooner you come up with it, the sooner we'll be on our way."

"You don't mean us no harm?" Vienna echoed. "You've already killed one of us, so get on your horses and get off this land, you murderin' bastards."

Bogart spoke softly to Wylie. "Back outta here and go around to the back." When Wylie began inching backward, Bogart called out again. "Lady, you ain't thinkin' straight. Me and my partner are gonna start shootin' that cabin to pieces if you don't come outta there right now, and that little shotgun ain't gonna do you much good."

"Is that a fact?" Vienna yelled. Then she moved up to the edge of the window and rested her rifle on the sill. "How 'bout a Winchester?" she asked as she fired off a round toward the sound of the voice. "Will that do any good?"

"You crazy bitch!" Bogart blurted when Vienna's rifle slug kicked up dirt a few feet from him, causing him to jump. Rapidly developing a rage, he pulled his rifle up and emptied the magazine, showering the window and door with lead that sent shards of wood flying from the window frame, and Vienna and Mary Beth to the floor for cover. By the time he finished reloading the empty magazine, he heard shots from Wylie's rifle at the back of the cabin. A few seconds later, answering fire came from the cabin from three different weapons: rifle, shotgun, and what sounded like a heavy revolver. There were at least three inside to contend with, and from the tracks he had seen in the garden, a couple of them had to be women. The one boot print had been not much bigger than the women's, from either a small man or a boy. It frustrated him to be held at bay by such a harmless bunch. Then, too, he had no way of knowing how many, and who, were already in the cabin. In frustration, he fired a few more rounds at the log cabin. *This ain't getting me anywhere,* he thought, so he backed away from the corn row and went to join Wylie behind the house.

Wylie had positioned himself behind a wood-pile at the back corner of the cabin. He jumped, startled, when Bogart suddenly dropped down beside him. "Whaddaya think we oughta do?" he asked. "We can set here shootin' till we use up all our cartridges, and we still won't get in that house."

Bogart thought for a minute. "Any shots come out the back at you?"

"Hell yeah," Wylie promptly replied.

"All right," Bogart said, still thinking. "They been shootin' from the front, from the back, and from that little window on this side, but they ain't nobody shootin' at us from the other side of the house." He gave Wylie a knowing smirk. "There ain't but three of 'em, that's why. They can't cover every side. That's how we'll get 'em. We'll slip in from the other side."

Wylie wasn't sure he agreed with Bogart's way of thinking. "Hell, I figure there ain't been nobody shootin' at us from the other side 'cause they can't see us from that side."

Bogart was so sure he was right, he decided to prove it. "Come on," he said, and moved from the woodpile to a wagon near the opposite corner of the house. When Wiley dropped down beside him, he pointed to the window on the side. "Now, throw a couple of shots at that back door and let's see what happens." Wylie raised his rifle and splintered the back doorframe. As soon as his rifle was silent, the door opened just wide enough to allow a rifle barrel to protrude, and his fire was answered by Vienna's Winchester. The slugs ripped great chunks of wood from the side of the wagon box, making it too hot to stay, so they retreated to a smokehouse several feet behind them to take cover. "See?" Bogart said. "Didn't nobody shoot at us from the corner of that side window. Only one of 'em shot at us, 'cause there ain't but three of 'em and the other two are scared of leavin' their spots, scared they'll get hit from the front if they do. I'm tellin' you, Wylie, they ain't got nobody coverin' that window on this side. That's where we'll get 'em before they know what happened."

Inside the cabin the besieged four awaited the next barrage of rifle fire. Vienna moved constantly from the front to the back, trying to determine where it might come from. Crouched by the front window, Mary Beth reported, "I don't have any more bullets for this old gun, just what's left in the cylinder. When I empty the cylinder, I'm out."

"Too bad it ain't a forty-four like mine," Vienna said, " 'cause I've got plenty of ammunition." She glanced in the bedroom at Doris, still kneeling before the window, the pistol she had given her held loosely in her hands. Looking back at Mary Beth, she said, "You might as well take my pistol when you give out. Doris ain't fired a shot." Mary Beth nodded, and Vienna asked, "Can you see the one out front?"

"No," Mary Beth answered, "but he hasn't shot for the last few minutes."

"He's most likely tryin' to figure a way to get closer," Vienna cautioned. "Keep your eyes sharp. That one in the backyard was behind the wagon, but I think I ran him outta there. I'll keep my eye on him." She called out then, "Jack, you still all right?"

"Yes, ma'am," came the reply from his post at the side window.

"Good boy. Keep your eyes peeled, 'cause they're gonna try to sneak in on us." She did not express her concern for the lateness of the hour, but it was her biggest worry. They would be unable to see their assailants when darkness fell, and she wasn't sure they could keep them out. There was nothing else she could think of to strengthen their defense. Concerned then that she had left her post at the back door too long, she went back into the kitchen. Unknown to her, she had already lingered too long checking on the others, for she got back to the door brief seconds after Wylie had made a dash for the corner of the house, and was even then crawling along the side wall toward the window, undetected by anyone inside.

Once he had reached the window safely, Wylie crouched underneath it and turned to signal Bogart, who was set to charge through the kitchen door as soon as Wylie started shooting at those inside. He waited for a few minutes, listening for sounds through the open window, and he soon concluded that the voices he heard evidently came from other parts of the cabin. It was obvious to him that the window was in a bedroom, or a spare room, and nobody was sitting there, watching. The windowsill was about head high, so he figured he could grab it with one hand and shinny up over it. With his pistol in his other hand, he could be ready to shoot at anyone in the room even before he was inside.

Still kneeling before the window, Doris had not moved from the trancelike position she had originally taken when Vienna led her into Mary Beth's bedroom. She continued to stare down at the revolver she held in her hands, her face streaked with the path of tears now finally stopped. A soft bump against the side of the cabin brought her out of the daze that had captured her mind and she lifted her head to look at the window.

With his pistol in one hand, the other clutching the windowsill, and the toes of his boots inching up the log wall, Wylie slowly raised his head until his eyes were level with the sill. Pulling himself a few inches higher, he was startled to discover the bereaved woman kneeling before the window. His initial impulse was to drop to the ground immediately, but she did not move, instead staring at him as if not seeing him at all. While he was deciding what to do, she slowly raised Vienna's pistol and fired at the face in the window at the same time he raised his gun and pulled the trigger. Screaming out in agony from the bullet that slammed through his teeth and tore a hole through his cheek, Wylie dropped to the ground and began crawling to the corner of the house on all fours.

Startled by the simultaneous gunshots from the

bedroom, Vienna and Mary Beth, with Jack close behind, ran to investigate, only to find Doris lying on the floor with a bullet through her heart. Jack cried out in horror and ran to his mother. Vienna's reaction was to check the window, where she had time to send one shot after the pair of boots just then disappearing around the corner of the cabin. Turning back to Doris then, she saw at once that there was nothing to be done to save her. Before she could say anything, they heard the sound of the kitchen door as it shattered under Bogart's powerful body.

"Shut the door!" Vienna screamed, and Mary Beth quickly slammed the bedroom door and bolted it. Trapped in the bedroom now, there was immediate panic, so the two women tried to think what to do other than standing there with their weapons aimed at the door. The boy knelt at his mother's side crying. Finally Vienna acted. "If he broke through the kitchen door, this little ol' door ain't gonna slow him down. We've got to get outta here!" She stepped quickly back to the open window and looked out. Seeing no sign of Wylie, she told them, "Out the window. Run to the new field and into the woods at the lower end. You first, Mary Beth, then you, Jack. If he comes through that door, I'll blow him to hell." They could hear him now, stomping through the kitchen, throwing chairs and the table aside as he stormed into the front room, yelling obscenities and threats. "Go!" Vienna cried when Mary Beth hesitated.

"You go," young Jack suddenly ordered. "I'll kill the son of a bitch. He killed my ma and pa." He picked up the revolver by his mother's side and got to his feet, facing the door.

"You can't face him, Jack," Vienna pleaded. "Maybe we can all get out the window and get away."

"The hell I can't stop him," Jack shot back. It was obvious that he had become a man in those brief terrifying seconds. Then seeing Vienna balking, and knowing that time was running out, he told her, "I'll be right behind you. Get goin'."

There was no time to argue. Vienna turned to Mary Beth. "Go!"

Mary Beth went out the window, and Vienna followed right behind. Mary Beth stumbled upon landing on the ground, but Vienna grabbed her under her arm and pulled her to her feet, and they ran into the field. It was too early in the summer for the corn to have grown high enough to hide them, so they forced themselves to run as hard as they could to reach the lower end. Behind them, they heard a burst of gunshots. Looking back, they discovered then that Jack was not following. Vienna started to turn back, but Mary Beth stopped her. "It's too late now," she insisted, for all was quiet in the cabin then. "Whatever happened is over, and you might be running right into your own death."

Even in that chaotic moment, Vienna realized that Mary Beth was right; it served no purpose. "Poor Jack," she moaned. "I hope he came out on top." It was a sincere wish, but she had no faith in it.

Inside the cabin, the lull in the sound of gunshots left uncertainty for both parties, for the volley had claimed no victim. Young Jack Freeman stood facing the bedroom door, now splintered on both sides from the rapid fire on either side. He hurriedly spun the cylinder of his pistol, reloading as fast as he could, uncertain if more than one or two bullets had penetrated the plank door. With his revolver reloaded, he was about to empty it again into the door, but he hesitated when there were no more shots from the other side. He waited. The long moments passed with still no sound from beyond the door. Then from the backyard, he heard his mother's murderer moaning and cursing, complaining that he was wounded. When several more moments passed with still nothing on the other side of the door, he assumed that one of his bullets had found the mark. Either that or the murderer's partner had gone to help the wounded man. Either way, Jack felt he had to act quickly to finish them both off. He threw the bolt on the door and jerked it open to find a smirking Bill Bogart waiting, his rifle aimed waist-high. The boy dropped to the floor with two slugs in his gut, his reflexive action causing him to fire a bullet into the floor as he fell.

Bogart stepped up to kick the pistol away from the boy's hand, then quickly scanned the small room to make sure there was no one else there. The open window told him what had happened to the others. After making sure Jack was dying, he stepped over his body to look at the woman's body lying by the window. His initial reaction was anger over Wylie's careless shooting, but then he realized that the woman was not the one he lusted for. *I reckon Wylie got this one before one of 'em got him,* he thought. *Too bad she got shot before we could have gotten some use out of her, though.* He cautiously poked his head out the window to look around in the fading afternoon light. No one was in sight. Then he heard Wylie's pitiful call for help. He looked back at Jack and said, "You're the one that made them little boot prints, so whoever jumped out the window are women and I know that pretty little honey is one of 'em." Knowing they were running, he felt assured he had nothing to fear from them for the time being, so he walked back into the front room, pausing only a moment to put a bullet in the boy's head.

"Quit your damn blubberin'," Bogart said when he walked out the back door to find Wylie sitting with his back propped against the wall of the cabin. "Lemme take a look at you—couldn't be too bad, or you wouldn't be able to cry like a baby."

"I reckon that's easy enough for you to say," Wylie complained, his voice strained with the pain and his words slurred by the destruction Doris's bullet had caused. His mouth and the left side of his face were covered with blood, and he was holding a blouse he had pulled from the clothesline pressed against his cheek in an effort to slow the bleeding. "I need a doctor," he mumbled, unable to speak clearly. "I'm hurt bad."

"Well, now, that'd be a problem, wouldn't it?" Bogart replied, with no show of sympathy. "Where in hell would we find a doctor around here? Even if we did, how we gonna explain how you got shot?"

"All I know is I'm hurtin' somethin' fierce," Wylie moaned while trying to talk without moving one side of his mouth. "We've got to do somethin'. I think I swallowed half of my teeth."

"Lemme see," Bogart said, and pulled the blouse away from Wylie's face, causing the wounded man to yelp with pain. He stared at the gaping rip in Wylie's cheek and the stumps of teeth on that side of his mouth. "Damn," he murmured, "sure made a mess of it. Who shot you, the boy?"

"That damn woman," Wylie said, his words

almost unintelligible, "but I think I put one in her, too."

"Yeah, she's dead," Bogart said, "and I know there was two more women in there, but they went out the window and took off—most likely still runnin'." He paused to take a look up at the sky. "We need to look for that damn money while there's still light enough to see."

"I need some doctorin'," Wylie protested.

"We ain't got no time for that, and I ain't aimin' to hang around here too long. I don't know where the nearest house is, but somebody mighta heard all the shootin' and come to take a look. Them women that got away are most likely on their way to get help, so we got to turn this place upside down and find whatever it is they're hidin', before we can get the hell outta here."

"I can't help you," Wylie insisted. "I'm hurt too bad. Dammit, I've got the side of my face blowed off."

Already disgusted with his partner for getting himself shot, Bogart fired back, "Well, you shoulda watched what the hell you were doin'. I'm gonna turn up anythin' I can find." Even though his mind had been set upon finding the woman he had seen on the wagon at Fort Fetterman, his common sense told him it was best not to linger. "You'd best get up off your ass if you're thinkin' 'bout goin' with me, 'cause I ain't waitin' for ya." He left him where he was and returned to the cabin. Starting in the kitchen, he opened every drawer and every cabinet he could fine, dumping pots, pans, and utensils on the floor. When he could find nothing there, he went through each of the other rooms, overturning furniture, ripping open mattresses, searching through the clothes drawers, all to no avail. Angry and disgusted, he slammed a chair up against the wall. Storming back into the kitchen, he started to kick the stove over, but a thought struck him at that moment. *The smokehouse.* He hadn't searched there.

Out the back door he charged, passing Wylie as the wounded man staggered toward their horses still tied up at the corral. Without a word to his partner, Bogart strode to the small log building next to the outhouse. There was no meat hanging inside the smokehouse, and he was about to reverse his steps when he noticed several feed sacks stacked against the wall. His eyes opened wide in anticipation when he remembered what Lem Sloat had said, but could she have still left the money in a sack of grain, as Lem claimed? He wasted no time finding out. Not bothering to untie the sacks, he plunged his knife in each one and ripped them open, spilling feed and grain on the earthen floor. Only one sack held feed corn and Bogart's knife blade struck something hard when he thrust it in that sack. His head was pounding with the rapid beat of his heart as he raked the corn out, uncovering eight small cloth bags. "Hot damn! Hot damn!" he blurted over and over, his fingers fumbling with excitement as he tried to open the bags. "I found it, Wylie! I knew there was money here!" It was too dark to count the money in the smokehouse, so he hurried outside and sat down on the ground to count his treasure. Seven of the bags contained five double eagles each. The eighth one held an assortment of silver coins. The huge man dumped them in his lap and grinned like a child at Christmastime. He enjoyed his find for a few moments more before calling his mind back to reality. Now that he had found what he had come for, the next thing was to get away from there before a posse of angry farmers appeared. Cradling the money up in his hands, he stalked toward the corral. "Wylie," he called out, "I got what we came for."

He found the wounded man sitting in the saddle, leaning forward on his horse's neck. "You found the money?" Wylie asked painfully. Bogart's announcement was enough to bring him back from the dead. "How much was it?"

"A couple hundred apiece," Bogart replied, thinking quickly.

"Gimme mine," Wylie rasped.

"Gimme a minute to put 'em down before I drop 'em," Bogart replied, and dropped all but two of the cloth bags in his saddlebag. "There you go," he crowed as he stuffed the two bags in

Wylie's saddlebag. "Now I expect it'd be healthier for us to get as far away from this place as we can." He climbed up and settled his heavy bulk in the saddle, but hesitated before turning his horse away from the corral rail. "I wonder about them other two women, though. If I had to run for it, I'd sure as hell take anythin' valuable I had. It would be mighty interestin' to find out what they grabbed before they jumped out that window."

Wylie didn't really care at that point. "We found the damn money," he mumbled painfully. "You just wanna get your hands on that damn woman. We need to get outta here."

"Maybe I will get my hands on that pretty little body before this is over," Bogart said. Wylie was right, he wanted the woman. She had burrowed into his lustful mind like a weevil. The thought that Luke Sunday might have had his way with her brought a greater desire to kill the sandy-haired Indian.

CHAPTER 13

The night was long and sleepless for the two desperate women huddled together under the steep bank of the river. Afraid to start a fire, even had they the means to start one, they spent the slowly passing hours listening for any sound that might announce the approach of the two killers. The river was quiet, except for the occasional splashing of a fish or a muskrat, or the croaking of a frog, but they were never certain that it was a fish or a muskrat and not something else. It was with mixed emotions that they greeted the first rays of light. They had survived the night, but the breaking day would provide light for anyone searching for them. They both felt that it would be hard to find them, for they had run a long way, making their way through thick patches of bushes and cottonwoods, along the river bluffs, and down countless gullies until they fell exhausted in a washed-out hole in the bank.

"Surely after all this time, they must have ridden on," Mary Beth said.

"Unless they've been waitin' for daylight to come after us," Vienna replied. "We shoulda found us a good place close to the cabin to ambush 'em last night, if they were of a mind to come after us." She was a little disgusted with herself for being so frightened during the night just passed, but she had never been exposed to such conscienceless murder before. Even encounters with hostile Indian war parties did not seem to be so terrifying as these two murderers. Resigning herself to regain her usual bluster, she announced, "I've had enough of this rabbit streak runnin' down my back. I'm goin' back to my cabin."

"Do you think it's safe to go back now?" Mary Beth replied, not so sure it would be a wise thing to do.

"Safe or not," Vienna stated, "it's my damn house those murderers are tearin' up, and they've killed an entire family of my friends. I'm goin' back, and if they're still there, well, then there's gonna be hell to pay." She cocked her rifle to emphasize her resolve. The cocking of the rifle was followed by another sound, this one from the bluff above them. Both women froze, for judging from the rustle of bushes, something or someone had found their hiding place. Vienna immediately backed up against the side of the hole and motioned for Mary Beth to get down. She trained her rifle on the edge of the overhanging bank, determined to shoot at whatever showed itself. They both jumped when they heard the voice.

"Ma'am, be careful with that rifle."

Crouched on her heels until that moment, Mary

Beth sprang up and ran out to the water's edge. Too late to stop her, Vienna could only gape at the woman who had seemingly lost her mind. A moment later, she saw Mary Beth's glad smile and heard her say, "Luke Sunday."

"Are you all right, ma'am?" Luke asked.

"Now that I'm looking at you, I am," Mary Beth admitted.

Vienna came out from under the bank to join them. "I've never been so glad to see someone in my entire life," she exclaimed when the tall white warrior made his way down through the gully. "I guess you saw what happened at my cabin."

"Yes, ma'am," Luke replied. "I'm real sorry for your friends. I didn't see anybody around, and I found your tracks leadin' across the field, so I came lookin' for you. I didn't see anybody's tracks chasin' you." His typical unemotional speech belied the anguish he had experienced when coming upon the ghastly scene at the cabin, as well as the joyous relief he felt upon finding Mary Beth safe.

"Is my house still standin'?" Vienna asked, afraid that the two assailants might have burned it down. Luke assured her that both houses were intact although there appeared to be quite a bit of destruction to the furnishings. "Well, at least they left us a roof over our heads," she said.

Answering his question, the women told him of the two men who had appeared at the edge of the road, and the futile attempt they had all made to defend themselves after John was shot down in cold blood. When Mary Beth described the two men, and said that the big one reminded her of one of the scouts she thought she had seen at Fort Fetterman, Luke had no doubt who the killers were. "Bogart," he muttered, for the huge man came to mind immediately. But how, he wondered, did Bill Bogart happen to be here on the Yellowstone, and not with the soldiers now chasing the splintered parties of Sioux and Cheyenne? Mary Beth told him about the demands they had made for the money they said they knew was hidden somewhere in the house. It seemed more likely then that someone at Fort Fetterman had found out about Mary Beth's sack of corn. And from her description of the men that attacked them, that man had to be Bogart. Still showing no outward emotion, he said, "Well, they're gone now, so we best be gettin' back. We've got bodies to bury." He took a long look at Mary Beth's eyes, now somewhat strained and weary, and said, "I expect you two could use some rest and maybe somethin' to eat."

"I could eat," Vienna replied immediately.

At Luke's insistence, the two women rode back to the cabin on his horse while he ran a few yards in front, trotting at a pace that dictated a fast walk for the paint gelding. It was a distance of a little over two miles, but it had seemed twice that in the darkness of the night before. Upon reaching the cornfield, Luke halted the horse, telling the women to remain there until he took a precautionary look around. "A man like Bogart might take a notion to come back lookin' for you," Luke said.

"Well, that's comfortin', ain't it?" Vienna asked facetiously.

"Don't hurt to be careful," Luke said, realizing then that it might not have been the right thing to say.

After a brief look around, Luke signaled for them to come in. Mary Beth and Vienna went directly to the bedroom, where they found Doris's body just as it had been when they escaped through the window. In the doorway of the bedroom, they found young John Edward Freeman Jr., called Jack by his parents, his body drawn up in the fetal position, a result of two gunshot wounds in his gut. A third wound in the side of his head must have slammed death's door on the dying boy. "Those bastards," Vienna spat. "They couldn't just rob us and leave us in peace. What kind of animal does this?"

"You women do whatever you want to get 'em ready to bury," Luke said. "I'll go up by the road and get John's body. Then I'll dig a grave."

"I'll take care of this," Vienna told Mary Beth. "Why don't you get a fire goin' in the stove and see if you can find something to cook? We're all about to starve." She looked through the doorway toward the kitchen. "They sure made a mess of the place. They probably didn't leave us a mouthful of food."

"I've got plenty of meat on my packhorse in the barn. I was bringin' it to you," Luke said as he was going out the front door.

"You always do," Mary Beth remarked. "Whenever we need food, you find a way to get it." Luke was not sure how to respond, so he didn't. Mary Beth watched him as he stepped off the front porch on his way to get John's body. She turned and started toward the kitchen, only to think of the one thing she had not checked on. She passed through the kitchen and out the back door, an anxious frown fixed on her face. Frozen in the door of the smokehouse, she stared at the gutted sacks against the wall. The one she was most concerned with sat almost empty, a pile of corn before it, the top of the bag collapsed upon itself, a signal to her that everything she had was gone. Knowing it to be a useless endeavor, she rushed to kneel before the gutted sack and scattered the pile of corn in desperate hope they might have missed a bag or a coin. *What a fool I am,* she silently berated herself for having thought the sack of corn the perfect hiding place. After a few moments of chastising herself, she told herself, *What's done is done. There's nothing I can do about it now.* And she once again despaired over David's and her fatal decision to come west in the first place. Pulling herself together, she got up to return to the kitchen to see what she could find to feed them, dreading to tell Vienna that the money she planned to spend on their farm was gone.

What Bogart and Wylie had not stolen, they had destroyed, but Luke supplied the women with enough meat, coffee, and beans to tide them over for a few days until they could go to town for more supplies. The money to buy those supplies was also furnished by Luke, who volunteered the balance of the one hundred dollars Mary Beth had paid him, sixty dollars to be exact. Mary Beth made a mild protest, but knew that she and Vienna had little choice but to take his money. Luke insisted that he was accustomed to being broke, so he would hardly miss it. "If I ain't got it, I won't have to worry about losin' it."

Mary Beth would always remember the sadness of the day when they buried John, Doris, and their son in one common grave. It had been a gray day from the beginning, and as soon as Luke had finished digging the grave, a light rain began to fall. It was as if God saw fit to personally express His sadness over the brutal murder of a young and promising family. There was little ceremony. Vienna beseeched God to please accept them lovingly. "They're good people," she implored, "the kind we need more of." She ended her prayer with one more request, since she had the Lord's ear, and that was to strike down the devils who had destroyed the family.

"Amen," Mary Beth offered.

The meal that followed was almost as sad as the funeral with all three eating in silence until Vienna commented that at least the rain had let up. "It wasn't enough to do the corn any good, but at least we got John and his family in the ground." Her comment seemed to end the mourning period and signal the need to plan for the future. "We need to get all that deer meat in the smokehouse and start drying it. Then we'd best get this place straightened up. After that, we can take care of John and Doris's house."

"I'll be leavin'," Luke announced quietly.

"Why?" Mary Beth quickly responded, her fears at once returning. "Where are you going?"

"I need to go while I've still got a trail to follow," he replied. "They didn't bother with coverin' their tracks."

Mary Beth was at once alarmed. "We need you here." She paused when both Vienna and Luke gave her a look of astonishment. "For a while, anyway," she continued. "What if those men come back?"

"That's why I've got to go after 'em," Luke said, "to make sure they don't." He glanced at Vienna, and she nodded in agreement. "One of 'em's hurt. I found a lot of blood on the ground back of the house. Maybe they'll be travelin' slow. I need to get after 'em before we have more rain and I lose the tracks."

"What about the law?" Mary Beth asked. "Shouldn't that be the law's responsibility?"

Her questions drew expressions of astonishment once again from both Luke and Vienna. "What law?" Vienna responded. "There ain't no law closer than Bozeman, and that's about a hundred and fifty miles from here. An eye for an eye, that's the law in this territory, and it's up to ordinary folks to protect themselves from predators like the ones responsible for our trouble." She left little doubt where she stood regarding punishment for the two men who had killed John, Doris, and Jack. "Ain't no different from shootin' a couple of coyotes raidin' the chicken coop."

"I guess you're right," Mary Beth conceded, "when you put it like that." She frowned and shook her head. "It's just that there's so much killing."

"That's just the way it is out here, ain't it, Luke?" Vienna remarked. "And it's the way it's gonna be until Coulson gets big enough to hire a sheriff. So good huntin', Luke," she blurted. "I hope you find 'em quick and send 'em to hell, where they belong." Seeing the concerned frown still in place on Mary Beth's face, she said, "We'll be all right. We'll get this place back in order, and me and my rifle will take care of anybody tryin' to bother us. Ain't that right, Mary Beth?"

Mary Beth smiled sheepishly. "That's right. We'll take care of ourselves." Her frown returned momentarily. "But, damn it, Luke, you be careful. Those men are dangerous."

"Yes, ma'am," he said as he turned to leave. They stood by the door, watching him until he disappeared into the barn to saddle up.

From the trail leading from the back of the barn, Luke could see that the two he followed were each leading a packhorse, making the tracks that much easier to follow. In addition, all four horses were shod, which helped as well. They led him to the common trail referred to as the river road by the settlers, and although there were many old tracks, those he trailed were much more recent than the others. As he rolled with easy grace to the paint's steady pace, he thought about the men he pursued. There was no doubt that the huge man the women had described was Bogart, and he wondered why fate seemed intent upon crossing their two trails again and again. It seemed that fate, or whatever, had decided that it was up to him to rid the world of the menace that was Bogart, so the sooner he could get it done, the better. He thought of the family he had just buried, and he knew there would be other innocent people to receive the same fate if he didn't stop Bogart.

When he reached the trail that forked off the river road and led into Coulson, he pulled his horses to a halt. The tracks he followed indicated that Bogart and Wylie had stopped here for some reason, telling Luke there was some discussion between the two. One of them had dismounted, for there were boot prints as well, large boot prints. Luke guessed they were Bogart's. Then the horses' tracks split, one set left the river road and headed down the trail to Coulson. The other set continued along the river. A small spot of blood on the ground told him that the wounded man took the trail to town. Luke had a feeling that the wounded man was Wylie, and not Bogart. He had a decision to make. If he chose to go after Wylie, it would give Bogart more time to put distance between them. It was a tough decision to make, because Bogart was the man he wanted most to stop. But, he told himself, Wylie was every bit as guilty, and since he was wounded, he should be easier to trail. *I'll go after him first,* he decided.

George Wylie was suffering. Sitting in the stable with his back up against the wall of a stall and one of Vienna Pitts's blouses wrapped around his head, he waited for Doc Gunderson to return from an overnight visit upriver. *And he ain't even*

303

a real doctor, he thought. *He's a damn horse doctor.* But Gunderson was all Coulson had to offer for folks in need of a doctor. While Wylie sat there trying not to think of the pain that encircled his head, he was deep in regret for ever having joined up with Bill Bogart. Sleep had been out of the question, so he had been forced to sit up all night, enduring the pain. Being in poor condition to defend himself should there be a call for it, he placed his rifle across his lap, cocked and ready to fire. Next to him lay his saddlebags. He had been in too much pain to unsaddle his horse, but he was not willing to risk leaving the saddlebags with two hundred dollars in gold coins inside.

Bogart had left him at the crossroad, left him to seek help on his own. Wylie would have shot him if he had possessed the strength, even knowing Bogart probably hoped he would try. At least he had the money. The thought created a desire to feel the weight of the gold coins in his hand and maybe take his mind off his wound for a few minutes. Fumbling with the left-side pocket flap, where Bogart had dropped the two small bags, he thrust his hand inside. The bags were not there. In a panic, he pulled the saddlebag across his legs to get to the other pocket, thinking he must have remembered incorrectly. As before, he found no gold coins in the pocket. Bogart had cheated him! But how? Wylie had seen Bogart drop the two bags in the saddlebag with his own eyes. He was sure the money was in his saddlebag. Then he remembered. At the crossroad, where he had left him, Bogart dismounted to talk to him, standing next to his horse. Bogart had to have taken the bags then when he had been hurting too badly to know he was being robbed. The realization of it caused his wounds to scream out in agony, and he leaned his head back against the board partition and silently pleaded for the strength to heal enough to track Bogart down and kill him. His fear returned then that he was not going to make it if the doctor didn't get there soon. Silently, he implored, *God! How much longer?* In immediate response to his plea, he heard a horse enter the stable, and a voice say, "Back yonder in the third stall."

"Buster said you're waitin' to see me," Doc Gunderson said upon entering the stall to find Wylie sitting there with what once was a woman's blouse wrapped around his head, now so blood-soaked as to be unrecognizable.

"I need doctorin'," Wylie said, his words garbled and almost incoherent, from his effort to talk with the teeth remaining on the other side of his mouth clenched against the pain.

"Well, let's take a look and see if I can help you," Gunderson said, and knelt down before him. Very carefully, he unwound the clumsy bandage to reveal the ghastly destruction of Wylie's mouth and jaw. "Good God, man!" Doc Gunderson exclaimed. "What the hell happened to you?"

Wylie painfully replied, "I was cleanin' my pistol, and it went off."

"That's as good a story as any, I reckon," Doc said, not wishing to know any further details. He remained kneeling before Wylie for several minutes while he studied the wounds and tried to decide what he could possibly do to treat them. "I'll be honest with you, mister," he finally said. "I don't rightly know if I can help you or not. That's a helluva hole in your cheek, and it looks like your jawbone is smashed. Tell you the truth, I'm tryin' to find somethin' to sew together." He shook his head apologetically. "You know, I ain't no physician. I'm a veterinarian."

The prognosis was not what Wylie had hoped to hear. "What would you do if I was a horse?" he sputtered.

"Shoot you," Doc answered.

"Damn you . . . ," Wylie started and clutched his rifle.

"Hold on!" Gunderson quickly interrupted. "I ain't said I wasn't gonna try to help you. Don't get all riled up. That sure ain't gonna help none. From the looks of it, you've already lost more blood than you needed to. There's some things I can do to make it easier on you, some medicine to help with the pain for one thing. Just sit tight, and I'll be back in a minute." He got to his feet and left the stall to retrieve a bottle of laudanum from his medicine cabinet in the tack room at the back of the stable.

Left to fret over the desperate situation he found himself in, Wylie groaned with the discomfort. Angered over Doc Gunderson's inability to fix his problem, he promised himself that he was going to shoot him if he didn't give him adequate treatment. Then the thought of Bogart riding away free and easy while he suffered almost gave him the strength to overcome his wounds. Lost in thoughts of a showdown with his ex-partner, he wasn't certain the voice was real when he heard it.

"You ain't lookin' too good, Wylie." Wylie jerked his head up, looking for the source, and finally located it at the door of the stall in the lethal form of Luke Sunday. "I've come to settle with you for those folks you killed back at that farmhouse."

"Sunday!" Wylie blurted, jerked his rifle up, and fired. His hurried shot missed wide, burying itself in a post by the door. Before he could cock the rifle again, Luke's patiently aimed shot hit him square in the chest, and he slumped over, fatally wounded. Luke chambered another cartridge and walked into the stall to make sure there was no more danger from Wylie. He picked up the saddlebags draped across Wylie's legs, turned them upside down, and raked out the contents on the floor of the stall. There were no little cloth bags with double eagles, so he did a quick check of Wylie's pockets and came up empty again. *Bogart's got Mary Beth's money,* he thought, and turned to face the door of the stall again, in case there was something to anticipate from Wylie's doctor. When no one came, he calmly walked out of the stable, climbed into the saddle, and rode out the front door.

Doc Gunderson, being a practical man, had quickly closed the tack room door behind him at the sound of the first gunshot. It was fully fifteen minutes after the second shot before he heard Buster Carter knock on the tack room door and tell him that it was safe to come out. Still a little leery, afraid that someone might be holding a gun on Buster, Doc cautiously pushed the door ajar. "He's gone," Buster exclaimed as he and Doc hurried to the stall. "I saw the whole thing. I was up in the hayloft when that feller came in. I was climbing down the ladder to see what he wanted when I heard the first shot. Then I heard the second shot. I was scared to death. I was still hangin' on to the ladder, halfway down, when he walked out—calm as you please—wild-lookin' feller, like one of them trappers that live up in the mountains. He looked at me and just nodded, like 'howdy-do.' I near fell off the ladder."

They stood looking at the late George Wylie, slumped against the wall of the stall. "Wasn't nothin' I could do for him, anyway," Doc said. "I was gonna try to dose him up on laudanum, but I doubt if he was able to swallow anythin'. I'da most likely had to pour it down him to get any in him. I'da been surprised if he coulda et anythin', either, the way his teeth and mouth was tore up. He mighta starved to death before he got well enough to eat."

"Wonder if that was the feller that shot him in the mouth," Buster speculated.

"Wouldn'ta surprised me none," Doc said. "Well, let's drag his carcass outta here and plant him in the ground. Right nice-lookin' rifle there. Winchester, ain't it?"

"Looks like we got us a couple of horses," Buster said, "and one of 'em's carrying packs."

Back at the fork on the river road, Luke knelt to carefully study the tracks of the two horses that had continued on after Wylie turned off to Coulson. He wanted to become as familiar with them as possible, noticing any small nicks or rough edges that would set them apart from others. There was no telling where Bogart might be heading, and Luke hoped not to lose the tracks if they became mixed in with any other recent travelers on the road. No marks were outstanding except for a small V, cut with a file on one shoe of one of the horses. *It might be like looking for a needle in a haystack,* he thought, *but at least it's something.* His scouting skills, honed in his years with the Crows and Cheyenne, would be put to the test. With confidence that those skills would not fail him, he climbed aboard the paint and headed west, following the common trail along the Yellowstone.

He knew it would be difficult to track a horse, even one with a V-notch in its shoe, for any great distance on a frequently traveled trail. So he was counting on luck and hoping he could overtake Bogart before the tracks became too old. He kept the paint at a steady pace, reasoning that Bogart was heading to Bozeman or Helena, someplace where he could spend the money he stole. He was also counting heavily on the assumption that Bogart wouldn't know he was being tracked. Solely to reassure himself, he stopped at every stream or creek that emptied into the river to check the hoofprints left in the soft sand and soil of the banks.

He came upon Bogart's first camp about a half day's ride from the Coulson fork. With plenty of daylight left, he continued on until darkness forced him to stop. At the end of the second day, when he'd found Bogart's second camp, there was little daylight left. It told him that the bloody killer had pushed his horses harder than the day before. Why, he wondered, was he now in a hurry to get somewhere? It meant that Luke was going to push the paint even harder, so he made his camp near the bank of a wide stream to rest the horse and wait for morning light to search for the V-notched horseshoe.

It had been a long time since he had been in this part of the country. It was a country of sweet grass valleys, formed by the Yellowstone and Boulder rivers, a land where he had hunted and trapped. He did not doubt that he might have remained there had not the cattlemen and the sheepherders discovered it. The thought brought a moment of regret when he remembered the beauty of the mountains on three sides of the rich grass prairie. He had considered making his life in the mountains: the Absarokas or the Beartooths. If he had done so, he now reminded himself, he would never have known Bogart or Wylie—or Sonny Pickens. And it would have been a happier world. But he would not have known Mary Beth Freeman, either. That thought caused him to frown, for it always troubled his mind, and he didn't know why. *Best to clear my head and get some sleep.*

At first light, he prepared to ride again, planning to wait for coffee and something to eat until he stopped to rest his horse. As before, Bogart's tracks were more easily read at the stream crossing, but this time there were many other tracks to add to the puzzle, some that even looked to be cow tracks. It called for a much closer inspection to distinguish Bogart's tracks from the others. All of the prints were recent, and all led to the north following the stream away from the river. Thinking that maybe he had picked someone else's trail by mistake, he made a more thorough search until he found the V-notched hoofprint among those that had deviated from the original trail. Still on one knee, he traced the imprint of the hoofprint with his finger while he considered the possible reasons for Bogart to change his mind. He looked up then, staring as far along the course of the stream as he could see. From memory, he knew there was nothing but grassland prairie between the Yellowstone and the Crazy Mountains, a distance of only about a half day's ride. What a man like Bogart would be looking for in those rugged mountains was impossible to guess. It occurred to him then that Bogart might have suspected he was being followed, and might have left the trail to see if anyone showed up. *If that's the game,* he thought, *then the sooner we get to it, the better.* He stepped up into the saddle and continued on, a bit warier now.

CHAPTER 14

Fred Gentry sat on his horse at the crest of a low rise in the prairie. On the other side, at the base of the slope, his partner was finishing packing up their camp in preparation to drive a group of twenty-three stray cattle back to join the main herd. "Somebody's comin'," Fred called down to Pete Scoggins. "Looks like an Injun, but he's all by himself. I don't see no others."

Pete climbed onto his horse and rode up to join his partner. In a few minutes, as the rider came closer, he stopped, obviously looking the two of them over. Then after a short pause, he continued toward them. "I ain't so sure it's an Injun," Pete said. "Might be just a drifter."

"Maybe you're right," Fred conceded. "The second one this week. I swear, it's gettin' down-right crowded around here."

It was obvious to Luke that neither of the two he saw on the rise was Bill Bogart, but since his tracks led this way, they might have seen him, so he guided the paint toward them. When they cautiously parted a few yards as he approached, he couldn't blame them for being wary. They watched silently, each with a rifle now cradled in his arms. "Mornin'," Luke called out as he rode up before them. "I'm lookin' to catch up with a feller. Any chance you mighta seen him?"

"Don't know," Fred answered. "We ain't seen but one feller, and that was back by the river yesterday. Was he a friend of yours?"

Luke was a little confused by the response. "You say back by the river? Was he a big man with a big bush of whiskers?"

"That sounds like him, all right," Pete said. "How come you're lookin' for him?"

"He killed some folks back in Coulson and stole their money," Luke replied.

"Damn," Fred muttered incredulously. He shot a glance of relief in Pete's direction. "It's a good thing we kept an eye on that feller." Looking back at Luke then, he said, "Hell, we ate breakfast with that feller. I'm settin' on his horse right now." Judging by the expression on Luke's face, Fred guessed his confusion. "He wanted to trade horses. This one had a loose shoe. He offered me forty dollars cash to trade with him. Hell, mine was a good horse, but it wasn't worth forty dollars' difference. I'da traded for twenty. Pete fixed the shoe twenty minutes after he left."

Immediately taken aback, Luke felt his mind racing with the thought that Bogart had fooled him. He had wasted time following the wrong horse—even more annoying to realize he no longer had a way to identify Bogart's horse. Maybe luck would favor him, and the V-notched shoe would be on Bogart's packhorse. "Mind if I take a look at that horse's hooves?" Luke asked.

Pete and Fred exchanged puzzled glances. "I reckon not," Fred said, "but I traded a good horse for this one, and if you're gonna try to tell me he stole this horse, well, that's just tough luck for the owner, 'cause it belongs to me now."

"I don't want the horse," Luke said. "I just wanna look at his hooves."

Still suspicious, but figuring Luke couldn't pull any tricks with the two of them watching him, Fred told him to go ahead and look. He lifted only two of the horse's hooves before he found what he hoped he wouldn't, the shoe with the V notched in the front. There was no longer any way to pick Bogart's tracks out from all the others. Suddenly he was struck with a feeling of dire urgency. "Which way was he headin' when he left you back by the river?"

"East," Pete answered.

"East?" Luke questioned. "Back the way he came from?" He didn't like the picture that was forming in his mind.

"I don't know which direction he came from," Pete replied. "But when he left us, he was headin' east."

"What color is the horse you traded?" Luke asked.

"Red roan," Fred replied, "a workin' horse, built more for endurance than speed."

Luke's mind was racing now as something Vienna had said returned to haunt him. *"It's a good thing those two didn't get a look at Mary Beth,"* she had said. *"A pretty young thing like her is liable to start men like that to thinkin' bad things."* Bogart *had* gotten a look at Mary Beth, back at Fort Fetterman, and Luke could not help the sudden notion that the murderer was heading back to finish the evil business he had started. All at once, Luke was overwhelmed by a feeling that he had to get back to Coulson. If his gut feeling was wrong, then so much for the better. He had to know that Mary Beth and Vienna were safe. Nothing else mattered.

Without another word to either of the two men, Luke climbed back in the saddle and wheeled the paint back the way he had come, leaving Pete and Fred to stare incredulously at each other. "If that don't beat all," Fred remarked. "He's a sociable cuss, ain't he?"

"I'm tickled he ain't after me," Pete responded.

It was difficult to hold his horse to a comfortable lope, but he knew if he asked the paint for more speed, the horse would willingly oblige, and he would run the risk of breaking its wind. So he held him in the same rapid lope, pulling him back to a fast walk periodically until he thought he had to stop and rest him. The fact that he and Bogart had evidently passed each other, riding in opposite directions without either man realizing it, could only have been bad luck on his part. There were many long stretches where the trail that followed the Yellowstone was more closely akin to a common road, used by many travelers—settlers, Indians, gold miners, soldiers. But there were also many miles where there was more than one trail through thickly wooded patches and broken bluffs, and one of these patches was undoubtedly where they had passed, probably at a distance of less than a quarter mile. It only added to his anxiety to think about how close they had come.

According to what he had been told by the two drovers, he was starting out a full day behind Bogart. He hoped, by riding day and night, he could catch up to him before Bogart got back to Coulson. Since the ride west had taken two days, he thought his chances were good, even allowing time to rest his horse. On through the day he rode, stopping at dusk to give the paint a longer rest. When the moon rose high above the Yellowstone, he saddled up and headed out again, pushing on at a more cautious pace, leery of holes and gullies hidden in the shadows, knowing that if the paint broke a leg, they were both finished. By the time the moon sat down behind the hills to the west, both horse and rider were showing signs of weariness. So when he came to a suitable campsite, he stopped, unsaddled the paint, and built a small fire. After a meal of coffee and deer jerky, he closed his eyes for a few minutes' rest, confident that sleep was impossible even had he wanted to. It was daylight when he opened his eyes again. Scrambling to his feet, he cursed his squandering of precious time. Hastily packing up his camp, he was soon under way once more.

"I sure as hell miss that boy Jack," Vienna lamented, standing in the backyard by the pump and gazing out across the cornfield. "He used to keep that corn free of weeds. Now it looks like the weeds are catchin' up." She looked at Mary Beth and uttered a long sigh. "That ain't the only reason I miss the boy, but we're gonna have to do the work he and his daddy did—as soon as we get the houses fixed up again. It'll help a helluva lot when Luke gets back."

"If he comes back," Mary Beth responded. "You know my only agreement with Luke was for him to take David and me to Coulson, so he's fulfilled his part of the bargain." She laughed. "Besides, can you see Luke Sunday working a farm? You might as well hitch an antelope to the plow. I'd be surprised if he came back here again."

Vienna did not miss the faraway look in Mary Beth's eyes when the young woman made the comment. "He'll be back," Vienna insisted. "He left that spotted gray packhorse he thinks so much of." She studied her younger friend's face for a moment, a tight little smile upon her face. "You know, it wouldn't be a bad idea for the two of you to pair up. We need a good, strong man around here if we're gonna make it."

The suggestion made Mary Beth blush. "Why, Vienna Pitts, bite your tongue. What a ridiculous thing to say, and me widowed for only a little over a month."

"Out here in this country, there ain't no time for proper doin's," Vienna scoffed. "A body can go under waitin' for the proper time to pass."

"Well, I think we have to plan on something besides the taming of Luke Sunday," Mary Beth declared.

"Well, if you ain't gonna do nothin' about it, can I have him?"

"Vienna Pitts!" Mary Beth exclaimed again in mock alarm. "Don't you have any shame?"

"I reckon not," Vienna said with a laugh. "Never had time for it."

"You know, there's such a thing as two people being in love before there should be any talk about getting married," Mary Beth lectured.

"Horse dung!" Vienna responded. "More folks have gotten themselves in trouble because of thinkin' they're in love. These young girls think they're miserable without some handsome fellow they're stuck on. They're miserable until they can tie the knot. Then after a month or two when the honeymoon's over, they're miserable for the rest of their lives."

Mary Beth shook her head, exasperated. "You can't make me believe you and your husband were miserable all your married life."

"Oh, hell no," Vienna quickly countered. "Not me and Vern, 'cause we weren't in love when we decided to get married. We talked it over and decided we could make a go of it as a team. And we did, till he up and got himself killed."

Mary Beth shook her head impatiently. "This is all the nonsense I've got time for. I'm going back in the house to finish nailing that table leg back on, then see if I can fix some of the other things those animals wrecked."

One of the *animals* Mary Beth referred to was at that moment kneeling just fifty yards away, watching the two women from a stand of cotton-woods on the creek bank. He was in no hurry to make his presence known, instead enjoying the opportunity to observe them as they went about their chores, unaware of the evil awaiting them. His memory had served him well, for the young one was a pretty little slip of a woman, and now with the chance to get a better look at her, his desire was stronger than ever. The only intimate relations he had ever experienced with women were all the same—give them the money first, keep your shirt and your boots on, and get it over with fast. And they usually complained the whole time about him being too rough and too in need of a bath, as if they were some kind of princess, instead of the painted-up hussies they were. *Well, it ain't gonna be like that this time,* he thought. A grin formed slowly across his whiskered face as he imagined the pleasure he anticipated. The older one would have suffered the same fate if the young one was not there, but he had already learned that she could be trouble—she of the sassy mouth and the Winchester rifle. So he planned to put a bullet in her brain first thing, and that would eliminate her as a problem.

Deciding he had waited long enough, Bogart rose to his feet. If Luke Sunday was still around, it didn't appear that he was going to show up before sundown. He felt certain that the two women were alone there, and he could deny his lust for Mary Beth no longer. About to fetch his horses, he stopped to listen. It was the sound of a horse's hooves pounding on the hard dirt of the path from the river road. A rider was coming in, and from the sound of the hoofbeats, he was in a hurry. Bogart moved up closer to the trunk of a large cottonwood to get a better look. As the rider charged into the yard between the barn and the house, Bogart peered around the tree. At once he froze, all the blood in his body seemed to drain to his boots. *Luke Sunday!* Bogart pressed hard against the tree, his mouth having gone completely dry, and his heart pounding as if about to burst out of his chest. He had boasted to George

Wylie about his desire to find Luke Sunday, and what he would do when he did. But now that he had suddenly appeared, he rapidly lost his nerve. The thought of facing him was paralyzing, for he could not forget his prior encounters with the white Indian.

He pressed even closer to the tree, inching around the trunk to keep it between him and the somber Indian scout as Luke rode down the path toward the house. And then it struck Bogart that Luke did not know he was there, and the opportunity he hoped for had presented itself. Sunday's back was an inviting target, and Bogart told himself he must act while the target was in short range. To get a clear shot, he had to come out from behind the tree. To steady himself, he dropped to one knee, but he was still trembling so much that he found it difficult to hold his front sight on the broad back riding comfortably on the paint pony. This feeling of uncertainty when about to back-shoot an unsuspecting victim had never occurred to him before, and he tried to tell himself to just calm down and pull the trigger.

Inside the house, Mary Beth glanced out the front door to see a rider coming down the path that led from the river road. She immediately recognized the familiar figure on the paint pony, and with a thankful smile of excitement, went out to meet him. "Luke!" she called out to him. At the same moment, she saw Bogart step out from behind a tree and kneel to take aim at him. "Luke!" This time she screamed his name in horror at the scene before her eyes. Luke reacted at once, but it was not soon enough, for Bogart's bullet was already on its way.

Almost beside himself with joyous excitement, Bogart realized he had won the final contest with the dangerous Indian scout as he watched Luke fall out of the saddle to land heavily on the ground. Unaware of the triumphant roar that burst forth from his mouth, he leaped to his feet. Still, ever cautious of the scout the Indians called Dead Man, Bogart warned himself to be wary of the man, although he had not moved since he had hit the ground. With his rifle still aimed at the body, he advanced slowly, alert to the possibility that Luke might be playing possum. There was no doubt that his bullet had hit Luke in the back, for he saw it tear into his shirt, but he wasn't sure whether Luke carried a pistol in his belt or not. *I'm gonna figure that you're lying there with your hand on a pistol,* he thought as he moved closer, planning to put another bullet into the fallen man.

Things had happened so fast that Luke wasn't sure of anything at first, except the fact that he found himself on the ground and in great pain. Bogart had beaten him. This was the first conscious thought that occurred to him as his ears seemed to be ringing with the sounds of the shot, mixed with Mary Beth's screams. Forcing himself to think, he knew that he had one chance, and one chance only, so he forced his hand down under his stomach to grasp the handle of the .44 revolver he had slipped inside his belt and waited for Bogart to come closer to gloat over his kill. But Bogart, ever wary of his dangerous foe, stopped short of the body, preferring to fire a precautionary shot at a safer distance.

Aware of the large circle of blood spreading on his shirt, the wounded man realized that his attempt to play dead had not tempted his assailant to come close to gloat. And time was now a determining factor, for he wasn't sure how long he might remain conscious before the loss of blood caused him to black out. He knew he had to act now, even if in total desperation. Calling on all the strength he could muster, he suddenly rolled over, pulling the revolver as he did, only to find that his vision was blurry and his head spinning. With no choice but to shoot, he pointed the pistol at the blurred object standing to watch him and pulled the trigger.

Bogart ducked automatically, but then realized that the pistol shot did not come within yards of him. It was then that he fully realized Luke Sunday was helpless, and he was in total control of his death. "What's the matter, you damn Injun lover?" Bogart roared. "Can't see where you're shootin'? I told you I'd fix your ass before it was over." He raised his rifle to administer the final strike. At that moment, Mary Beth screamed Luke's name again and ran from the porch to help the fallen man. Bogart found it amusing, and hesitated to pull the trigger, waiting to time the shot when she was only a few yards away from Luke. "You're too late, darlin'. You're gonna be spreadin' them pretty white legs for me tonight." The fatal shot rang out, but it was not from Bogart's rifle. The huge brute's head snapped back sharply and he staggered backward several awkward paces before crumpling to the ground, shot through the head.

"Damned if that's so," Vienna Pitts growled. She pulled the Winchester back from the porch railing that she had used to steady her aim and remarked, "Damn thing shoots a little high. I was aimin' at his chest."

"I swear, I'm right sorry to hear about John Freeman and his family," Doc Gunderson said. "They were mighty nice folks. We don't need to lose folks like that here in the valley. We've already got a gracious plenty of the other kind, like that big carcass lyin' in the path up yonder. Me and Buster can drag him up on the bluff and dig a hole for him, so you ladies won't have to look at him anymore."

"We'd appreciate that, Doc," Vienna said.

"What about the other carcass we got lyin' in the front bedroom. Are we gonna have to dig a hole for him, too?"

"Him? Nah, he's as strong as an ox. He ain't gonna be much use to you for a few weeks, though. He was lucky, if you can call gettin' shot lucky. I can't say for sure, but I'd guess that if that bullet had been an inch or two more toward the center, it'da got a lung. But he ain't havin' no trouble breathin' right now. I ain't a people doctor, but if he was a horse, I'd guarantee you, he'll be back to the stallion he was before." He nodded toward Buster Carter, who had come along to help. "Buster says he's the feller that killed one of my other patients." He laughed and shook his head. "He gave me and Buster a fright, I'll tell you." When he read concern in the eyes of both women, he continued. "From what you ladies told me about those two fellers and what they did to the Freemans, I don't see any reason to tell anybody about who killed who."

Buster spoke up then. "He's the same feller, all right, but looks like he had reason to do what he did." When Gunderson picked up his bag to leave, Buster followed him. At the door, he paused to offer his help around the farm to Vienna, who gladly took him up on the offer.

After they left, Vienna went back into the bedroom, where Mary Beth was standing by Luke's bedside. "Asleep?" Vienna asked. Mary

Beth nodded. "Well, looks like he might make it. At least Doc thinks so."

"He'll be all right," Mary Beth said. "I know he will."

"While you got him down, you oughta put your brand on him," Vienna advised with a naughty grin.

"I wouldn't, even if I wanted to," Mary Beth replied, blushing. "I doubt you could tame someone like Luke Sunday." She gazed at the sleeping man for a few moments before looking up to see Vienna still grinning at her.

"Hell," Vienna scoffed, "you'd be the one to do it. They tame wild mustangs all the time. We could use a strong man like him to help us run this place. We need all the help we can get, and it don't sound like a bad idea to have a man called Sunday workin' for us."

Mary Beth shook her head slowly as if exasperated with her partner. Then she took another look at the peaceful face of the sleeping warrior. "I wouldn't count on it," she said. But to herself, she thought, *We'll just have to wait and see.*

Center Point Large Print
600 Brooks Road / PO Box 1
Thorndike, ME 04986-0001 USA

(207) 568-3717

US & Canada:
1 800 929-9108
www.centerpointlargeprint.com